"VALE, HOW ARE THE KLINGONS DOING?"

"Not good," Vale said. "The birds-of-prey are gone. The cruisers are firing at the planet."

Riker immediately pictured Captain Picard and Deanna in the Tezwan capital, on the receiving end of a Klingon torpedo barrage. Then he made an educated guess about what another hit from Tezwa's planet-based artillery would do to the *Enterprise*.

"Helm," he said. "Set a course for the Tezwan capital. We're going in to get the captain."

STAR TREK®
A Time to Kill

DAVID MACK

Based on
STAR TREK: THE NEXT GENERATION®
created by Gene Roddenberry

POCKET BOOKS
New York   London   Toronto   Sydney

An *Original* Publication of POCKET BOOKS

POCKET BOOKS, a division of Simon & Schuster, Inc.
1230 Avenue of the Americas, New York, NY 10020

This book is published by Pocket Books, a division of Simon & Schuster, Inc., under exclusive license from Paramount Pictures.

ISBN: 0-7434-9177-7

First Pocket Books printing August 2004

10 9 8 7 6 5 4 3 2 1

POCKET and colophon are registered trademarks of Simon & Schuster, Inc.

Manufactured in the United States of America

For information regarding special discounts for bulk purchases, please contact Simon & Schuster Special Sales at 1-800-456-6798 or business@simonandschuster.com

The last temptation is the greatest treason:
to do the right deed for the wrong reason.
—T. S. Eliot, *Murder in the Cathedral*

A Time to Kill

Chapter 1
U.S.S. Enterprise-E

THE BLASTER PULSE STRETCHED with a surreal, elastic quality as it missed Commander William Riker, who had been pushed out of harm's way at the final moment by his father, Kyle Riker. The audible sizzle of the beam striking Kyle was muffled by the older man's agonized shout. Kyle fell, leaden and limp. His creased face was slackened and blank, the defiant spark of his life robbed from him by a bloodthirsty Bader gunman. Kyle struck the floor next to Will. His age-softened body landed with an unceremonious thud, the sickly-sweet reek of his charred flesh overpowering in the frigid, subarctic air. . . .

Commander William Riker shuddered awake from his nightmare. Hot tears of anger stung his eyes. The desperate expression of his murdered father's face haunted his sight like an afterimage.

He couldn't count how many times during his childhood his father had admonished him, "Boys don't cry, Will." For as long as he had strived to break free of his father's influence, he'd never been able to emancipate himself of the old man's damnable yoke of stoicism.

Not until now.

He turned his head and looked at Deanna Troi, his on-again, off-again, then on-again lover—and now his fiancée. She slept next to him, her cascade of dark hair spilling wildly across a pair of broad pillows. Her face was serene in the pale glow of starlight.

He checked the chronometer. It was just after 0400 hours. Taking care not to wake Deanna, he inched his arm out from under the covers. He gently folded back the sheets and sat up. He looked back at her. Her breaths were long and deep, her slumber untroubled. A more selfish man might have envied her; Riker took comfort in her peaceful repose and half-smiled, grateful for the good fortune that had brought his sweet *Imzadi* into his life.

Scratching at his beard, he stood and walked out into the main room. Closing his eyes, he stopped in front of the row of sloping, narrow windows in the ceiling and gazed at the cold, sterile beauty of the stars. He took a long breath, one deep enough that he could feel it press his chest outward. He held it, savored it for a moment, then let it go. He marveled at the feeling, at how he could take for granted the very tides of his own life and death. *A thousand times a day we breathe in and we're full,* he thought. *A thousand times a day we breathe out and we're empty.*

Empty was how he'd felt every day since he'd watched his father die. Since the moment he saw a lifetime of unfinished business become an eternity of missed opportunities.

Perhaps it had been irony—or an example of karmic balance—but less than a week ago, upon returning from his father's appropriately terse and unsentimental funeral, Riker had been contacted by Admiral Kathryn Janeway, who'd offered him the captain's chair on the *Titan*.

The ship, she'd said, was still in spacedock undergoing a final series of upgrades and mandatory inspections. It would be ready for active duty in a few months. Riker had asked for time to think it over, and she'd graciously agreed. But she'd also made it clear the offer wouldn't remain open indefinitely.

For most career Starfleet officers, an offer such as this was a once-in-a-lifetime shot at command. For those lucky few who were invited to take their place in the big chair, the very rarity of the offer made the decision to say yes easy and immediate. Riker, on the other hand, held the dubious distinction of having refused more offers of command than any other active Starfleet officer. Almost fifteen years ago, he'd chosen to serve as Captain Jean-Luc Picard's first officer aboard the *Enterprise*-D rather than take command of the *Drake*. Roughly eighteen months later, he'd declined Starfleet's offer to captain the *Aries*.

For most officers, refusing two commands in less than two years would be the end of their career track. But Riker was offered a third bite at the apple, during the Borg crisis of 2366, when Starfleet Command all but begged him to take command of the *Melbourne*. He'd passed up that chance, as well, but shortly afterward received a field promotion to captain of the *Enterprise*-D when Picard was captured by the Borg and transformed temporarily into Locutus.

A few days later, after Riker had risked everything to save his captured commanding officer, he'd heard the whispers of the *Enterprise* crew, most of whom couldn't believe he'd actually requested demotion to his former rank of commander so he could continue to serve as Picard's trusted Number One.

That was more than twelve years ago, and since then Starfleet had stopped offering him command posts. Until now.

He sighed and stroked his graying beard for a moment. *Why now?* he wondered to himself. *Why did it have to be now?*

He stepped over to the replicator. "Water, cold."

The singsong whine of the replicator crested, then faded. A faintly glowing swirl of atoms coalesced into a squat, square-sided drinking glass three-quarters filled with pure, cool water. Riker picked it up and drank half of it in a few gulps. He let out a satisfied breath, then downed the rest of it. He put the empty glass back in the replicator and pressed the matter-reclamation key. He turned and walked back to the windows as the replicator dematerialized the empty glass.

The timing of Janeway's offer couldn't have been more awkward, in Riker's opinion. The last few months had been unkind to the *Enterprise*-E in general, and to Captain Picard in particular. The Rashanar incident had led to a politically motivated tarnishing of the captain's reputation—and, by extension, a blemish on the prestige of the ship and its crew. Consequently, several dozen crew members and officers had made formal requests for transfer off the ship.

At the same time, the personnel sent recently to the *Enterprise* by Starfleet Command seemed to be individuals whose records were checkered with disciplinary problems, poor work evaluations, or borderline psychiatric profiles.

Riker and Troi had done everything they could to convince their shipmates not to leave, but, with only a few notable exceptions, they'd been unable to prevent the exodus of many of the ship's best department chiefs and noncommissioned officers. Every high-profile departure had been another blow to the esteem of the *Enterprise* and her captain, and Riker knew full well that rumors were spreading through Starfleet that the *Enterprise* had become a ship where failing careers were sent to die.

And now Starfleet was inviting its first officer to join the growing ranks of the *Enterprise*'s recently departed, accompanied by his wife-to-be, who was also the ship's senior counselor. If the two most vocal defenders of Picard's integrity left the ship for greener pastures, the damage to the crew's morale might prove irreparable. Picard's credibility as a commanding officer would be all but ruined by gossip and innuendo. Riker had to wonder if the timing of this offer from Starfleet had been intended to serve exactly that purpose.

Riker didn't want to abandon Picard at a time such as this; the captain had been more than a commanding officer to him, more than a comrade. He'd been a true friend, and, in many ways, like the father Riker had always wished Kyle could have been. But at the same time, this was the first offer of promotion Riker had received in more than a decade—and he had every reason to believe that if he refused it, it would also be the last.

He heard Troi's gentle footfalls on the carpet behind him a moment before she snaked her arms around him and embraced him. "Nightmares again?" she said, pressing against his back.

He nodded. "The same one."

She pressed her cheek against his shoulder blade. "I felt it. It's getting more vivid, isn't it?" He didn't answer her, but they both knew she was right. "Are you sure you don't—"

"No," he said. "I'll be all right. I'll work it out." He felt slightly guilty about the effects his nightmares had been having on her, even though he knew there was nothing he could do to prevent it. Her half-Betazoid ancestry had gifted her with empathic skills that, when she was awake, she could control or choose to ignore. But when she was asleep, some of her psychic control became dormant. As a result, when they slept in the same bed, she would often sense the emotional tenor of his dreams.

He turned to face her and held her close. Her hair was soft, and it had a sweet fragrance. It made him think of jasmine and honey.

She looked up at him. "Come back to bed," she whispered.

"I will." He kissed her forehead. "You go. I'll be there in a little while." She gave his hand a small squeeze, then smiled as she reached up and stroked his cheek with her fingertips. She turned and padded softly back into the bedroom.

He looked back out at the stars. For the last fourteen

years he'd had a number of things he'd wanted to say to his father—most of them words of spite. It wasn't as if he couldn't have tracked him down; Kyle had rarely kept a low profile. Riker now realized, to his shame, that the only thing that had prevented him from settling things with his father had been his own stubborn refusal to let it happen.

He looked toward the bedroom and considered going back to sleep. He closed his eyes. The memory of his father's face still lingered like a shroud in front of his thoughts. He opened his eyes, drew a deep breath, then let it ebb. He focused on the feeling of emptiness that was left behind, and he longed for a day when it wouldn't feel quite so familiar.

Chapter 2
Tezwa

PRIME MINISTER KINCHAWN adjusted the settings of his holographic display. The image was divided into two equal, wide rectangles. The top half showed the stern countenance of Bilok, his deputy prime minister. On the bottom was the broad, fleshy face of Koll Azernal, the chief of staff to the Federation president. Kinchawn didn't know when, exactly, Azernal had cultivated Bilok as a secret ally, but, knowing the Zakdorn's methods, it had likely been the same day he'd enlisted Kinchawn's help in the Dominion War. Regardless, it justified his eavesdropping now.

"You're quite certain this will work?" Azernal said. He sounded tense, but since he lacked nape feathers it was hard for Kinchawn to tell. It amazed the prime minister that so many humanoid species looked so much alike, yet so few shared his people's feathering; most had hair, which struck him as a poor substitute. He found their round irises to be an equally curious difference from the Tezwan norm.

Bilok nodded, swaying the gray and white plumage that framed his age-worn face. *"Kinchawn will not fire,"* he said. *"He will assume that if you put one of your own ships at risk, you must have withheld a secret defense against the pulse cannons."*

"And if you're wrong?" the Zakdorn said.

Bilok paused. *"He cannot declare war without majority approval in the Assembly. He will have to err on the side of caution."* Kinchawn was glad they were speaking candidly. It reassured him that they were unaware he had secretly ordered the military to intercept all of Bilok's private transmissions.

"Perhaps," Azernal said. *"Now, how do you propose we secure a long-term solution?"* Kinchawn never tired of the Zakdorn's gift for euphemisms. By "long-term solution," Azernal had, of course, meant the deposing of Kinchawn himself.

"The Assembly is almost evenly divided, and only the slightest plurality is aligned with Kinchawn," Bilok said. *"Once he stands down, he'll likely lose the support of a few of his most extreme partisans. At that point it should be fairly easy to pass a vote of no confidence and demand his resignation."*

The downy, pale brown feathers at the nape of Kinchawn's neck ruffled, betraying his rising ire. He had never trusted Bilok. Worse, he had long envied the elder statesman's influence. Bilok was one of the *trinae,* the high-mountain people. They were larger, stronger, and, some Tezwans believed, smarter than Kinchawn's people, the *elininae.* Power had always come easily to them. But what Kinchawn lacked in finesse he more than made up for in naked aggression, which had enabled him to soar ahead of Bilok to the top aerie of power.

"All right," Azernal said. He seemed suspicious. *"But can you keep the Assembly in line?"*

"With appropriate enticements," Bilok said. *"Easily."*

Azernal scowled, bunching the overlapping folds of skin that draped his fleshy cheeks like curtains. *"I ask because the cannons weren't supposed to go online. Yet here we—"*

"That was out of my hands," Bilok said. *"Kinchawn bypassed the Assembly and now issues orders directly to the army."*

Azernal raised one eyebrow, which, being composed of hair, looked as alien as anything Kinchawn had ever seen on a face.

"The Assembly doesn't know about the cannons?"

"No," Bilok said.

"Good. Keep it that way."

"For how long?" Bilok said. *"I fear Kinchawn plans to dissolve the Assembly and establish a military government."*

"Obviously," Azernal said. *"If we help you take Kinchawn out of play, can you control the commanders?"*

Bilok frowned. *"Difficult to say."*

Azernal was quiet but unyielding. *"How difficult?"*

"He replaced most of them over the last two years," Bilok said. *"They in turn replaced most of their immediate subordinates. I'm not sure how they'll react to his removal."*

"What about the general population?"

"His obsession with building up the military came at

their expense. They've been eager for his ouster for some time."

"*Good, good,*" Azernal said.

"*After we've unmade this crisis,*" Bilok said, "*how soon can your people get these damned cannons off my planet?*"

"*We'll have to be discreet,*" Azernal replied. "*Perhaps a few months, assuming your military doesn't interfere.*"

"*Excellent,*" Bilok said. "*We'll also need your commitment to provide doctors and civic engineers, to undo the damage of Kinchawn's misrule.*"

"*Of course,*" the Zakdorn said with a nod.

"*And our application for Federation membership?*"

"*Let's get the cannons back into mothballs before we open that discussion,*" Azernal said.

"*I understand,*" Bilok said, disappointed.

Kinchawn pitied Bilok's misguided fantasy of adding Tezwa to the Federation. Bilok clearly was ignorant of the fact that harsh economic struggles were threatening to splinter the Federation into two factions. Worlds that had been devastated by the Dominion War had been rebuffed when they asked those that hadn't suffered to assist in their costly reconstruction. In the midst of such a tense fiscal crisis, the last thing the Federation needed was to take responsibility for another impoverished planet, such as Tezwa.

"*All right, then,*" Azernal said, nodding. "*We can make this work, as long as you can keep his finger off the trigger. We just ended a war we're in no mood for another. If Kinchawn provokes the Klingons, you're on your own. . . . Azernal out.*"

The display flickered and went dark as Bilok and Azernal terminated their transmission. Kinchawn stood up from his desk and strode out onto the promenade that ringed his office. He surveyed the towers, spires, and domes of Keelee-Kee, Tezwa's ancient capital city. His dark gray eyes scanned distant features of the cityscape, some almost as far away as the horizon, which brightened with the promise of a golden dawn. The metropolis radiated out from the *Ilanatava,* or Prime Aerie, and spread across the plains with geometric precision.

A warm zephyr swirled around him, fluttering his purple robe and the tufts of feathers that covered his bare forearms. He drew a breath and swallowed his rage. *So he plans to depose me?* he mused. *With the aid of a defenseless Starfleet vessel and a Federation with no stomach for bloodshed?*

He locked his slender, bony fingers around the promenade's railing. *Not today,* he vowed.

Chapter 3
Earth

PRESIDENT MIN ZIFE, leader of the United Federation of Planets, turned his head to listen as his chief of staff leaned over and whispered discreetly in his ear: "Mr. President, Tezwa just threatened the Klingons."

Zife pushed away his half-finished plate of fettucine primavera. Without explanation or apology to the hundreds of VIP guests seated in the high-ceilinged, burgundy-and-gold main ballroom of Buckingham Palace, he exited the formal state dinner welcoming the newly elected members of the Federation Council. A politely hushed murmur followed him as he stepped off the raised dais at the front of the room. He, his six-person security detail, and Azernal marched down the broad aisle that separated the two parallel rows of banquettes. Their footfalls snapped sharply and echoed in the ancient, gilded hall.

They hurried out a side door, into a service corridor. They quickened as they moved toward an exit, which was flanked by a pair of uniformed Starfleet security officers. Azernal, though shorter and considerably more stout than Zife, moved at a much quicker pace than the middle-aged Bolian chief executive. The only thing that prevented him from drastically outpacing the president was the phalanx of plainclothes Federation security personnel that surrounded them. "How long ago?" Zife said, his voice pitched slightly from exertion.

"About six hours, sir. Prime Minister Kinchawn declared Tezwan sovereignty over the Klingon border colony of QiV'ol."

Zife frowned and loosened the top button of his shirt. Of all the protocols he'd learned to observe while on Earth, its native fashions had proved to be the most vexing. He blamed the constricting discomfort of the shirt's collar for the headache he'd been fighting off all evening. He often envied Azernal for the behind-the-scenes nature of his job, not least because it afforded him the luxury of wearing looser, more comfortable clothing.

They neared the end of the corridor. The two Starfleet officers pushed open the double doors and ushered them into the secure transporter station. A stocky, powerfully built human man with a high-and-tight haircut, a goatee, and three full pips on his Starfleet uniform collar stood at attention behind the transporter console. "Good evening, Mr. President," he said.

"Good evening, Commander Wexler," Zife said.

"Destination, sir?"

"Palais de la Concorde," Zife said with a flawless French accent.

Wexler nodded. "Aye, sir."

Zife shut his eyes and measured his breaths, in an effort to dispel his headache. He barely noticed the musical wash of white sound and the oddly effervescent tingle of the transporter beam. When he opened his eyes again, he was standing in his private transporter station at the Federation headquarters in Paris.

He and Azernal stepped off the transport pad and walked briskly toward the turbolift to his office, on the top floor. The plainclothes security detail followed them into the turbolift. The doors hissed closed, and the lift shot upward without any discernible sensation of acceleration.

Though Azernal didn't say a word during the ride upstairs, Zife recognized the feral gleam in the man's eyes. He'd seen his chief of staff sport that expression several times during the later stages of the war against the Dominion, while crafting one ruthlessly cunning battle plan after another. Though many members of the Admiralty and the Security Council had made valuable, high-profile contributions to directing the war effort, Zife and the senior members of the Federation Council knew that the war's true unsung hero had been Koll Azernal.

Zife was certain he knew what to expect when he saw Azernal's jaw muscles tighten and his brow furrow into dark knots: The irascible Zakdorn strategist had already settled on a plan of action.

The turbolift doors opened into a broad, windowless, crescent-shaped outer office. Opposite the turbolift, on the far left and right sides of the inner wall, were pairs of enormous, antique oak doors with brass fixtures. Each pair of doors was guarded by an armed plainclothes Federation security officer. Zife strode to the left pair of doors. The security officer opened the door for him and nodded curtly. "Mr. President."

"Thank you," Zife said, and entered his office without missing a step. Azernal followed close behind him. Zife's six-man security detail halted outside the door.

The door shut with a low thud, behind the chief of staff. Zife walked across the wide chamber to his desk and pivoted to face Azernal. "What the hell is Kinchawn doing?"

"It seems our old friend is no longer satisfied with dominating his own planet," Azernal said. When he spoke, the overlapping curves of carapace beneath his cheeks shifted against each other in a way that Zife still found distracting, even after more than a decade of relying on Azernal as his senior advisor. "He's acquired a small fleet of ships—twenty-four, according to a reliable source. Most likely from the Danteri, by way of the Orion Syndicate. Our best estimates indicate he'll be ready to deploy them in less than five days."

"Five days? The Klingons can hit Tezwa sooner than that."

"They're already massing a fleet in the Zurav Nebula," Azernal said. "Ambassador Worf is trying to convince Martok not to launch a preemptive strike."

"How would you rate Worf's chances?"

"I wouldn't," Azernal said. "When the Klingons get mad, all bets are off."

Zife narrowed his eyes. "Why now?" he said. "Why is Kinchawn forcing the issue now?"

"The Trill fiasco, I suspect," Azernal said. "Or maybe the Genesis wave or the holostrike or the Rashanar incident. Regardless, he's aware of the pressure we're under from the secessionists, now that the war's over."

Zife's face grew hot as his anger escalated. Despite the best efforts of his press secretary to downplay those incidents, it had been impossible to prevent the Federation News Service from reporting extensively on them.

Rashanar was just the most recent problem. Several months ago in the Rashanar Sector, a crisis situation, coupled with a case of mistaken identity, resulted in two Starfleet vessels, the *Juno* and the *Enterprise,* being attacked by allied Ontailian ships. The *Juno* was destroyed and lost with all hands before the situation could be defused.

With rumbles of discontent and secession already threatening to unravel the political fabric of the Federation, the decision was made to help the Ontailians save face and prevent a fracturing of the Federation Council. But the preservation of the Ontailians' honor had been achieved by unjustly laying all the blame for the *Juno* tragedy at the feet of Captain Jean-Luc Picard and his *Enterprise* crew.

Zife wiped a sheen of sweat from his ridged blue pate. "Dammit," he said. "Does Kinchawn know what'll happen if he attacks the Klingons?"

Azernal nodded. "Indubitably. But I think he expects us to pressure them into ceding QiV'ol to his jurisdiction."

Zife planted his hands on the polished black semi-

circle of his desk. "How could he possibly think we'd—"
Zife stopped in midsentence. He fixed Azernal with a
glowering look. "The guns."

"Yes, sir." Azernal's voice was heavy with regret.
"The guns. He's made them operational."

Zife sagged into his high-backed chair. He swiveled
slowly away from Azernal and scanned the Paris
cityscape behind his desk. One of the perks of the presidency was having an office with an unparalleled view of
Earth's famed City of Light. To his right was the
Champs-Elysée and the Arc de Triomphe; just shy of
the center of his three-hundred-degree view was the
Tour Eiffel, which shone against the night sky like iron
fresh from the forge. To his left was the spotlighted,
Gothic majesty of the ancient human temple of Sacre
Coeur. Most of the time his back was turned to it all—
partly to avoid distraction, but also because it made for
a "more presidential" backdrop when he greeted visi-
tors. Beautiful as it all was, none of it assuaged the sour
bile rising in his throat.

"We can't let him challenge the Klingons," Zife said,
turning his chair away from the city to face Azernal
again.

"No, sir, we can't. But I'd caution that we shouldn't
let him extort us into doing his dirty work for him."

"Agreed." Zife tapped his index finger on the desktop.
"Perhaps we could ask Ambassador Lagan to—"

Azernal interrupted with a raised hand and a shake of
his head. "I'm sorry, sir. Our diplomatic team was expelled from Tezwa just over an hour ago."

Zife leaned forward on his left elbow. "Not leaving us

many options, is he?" His left hand closed, almost reflexively, into a white-knuckled fist. "What's his real agenda?"

Azernal folded his hands behind his back and lowered his chin while he considered the question. "It could be a power grab. Or he might be trying to extort us into compensating his people, for putting them in harm's way during the war."

Zife harumphed. "They never saw a single day of the war."

"Regardless, they took a terrible risk—"

"They took a risk?" Zife bellowed. "What about us? If the Klingons find out we violated the Khitomer Accords by building an arsenal on their doorstep—"

"That won't happen, sir."

"If Tezwa attacks the Klingons, it'll be inevitable."

Azernal nodded in reply. "True. Which makes it imperative that we contain the situation at all costs."

Zife massaged his aching brow. "I knew it would haunt us."

"What would, sir?"

Zife glanced guiltily from beneath his hand, his face drooping with remorse and self-loathing.

"The plan. . . . The lies."

Azernal's voice grew sharp and cold. "The plan was sound, Mr. President. And there were no 'lies.' Simply necessary omissions."

"We should have told the Klingons," Zife said.

"At the time we thought they were the enemy," Azernal said. "And in any event, you'd have been telling the Dominion. Sisko and his crew didn't expose the

Changeling infiltrator until three months after we solidified the Tezwa agreement."

"We could have come clean then."

"And fractured the alliance we'd only just barely salvaged. No, Mr. President. I stand by what I told you then: There was no other way. And there still isn't."

Zife sighed heavily. "What's our strategy, then?"

"A show of force." Azernal reached into the folds of his robe and produced a padd. He tapped in a few commands. "The closest ship is the *Enterprise*. She could be in orbit over Tezwa in less than three days."

"One ship," Zife said. "Hardly enough to strike terror into the heart of a man who could blow it to smithereens."

"I think the Klingons could be convinced to lend us a few of their ships," Azernal said. He cocked his head to underscore his sarcasm. "Just to make sure Kinchawn gets the point."

"Martok won't like the idea of *his* fleet toeing the line behind one of *our* ships," Zife said.

"We'll make it worth his while." Azernal placed his hands on the back of a chair in front of Zife's desk. "We can renounce our claim on the Mirka colonies."

Zife raised an eyebrow. *"All* of them?"

The portly Zakdorn shrugged. "We only kept them because the Klingons wanted them. Now's a good time to cash them in."

Zife nodded. "That should buy us some breathing room."

Azernal gave him a reassuring nod. "A few days, at least."

"What if Kinchawn isn't bluffing?" Zife's stomach

gurgled loudly. A sick, queasy feeling in his gut grew stronger. "What if the Klingons provoke him? Those guns'll cut through their shields like—"

"He won't fire, sir," Azernal said. "I have that on the best authority." He tapped a few commands on his padd and handed it to Zife. The president took the data tablet in a shaking hand. He glanced at its display even as Azernal told him what it said. "We'll send Picard with an offer of aid—food, medicine, orders to initiate civic-engineering projects, the usual. That'll show Kinchawn we're not looking for a fight. But the Klingon fleet we send with the *Enterprise* will make it clear we're ready to win one, if that's what he really wants."

Zife put down the padd and nodded slowly. " 'A carrot and a stick,' as the humans say."

"Precisely, sir."

"And what if it's the Klingons who're spoiling for a fight?"

Azernal pursed his lips for a moment. "Picard and his crew will make sure they don't aggravate the situation."

"That's a fairly tall order," Zife said. "Are you sure Picard has the credibility to make it work?"

"I admit, I had my doubts about Picard during the Rashanar incident," Azernal said. "But his record certainly indicates he has a knack for dealing with the Klingons."

"I'm not questioning his record," Zife said. "I'm concerned about his reputation. The Klingons care a great deal about honor. After the Rashanar debacle, are they going to take him seriously?"

Azernal chuckled. "He preemptively destroyed a

threat vessel based on nothing more than the word of a trusted senior officer," he said, his tone a bit too smug for Zife's taste. *"We* might not have approved, but believe me, sir—the Klingons won't have any problem with what he did." Azernal flashed a predatory smirk. "Honestly? He's the perfect man for the job."

Chapter 4
Qo'noS

CHANCELLOR MARTOK'S VOICE rumbled in the dimly lit main chamber of the Klingon High Council. "Has Zife lost his mind?"

Worf—son of Mogh, former Starfleet officer, and the current Federation Ambassador to Qo'noS—stood alone in the musky heat of the newly erected Great Hall, weathering a storm of rancor from the leader of the Klingon Empire. Years ago, during the war against the Dominion, Martok had made Worf a member of his House. However, when Worf spoke here on behalf of the Federation, he knew his status as Martok's kinsman would not earn him preferential treatment. Now, as Martok spewed Klingon obscenities toward the roof, the ceremonial vestments Worf wore when visiting the Great Hall on official business seemed to grow heavy with the burdens of diplomatic probity.

"What does he think we are?" Martok roared from the raised dais on which his chair was mounted. "Mercenaries? Hired thugs? He interferes in the defense of the Empire, then has the gall to ask us to follow one of *his* ships to a parley?"

"Chancellor," Worf said, "the Federation has an equal interest in preserving the peace along our shared border." Bringing his hands to his chest, Worf clutched the inner edges of his bronze stole, which was draped evenly across his shoulders and down the front of his blood-wine-colored Cossack robe. "Our request of an escort for our flagship is not an indictment of the Empire's sovereign interest, but an urgent appeal for the support of our trusted ally."

"Don't insult me, Worf," Martok said, his voice underscored by a low growl of contempt. "Zife wants our ships to be the *Enterprise*'s lackeys." Worf admired the ragged patch of crudely grafted skin over Martok's left eye socket. The chancellor bore the old wound with the pride it deserved. He closed his right eye for a moment. When he opened it again, it burned with contempt. He bared his teeth and grunted. "Worst of all, he tries to bribe us—as if we were Ferengi!"

"The Federation's offer of the Mirka colonies is unrelated to its request," Worf said. He was simply repeating what he'd been told by Koll Azernal, the president's chief of staff. Worf couldn't be sure how much of his diplomatic briefing was actually true, but even he was galled by this transparently callous attempt to buy the Klingons' favor. Unfortunately, he didn't have the luxury of admitting it aloud. He had to relay the message as it had been given. "The current economic crisis in the Federation has made the sustenance of those colonies untenable," he continued. "For that reason, the Federation Council has approved President Zife's petition to remand the colonies to Klingon jurisdiction."

"Does Zife really believe he can buy us so shamelessly?" Martok pounded his fist on the arm of his chair. "Am I supposed to believe the timing of this resolution was a coincidence?"

"Regardless of what you believe," Worf said, "it is done."

"It makes no difference," Martok said. "Tezwa's threats are a matter of record. Its fleet is preparing to launch. The Empire cannot—will not—permit this challenge to go unpunished."

"Their challenge can be withdrawn."

Martok shook his head angrily. "Not good enough. We will not be seen as weak, Worf. . . . I will not be seen as weak." He lowered his voice. "You know as well as I do, this is a dangerous time for the Empire. The war cost us dearly, but the Empire must continue to grow. . . . Mercy is not an option."

"But prudence is." In defiance of protocol, Worf took two steps toward Martok. "The honor of the Empire can be preserved without the risks of war, if you permit Captain Picard to negotiate."

"Why should I put my trust in him?" Martok said. "How do I know he doesn't have an agenda of his own?"

"I served with Captain Picard for many years," Worf said. The words came out a bit more defensive-sounding than he would have liked. "He has always shown the deepest respect for our laws and traditions—and you of all people should know he has proved more than once that he is a true friend to the Klingon people."

Martok let out a contemptuous guffaw. "Why? Because he installed my predecessor? That incompetent narcissist Gowron? That act of friendship nearly led the Empire to its doom."

"Gowron's sins were his own," Worf said. "But if not for Captain Picard, the Empire would be in the hands of traitors."

"If you pledge to me that Picard's a good man, I'll believe you," Martok said. "But his first loyalty is to the Federation. If he's forced to decide between its best interest and ours, whose welfare do you think he'll favor?"

"Captain Picard is an honorable man," Worf said. "He will negotiate fairly, and honestly. And he will not let the Empire be betrayed—not by Tezwa, not even by the Federation. Of this I give you my word—as the Federation's ambassador, as your kinsman . . . as a Klingon."

Martok simmered for a long moment. He glowered with his one eye. Then he got up from his chair, stepped down, and stood in front of Worf. He flashed his jagged, sharp-toothed smile. "Your word was all I needed," he said. "Our fleet will escort the *Enterprise* to Tezwa." He reached out and grasped Worf's forearm. Worf returned the gesture, sealing the agreement. *"Qapla'!"* Martok said.

Worf nodded. He had faith that the crew of the *Enterprise* would defuse the crisis on Tezwa. And considering the situation's incendiary effect on Federation-Klingon politics, he knew he was the best person to help the two allies reconcile their often incompatible foreign policies. But he couldn't deny that he missed the days when he was able to solve problems with actions instead of words. He did not regret becoming a diplomat, but he was still a Klingon; the time he'd spent living on Qo'noS had reawakened the long-dormant fire in his warrior's heart.

And though he couldn't say so, had the decision been his to make, Tezwa would already have been destroyed.

Chapter 5
U.S.S. Enterprise-E

CAPTAIN JEAN-LUC PICARD sat in the quiet haven of his ready room. He sipped his freshly replicated Earl Grey tea while he scrolled through a classified report on Tezwa. The file, along with dozens of others, had been forwarded to him by Starfleet Intelligence. He'd read all the files several times over the past two days, since the *Enterprise* had received its orders to intervene in the Tezwa crisis. The reports were far more detailed than those he usually received on such short notice. Population reports, overviews of Tezwa's industrial output and political processes, and even statistical analyses of its meteorology and economic stability had been included.

What was conspicuously absent, however, was an explanation for why its prime minister, an outspoken nationalist named Kinchawn, believed he could challenge the Klingon Empire. And although the Starfleet Intelligence briefing contained superb technical schematics of Tezwa's recently acquired fleet of two dozen Danteri-manufactured starships, it failed to explain how the Tezwan government had convinced the Danteri to sell them the ships, how it had finagled the Orion Syndicate into acting as a broker, or how it had paid for the ships in the first place.

Equally troubling to Picard was why the Federation was now inserting itself into what was, as far as he could determine, an internal matter of the Klingon Empire. Tezwa was uncomfortably close to the Federation's border, but the Klingons were an ally; he couldn't ascertain why a Klingon military action in neutral space was deemed to be within the Federation's jurisdiction.

Nonetheless, it was not the first time he'd been asked to intervene in a foreign crisis to prevent bloodshed, even if he wasn't necessarily privy to the larger agenda of the Federation Council. His orders were clear: Convince the Tezwans to accept Federation aid rather than antagonize the Klingons by usurping their colony for its natural resources, and get them to make a formal apology to extinguish the Klingons' war lust.

Picard closed the Tezwa file and reclined slightly. He cupped his hands around the warm mug and swiveled his chair to look out the aft-facing window behind his desk. Beyond the window's ghostly reflection of his aquiline visage, the warp-distorted stars stretched away behind the *Enterprise,* which was flanked by half a squadron of Klingon warships of various sizes and classes. Four birds-of-prey were at station between the six larger battle cruisers and fast-attack frigates, all of which remained respectfully—if barely—aft of the Federation flagship.

Normally, he would have been reassured to have this

many Klingon ships at his back. But he knew full well that the crews of those ships were escorting the *Enterprise* only grudgingly. No doubt they were seething over the order from Chancellor Martok, and deeply resentful of the *Enterprise*'s presence. He understood the Klingons well enough to trust them to obey their orders, but he knew that if Tezwan Prime Minister Kinchawn provoked them, the Klingons' reprisal would be swift and terrible.

He also knew enough by now about Klingon fleet operations to be certain that if he saw ten Klingon vessels, there were at least a few more he didn't see, traveling under the protection of their cloaking devices. The Klingons had not specified the number of ships that would escort the *Enterprise* to Tezwa. They had said only that it would be sufficient to "send the correct message."

Picard finished the rest of his tea and walked over to the replicator. As its matter reclamator dissolved and re-absorbed the empty mug, he wondered to himself why he felt so optimistic about being used as a bulwark between the Klingons and a battle. Then, after a moment of introspection, he realized what felt different today: This felt like a mission that mattered.

After several months of being personally pilloried in the court of public opinion, and seeing his ship and crew detailed to a series of ostensibly low-profile assignments, it felt good to finally return to more serious duties. This seemed to Picard like a chance to get back to the way things used to be. It could be a prime opportunity to cleanse the *Enterprise* and its crew of the stigma that had haunted them since Rashanar.

But hopeful as he was, he knew that one successful peace negotiation wouldn't mend all the fences that had recently been broken.

No amount of diplomatic finesse he could wield on Tezwa would convince Admiral Nakamura to allow Data to reinstall his emotion chip; he had blamed the mysterious piece of technology for impairing the android's judgment and instigating the Rashanar crisis.

And even if Picard could coax the Klingons into forgiving the Tezwans for making a hasty threat on their territory, he was unlikely to secure such charitable feelings from Dr. Beverly Crusher. She had seemed colder toward him, in some subtle ways, since the mission to Delta Sigma IV. He wondered if she had resented his trumping of her medical authority on that assignment. It seemed unlikely to him. He had made many such command decisions over the years; none had provoked this kind of reaction from her. He wanted to think that this communication breakdown was all in his imagination, but they had not met for breakfast since the *Enterprise* left Delta Sigma IV, and their conversations had grown strained and awkward.

The bitter irony of his situation pulled the corners of his mouth into a wry grin. To bridge a chasm of loathing between two worlds and peoples would be all in a day's work, but to rebuild the damaged foundation of his decades-long friendship with Beverly seemed maddeningly beyond his abilities. One detail that was feeding his own resentment was that she had yet to confide in him that she had received an offer from Dr. Yerbi Fandau, the head of Starfleet Medical, to take his place when he retired. Picard had learned of the offer from

Dr. Fandau himself, in a standard-protocol written brief. Now he found himself torn between wishing her well, and not wanting her to go.

Perhaps I'm just getting old, he chided himself. After the Rashanar debacle, he had been ordered to undergo a complete competency evaluation. During those tests, more than one person had questioned whether he was still fit for the captain's chair.

The warble of the com broke the silence. *"Riker to Picard. We've just entered communication range, and we're being hailed."*

Picard strode quickly toward the door, which swished open. He stepped onto the bridge, walked directly to his tall faux-leather seat, and sat down. The chair welcomed his lean, toned physique as if it had been made just for him. Riker, seated on Picard's right, looked up from his command console. "Prime Minister Kinchawn is waiting for us to respond."

"Patience, Number One," Picard said. "Let him wait a few moments." Noticing Riker's glance, he added with a bemused grin, "An old trick I learned as a young suitor: The one who makes others wait is the one who's in control."

The command deck of the *Enterprise*-E was relatively quiet. Soft, electronic tones served as an innocuous form of active feedback for the dozen or so officers working at various stations along the bridge's aft bulkhead, just behind the captain's chair. Though the bridge was dimly lit, the glow of active panels was strong enough to illuminate their users' faces. Data's silvery, synthetic skin shone in the light of the ops console, which was located to Picard's left, in front of the wraparound main viewer, which showed stars elongated by the ship's faster-than-light transit.

Next to Data, at the helm, was Lieutenant Kell Perim. Perim was an unjoined Trill woman whose angular features were subtly complemented by two rows of distinctive, oddly shaped beige markings. The spots began above her temples, somewhere beneath her tawny hair, and traced a straight line over the corner of her jaw, down the side of her neck, and under the collar of her uniform.

The turbolift door opened. Counselor Troi stepped out and took her post in the seat to Picard's left, opposite her fiancé. Picard greeted her with a brief nod, then stood and pulled down the front of his uniform jacket, smoothing its random wrinkles. He turned to Christine Vale at tactical. "Open the channel."

Vale punched a command into her panel. The warp-distorted starfield was replaced by a live transmission from the floor of the Tezwan Assembly Forum. Hundreds of Tezwan government representatives were crowded into the ancient-looking meeting hall. They sat in a seven-rowed semicircle, all of them facing the high, multilevel dais located front-and-center before them.

Occupying the topmost level of the dais was Prime Minister Kinchawn. The Tezwan head of state was more than two meters tall and slightly built. His sand-colored crown of plumage contrasted with his dark bronze skin. His charcoal-hued eyes were piercing in their intensity. His mouth was twisted into the least-sincere smile that Picard had seen in more than five decades of diplomatic assignments with Starfleet.

"Captain Picard, on behalf of myself, Deputy Prime Minister Bilok, and the ministers of the Tezwan Assembly, I welcome you and your distinguished Klingon allies to Tezwa."

"Thank you, Prime Minister," Picard said. "On behalf of the United Federation of Planets, I request the honor of a formal parley, in the hope that we might avert an unnecessary conflict."

Kinchawn nodded. *"A most amenable proposition, Captain,"* he said. *"I offer you my assurance of safe passage and invite your vessel and its Klingon escorts to make orbit."* Kinchawn spread his arms in what Picard guessed was a clumsy imitation of the human invitation for an embrace. *"We would be honored if you and an entourage of your choosing would join us here at the Forum to reopen the discussion of diplomatic options."*

"With your permission, Captain Logaar of the *I.K.S. meQ'chal* will join me, on behalf of the Klingon Empire."

"Of course, Captain," Kinchawn said. *"Signal us when you're ready to receive beam-down coordinates for the Assembly Forum."*

Picard cracked a polite smile. "Thank you, Prime Minister. We'll contact you after we make orbit."

"Very good. Kinchawn out." The transmission terminated, and the main viewer reverted to the image of the warp-speed starfield. The point of light that was Tezwa had grown a tiny bit larger and brighter.

Riker and Troi turned toward Picard. "Two days ago he was ready to fight the Klingon Empire," Riker said. "Now he talks like he's backing down. I don't buy it."

"It does seem unlikely," Troi said. "But it's also possible he's not prepared for a war on two fronts."

"What was your impression of him, Counselor?" Picard said.

"Confident," Troi said. "Aggressive."

"Did he seem to be hiding anything? Concealing an agenda?"

"Hard to tell, Captain," she said. "He is, after all, a politician on the brink of war."

"Point taken," Picard said. He rose from his chair. "Number One, you have the conn. Maintain yellow alert and have a security team meet me in transporter room one. Counselor, you're with me."

Chapter 6
Tezwa

AFTERNOON SUNLIGHT SLANTED through the broad, tinted windows of the Assembly Forum. The sunbeams angled down from behind the uppermost tier of seats, just beneath the ceiling dome, and painted the vast room with warm, reddish-orange hues. Commander Deanna Troi wondered whether the late-day Tezwan sun was also the reason the room seemed to be growing warmer, or if her empathic talent was merely responding to the rising emotional temperature in the spacious meeting hall.

The reciprocal hatred that filled the Assembly Forum was so powerful, so undiluted by reason, that Troi perceived it as an almost physical presence. It was like a pair of tidal waves breaking against one another, over and over. However, the animosity wasn't rooted between the Tezwans and the Federation-Klingon diplomatic team that had come to negotiate with them, but rather between two obviously bitter rival factions within the Assembly itself. For Troi, it was like being in the midst of the fractured Council on Delta Sigma IV all over again.

As the ministers bickered in hushed tones behind her, Troi struggled to keep her attention focused on the tall, tiered dais that towered above her. Prime Minister Kinchawn—garbed in flowing purple robes and holding a metal-banded wooden staff topped with a jeweled headpiece—stood atop its uppermost level, a dozen meters above them. On the level below him stood his deputy, Bilok. Both men's tiers had exclusive entrances and gilded railings. On the three tiers below Bilok sat other senior members of the Assembly. Tezwan armed guards were stationed around the periphery of the room, on the top and bottom levels.

As "honored guests," Troi, Picard, and Klingon Captain Logaar had been seated at a long table situated between the tiers of the General Assembly and the dais of the Assembly Leadership. Behind them stood four Starfleet security officers, all of whom were even more tense than usual because Tezwan law had required them to forgo carrying weapons in the Forum.

Troi sat to the right of Picard. On Picard's left was Logaar, who stood and slammed his fist on the polished black stone tabletop. "Lies! Tezwa has no claim to QiV'ol!" The irate Klingon scooped up a sheaf of papers and clenched his fist around them. "This survey report is a fraud!" He threw the crumpled wad on the floor. "You sent no probe there!"

"Typical Klingon arrogance," Kinchawn said. "You ignore evidence, you ignore the law, then dare to stand in our sacred hall and call us liars." The chatter of arguing voices in the Assembly began to grow louder. "Are you the best your chancellor can send? An ill-tempered barbarian?"

"Are you the best your people can do?" Logaar thundered. "A lying simpleton?"

"Gentlemen!" Picard said, his voice hoarse from more than an hour of shouting down the escalating arguments between Logaar and the prime minister. "Personal insults help no one. . . . Prime Minister, the Klingon colony on QiV'ol has been thriving for well over four decades. It's officially recognized by the United Federation of Planets, the Romulan Star Empire, and the Tholian Assembly as a legitimate holding. Despite your allegations of sovereignty over QiV'ol, the fact is you never sent any of your people there. And your claim of having sent an automated probe cannot be verified."

A voice rang out from a high tier behind Troi and Picard. "Because the Klingons destroyed it!" Angry shouts of assent were met by equally clamorous rebuttals. Troi could sense Picard's patience waning. The captain seemed about to dispute the shouted assertion, but he paused as Deputy Prime Minister Bilok stepped forward and leaned over the railing of his tier.

"Captain Picard is right," Bilok said. His voice filled the room. Its echoing rumble dulled the susurrus of the Assembly's debate. "The law is not on our side. QiV'ol is not ours to take."

"Silence, Bilok!" Kinchawn said. "Spare us your treasonous—"

Bilok confronted Kinchawn. "Has truth become treason?" He looked back at the Assembly and pointed upward. "A fleet hovers over our world, poised to strike. Why?" The elder statesman pointed at the now-fuming Kinchawn. "Because he led us to the edge of war!" Bilok turned back to face Kinchawn. "A true leader puts the good of his people ahead of his own ego, Kinchawn. A prime minister worthy of the title knows when to negotiate."

The Forum erupted with furious voices. Troi's temples throbbed with pain as the climate of rage around her swelled. She squeezed her eyes shut and tried to focus on Logaar, Picard, and Kinchawn. High above, the prime minister and his deputy traded vehement insults. Next to her, Logaar and Picard looked around, both equally concerned by the erupting verbal conflict that surrounded them.

The chaotic shouting diminished as Kinchawn repeatedly slammed the base of his staff against his platform.

"Silence! Order!" He repeated himself until the room fell quiet. "Let us put the matter to an open vote." Kinchawn raised his staff and pressed a trigger on its side. A holographic display consisting of two huge, matching symbols—one red, the other blue—appeared in midair between the dais of the Assembly Leadership and the tiers of the General Assembly. "All those in favor of making a formal state apology to the Klingon Empire, vote yes. All opposed, vote no."

A series of changing symbols that Troi surmised was a countdown appeared above the two identical symbols. About a minute later the timer stopped. The two symbols beneath it changed and were no longer identical.

Kinchawn rapped his staff against the dais. "The motion is rejected. There will be no state apology."

Logaar stood up quickly, knocking over his chair. "This insult will be avenged, Kinchawn!" Picard stood and tried to interpose himself between the Klingon and the prime minister.

"Prime Minister, please," Picard said. "Don't force this confrontation. The Federation is prepared—"

"To bribe us," Kinchawn said with a sneer. "With goods and services it wouldn't provide when we were peaceful. What do you call that annoying law of yours? Ah, yes. The Prime Directive. The policy of noninterference. When we needed and wanted your technology, you refused to share it. But put a gun to your head and you offer us everything we ask and more. If you'll do this before blood is shed, what will you offer when we make you sue for peace?"

"Prime Minister!" Bilok said. "Be reasonable! We can't stand against both the Federation *and* the Klingon Empire!"

"You'd rather I surrender, Bilok?" Kinchawn gestured toward Picard, Logaar, and Troi. "Put myself at their mercy?" Kinchawn stiffened his posture imperiously. "Not today. . . . Not ever."

"You *must* issue the state apology," Bilok said. "It's the only way to avert disaster—and you *know* it."

"What I *know*, Bilok, is that I don't take orders from you."

Troi, sensing an imminent disaster, gripped Picard's arm. Her voice was a frightened whisper. "Captain," she said, "we have to get—" Another sharp crack of Kinchawn's staff cut her off.

"Seize them!" Kinchawn said. Armed Tezwan guards moved in from all directions, their long, slender limbs propelling them in large, swift strides. The four Starfleet security officers immediately closed ranks and assumed defensive postures around Picard, Troi, and Logaar.

"Stand down!" Picard ordered. "Don't resist." The captain reached up to tap his combadge, but stopped as a Tezwan guard with gleaming black plumage aimed a compact-looking rifle at him. The Starfleet security team reluctantly allowed the Tezwan guards to restrain their hands with magnetic manacles.

"After all your decades in the Assembly," Kinchawn said to Bilok, "how ironic that it now falls to me to show you what it means to lead." Kinchawn leveled his staff at Troi and the others. "Take them to the detention—"

"You can't declare war without a vote of the Assembly!" Bilok interrupted. "This is illegal! I demand—"

"Silence! Don't test me, Bilok! I control the majority vote, and if I say we're at war, *we're at war!*"

Troi felt Logaar's surging fury as a Tezwan guard reached to snap a pair of magnetic manacles onto the Klingon's wrists. Just before the manacles closed, Logaar turned and struck the guard in the chest with his palm. The guard's sternum and ribs broke with a sickening crack, and the tall, long-limbed Tezwan was hurled several meters through the air. The planet's slightly lighter-than-Earth gravity clearly had made the Tezwans' bones less resilient than those of other humanoids, and afforded the Klingon a distinct advantage in hand-to-hand combat.

Which, Troi understood full well, was why three other Tezwan guards, who had been standing out of melee range, opened fire on Logaar and vaporized him. Not a single mote of dust remained to sully the floor of the Assembly Forum as his glowing silhouette faded and vanished. The Tezwan guard-in-charge gestured with his rifle at the Starfleet personnel. "Toss your combadges to me."

Troi and the security personnel all waited until Picard removed his combadge, then did likewise. Troi triple-tapped the back of her combadge to deactivate it—and, more important, to activate the hidden backup subspace transceiver concealed in the heel of her shoe. The precaution that she had called "paranoid" when Riker insisted upon it an hour ago now seemed prescient. She lobbed the metallic arrowhead-shaped combadge to the guard. As he collected them, the six officers were manacled and grouped together. Above them, Kinchawn chortled with satisfaction.

"Take them to the detention center," he said. Troi winced as a guard's rifle poked her between her shoulder blades, prompting her forward. She walked toward the exit.

As she neared the door, Kinchawn's voice echoed from atop the Assembly Forum. "Ministers of the Assembly," he declared, "prepare to behold the beginning of a new chapter in our history, as I demonstrate the true power now at our command." Troi glanced sideways at Picard, whose stoic expression concealed the seething anger evoked by the prime minister's next words: "Watch with me now, as we destroy the enemy fleet in orbit above our world."

Chapter 7
U.S.S. Enterprise-E

RIKER LOOKED AWAY from the image of Tezwa on the main viewer and activated his tactical console to study the Klingon fleet's movements. As soon as the negotiating team had beamed down, the ten Klingon ships had gradually dispersed. Six were now positioned at roughly equal intervals around the equator of the planet, while the other four had split off into two pairs, one above each planetary pole. He could only speculate about the location of the cloaked vessels that he assumed must be reconnoitering from high orbit. The formation might look innocuous to an untrained observer, but Riker knew the Tezwans would recognize its purpose as clearly as he did. The Klingon fleet had deployed to optimize its surface attack.

Data responded to a chirp from his ops console. "Commander, we just lost the away team's com signals," he said as he keyed in new commands. "I am scanning for their backup transceivers."

Lieutenant Vale tensed as she responded to an alert on

her tactical console. "Sir, the Tezwans just activated an energy shield over the capital."

"Red alert," Riker said. "Tell the Klingon fleet—"

"Incoming!" Vale said, cutting him off.

"Shields!" Riker said. "Helm, evasive!"

The shallow curve of the planet on the main viewer rolled erratically between vertical and horizontal as Perim increased the ship's speed and initiated defensive maneuvers. Riker watched the first volley of bluish white energy bolts race upward from the planet surface toward the orbiting fleet. One of the large Klingon battle cruisers, unable to raise its shields in time, exploded instantly. The other cruisers and all four visible birds-of-prey were hit as a shot struck the *Enterprise*.

The blast force lifted several personnel into the air and tossed them forward toward the main viewer. The overhead lights blinked out as the main viewscreen flared white with painfully bright static. Caught in its disrupted flicker, the bodies seemed to tumble back to the deck in jerky slow motion. Sparks and smoke spewed from several overloaded consoles.

Riker coughed and waved a veil of acrid smoke from his eyes. "Damage report!" In the hazy half-light of the wounded bridge he saw Vale and Perim clinging to their consoles.

"Shields are down," Vale said. "Torpedoes are offline."

"Helm damaged but functional," Perim said.

Riker coughed. "Vale, how are the Klingons doing?"

"Not good," Vale said. "The birds-of-prey are gone. The cruisers are firing at the planet."

Riker immediately pictured Captain Picard and Deanna

in the Tezwan capital, on the receiving end of a Klingon torpedo barrage. Then he made an educated guess about what another hit from Tezwa's planet-based artillery would do to the *Enterprise.*

"Helm," he said. "Set a course for the Tezwan capital. We're going under their shield to get the captain."

"Aye, sir," Perim said as she plotted the course and began the rapid dive toward the planet. "ETA, twenty-one seconds."

Data keyed in more commands at his station. "Rerouting shield power to navigational deflectors to protect the hull."

Vale tapped targeting orders into her console. "Standing by to neutralize the capital's interceptor drones."

"Good work," Riker said. "Riker to transporter room."

"Go ahead, sir," Transporter Chief T'Bonz answered.

"Start scanning for the away team's backup signals. Energize as soon as you have a lock."

"Acknowledged. Transporter room out."

Riker watched the details of the planet's surface sharpen on the still-staticky main viewer. *Here's where the fun begins,* he mused cynically. As the *Enterprise* leveled out from its steep descent, he saw countless telltale flares of Klingon torpedo detonations beyond the horizon, on the nightside of Tezwa. Directly ahead and growing larger by the second was Keelee-Kee, the planet's capital. Between the *Enterprise* and the city was a cluster of small, fast moving attack drones racing toward them.

"Helm, all ahead full," Riker said.

"Slipping under the city-shield in five seconds," Perim said as the twelve drones grew larger on the main viewer.

"Interceptors are locking weapons," Vale said.

"Fire at will," Riker ordered.

Phaser beams from the *Enterprise* lashed out at the uncrewed attack ships, which crisscrossed to evade the starship's preemptive volley. Two were sliced in half by the phaser attack, while the others swarmed around the large, *Sovereign*-class starship. A shuddering boom of impact resounded through the deck as muffled explosions peppered the outer hull.

"Report!" Riker said.

"A drone rammed our torpedo launcher," Vale said. "Damage and casualties in engineering, decks twelve and thirteen."

"We're under the shield," Perim said. On the viewscreen, the cityscape rolled like a kaleidoscope of metal, stone, and glass as she piloted the ship sideways on its center axis over the city's main boulevard. Riker was used to watching stars spin on the viewer, but this spectacle was vertigo-inducing.

"Riker to transporter room. Let me know the second you've got them."

"Still scanning, sir." Another explosion shook the ship. Half a second later came the screech of the ship's phasers being discharged in an atmosphere.

"Watch your targets, Lieutenant," Riker said. "These are civilians down here."

"I'm aware, sir," Vale said. Riker smiled grimly at Vale's implicit rebuke.

"Riker to engineering."

The chief engineer's voice crackled over the com. *"La Forge here."*

"Geordi, get ready to give me warp power," Riker said.

"Ready when you are, Commander," La Forge said.

An exploding com panel to Riker's left sent sparks and flames dancing across the bridge. Smoke stung his eyes as tongues of fire licked at his fingers.

"Transporter room to bridge. Energizing now."

"Acknowledged," Riker said. A security officer extinguished the fire at the first officer's feet, then moved to squelch the blaze inside the ruined com panel. Another round of detonations rattled the ship. "Helm, initiate a point-nine-eight warp field and head for orbit, best possible speed."

"Aye, sir," Perim said. "Hang on to something, folks," she added, to no one in particular.

"All hands," Vale broadcast over the ship's com. "Brace for impact." Riker clutched the arms of the captain's chair as the ship angled skyward and accelerated away from the city. The ship lurched and quaked as it punched through the city's defensive screen. As Riker had hoped, the *Enterprise*'s near-warp subspace field had enabled it to pierce the capital's shield and make a direct ascent to orbit, rather than spend precious seconds trying to maneuver clear of the energy barrier. Now all that remained was to escape the planet's gravity and evade its lethal artillery long enough to go to warp speed.

The cinnamon-colored sky thinned and faded to reveal the star-speckled curtain of space. Several smoldering clusters of wreckage drifted derelict in low orbit. Only one Klingon vessel, a cruiser, was still even partially intact. Riker concluded it had been part of the Klingons' cloaked detachment. Its hull was riddled with damage, and it was venting charged plasma from its ruptured warp nacelles. Its maneuvering engines were dark.

"Data," Riker said. "Get a—"

"Tractor beam locked," Data said.

"Warp field extended," Perim said.

"Incoming!" Vale said.

"Get us out of here."

"Aye, sir," Perim said as she engaged the warp drive, catapulting the *Enterprise* and the towed Klingon cruiser beyond the reach of Tezwa's artillery.

Chapter 8
Tezwa

As Kinchawn's declaration of war was belatedly approved by a narrow vote split precisely along partisan lines, Bilok could barely contain his anger. He had always known Kinchawn was a rabid nationalist, but until this moment he hadn't realized how radical and dangerous the man truly was. How many Klingon lives had Kinchawn just snuffed out on those ships? Five thousand? More? How many hundreds of thousands of civilians had just perished in the Klingon counterstrike? Contemplating the scope of the atrocity he'd just witnessed made Bilok ill.

"You imbecile," he said to Kinchawn. Bilok tried to keep his voice down, tried to mask his rage, but even a whisper would have been audible in the stunned silence of the Assembly Forum. "You've no idea what you've just done."

The prime minister dismissed him with a haughty wave of his slender hand. "Spare me your alarmist pessimism," he said. "I've guaranteed our independence with this victory."

"Victory?" Bilok said, his bitterness unconcealed. "The Klingons annihilated our defense forces!" He pointed to several blinking points on the holographic tactical display hovering over the Assembly. "Our bases, our starports—gone! It'll take us weeks to count all our dead." He lifted his arms in frustration. "This is your definition of victory?"

"All irrelevant," Kinchawn said. "Our fleet is intact, its crews are safe, our capital is undamaged—and our new network of defensive artillery has made us unassailable from space."

"Wrong," Bilok said. "They'll make an invasion costly, but they didn't stop the *Enterprise* from buzzing our capital. And they certainly won't stop the Klingons from landing an army."

"Don't be absurd," Kinchawn said. "Even if they send twenty ships, we can pulverize them within minutes. Their troops would never reach the surface."

Bilok couldn't suppress an angry chortle. "What makes you think they'll send only twenty ships?" he said. He turned to face the Assembly. "They will commit as many ships, sacrifice as many troops as are necessary, to crush us for this."

Several members of Kinchawn's *elininae*-dominated *Lacaam* Coalition jeered Bilok. "Coward," one recently elected minister shouted. "Leave the wars to us, grayfeather," another slightly more experienced *Lacaam'i* heckled. Bilok knew better than to expect verbal support from his own *trinae*-controlled *Gatni* Party, which for several years now had been harshly cowed by the almost irrational aggression of the *Lacaam'i* plurality.

He glowered back up at Kinchawn, who gloated over his faction's unrepentant, if narrowly held, dominance of the Assembly. "If you don't think the Klingons will retaliate," Bilok said, "then you don't understand them at all."

"I think we understand the Klingons better than you do," Kinchawn said, sweeping his arm toward the bloc of *Lacaam'i* ministers on his left. "We know they respect strength."

"Wrong again," Bilok said, his voice dark with anger. "You've confused your values with theirs. They don't respect *strength,* they respect *honor.* And I guarantee you they'll consider your sneak attack on their fleet to be both dishonorable and cowardly."

"You should choose your words with care, Bilok," Kinchawn said, his tone laced with menace. "You wouldn't want to invite charges of treason during a time of war." Kinchawn rapped the bottom of his staff on his dais. The sharp noise hurt Bilok's ears. "Minister Xelas, keep the artillery on full alert. Order all starship personnel to report for duty, and deploy the fleet to repel any Klingon or Federation counterstrike." Kinchawn struck his staff twice more in quick succession. "This session of the Assembly is now closed. All ministers are to remain in the capital until further notice. *Aleem no'cha.*" Ending the session with the quasi-religious benediction was a *Lacaam'i* affectation that had rankled Bilok since its first utterance.

The *Lacaam'i* ministers returned the traditional response of *Aleem neel'ko* and shuffled out of the chamber. Kinchawn turned and stepped toward his private portal, which slid open without a sound and closed behind him after he stepped through.

Bilok remained motionless on the second dais, staring down into the Assembly Forum. A trio of *Gatni*-aligned senior ministers looked up and met his gaze. With a curt tilt of his head, he summoned them to reconvene in his office.

Several minutes later, Bilok waited on his private balcony and watched the sun set. The horizon was aglow with the fires of far-off devastation wrought by the Klingons. He heard the three *Gatni* ministers enter his office behind him. He turned and greeted them. "Thank you for coming," he said. It was an empty pleasantry; Bilok was the head of the *Gatni* Party, so they had little choice but to comply with his invitation.

"Of course, Deputy Prime Minister," said Elazol, the most senior of the three, and Bilok's oldest friend in the Assembly. Before Kinchawn had assumed power seven years ago, Elazol had been the minister of intelligence. Now, at Kinchawn's behest, he supervised the largely ineffectual Ministry of Agriculture.

Accompanying him were Neelo and Dasana, the ministers of trade and education, respectively. Like Elazol, they had been removed from more prestigious posts during Kinchawn's wholly unprecedented reorganization of the government, during which he had placed members of his *Lacaam* Coalition into all the most influential military, economic, and diplomatic offices. Neelo had been coerced into resigning her office as minister of the army, and Dasana had been ousted without explanation or apology after she had served as Tezwa's foreign minister for more than eight years. To say that the three veteran politicians remained bitter over the blatantly political usurpation of their offices would have been a gross understatement.

"Please join me on the balcony," Bilok said. Neelo and Dasana followed Elazol onto the open-air terrace that overlooked much of the capital city. The skyline was abuzz with hovercraft traffic. "Close the door," Bilok said. Dasana slid the transparent portal shut. Bilok rested his weight on the sturdy metal railing. "We need a plan of action right now," he said.

"We don't have enough votes to push him out," Dasana said.

"What about a coup?" Bilok said to Neelo. "Do you have any pull left with the officer corps?"

"Not really," Neelo said. "He demoted or cashiered almost every *trinae* officer."

Bilok looked at Elazol. "Covert options?"

"Pointless," Elazol said. "The *Lacaam'i* would just elect another of their own, probably Ilokar. He'd have us at war with the rest of the quadrant within an hour of his inauguration."

Bilok let out a heavy sigh. He had hoped that this crisis might be handled internally, that there might be some means of averting a war without compromising Tezwa's sovereignty. But as the inevitably brutal Klingon reprisal drew closer, he knew his only hope for saving his people was to enlist the Federation's aid in deposing Kinchawn—even if it meant surrendering Tezwa indefinitely to foreign control.

He dreaded asking Koll Azernal for help. The irascible

Zakdorn was certain to excoriate him for misjudging Kinchawn's resolve. Had the *Enterprise* not escaped the prime minister's ambush, Bilok wouldn't dare ask the Federation for anything. If the Starfleet ship had been destroyed, he and many of his allies in the Assembly would, in all likelihood, be engaged in a desperate search for clandestine transport off-world. Of course, if Azernal refused his request for help, flight was an option he was still willing to consider.

The three ministers awaited his decision. "I'm going to explore one last option," he said finally. "If it's to succeed, all of our *trinae* allies need to stand ready for my order."

"To do what?" Dasana asked in a nervous voice that implied she already knew the answer.

Bilok's browfeathers furrowed as he suggested the unspeakable: "To take back the Assembly by force."

Chapter 9
I.K.S. Taj

RIKER LED THE STARFLEET search-and-rescue team through the narrow passages of the crippled battle cruiser *I.K.S. Taj*. So far he'd seen five decks of tragically repetitive carnage and wreckage, including several compartments of dead Klingon ground troops. The lightless corridors were thick with smoke from plasma fires that had just been extinguished. The air was tinged with the stomach-turning odor of death. Through the soles of his boots he felt the squelched fires' residual heat radiating from the deck. He stepped carefully over another charred corpse and aimed the beam from his palm beacon ahead of him.

The intersection in front of him was strewn with Klingon bodies. He stopped and scanned them with his tricorder, but, as he feared, there were no life signs. Stepping closer, he saw the damage the fire had wrought to their bodies, their hair gone, their flesh reduced to brittle paper-white husks. He noted the engineering equipment still clutched in their hands, and realized they had probably been working to repair the fire-suppression system when they had been killed.

He looked back and shielded his eyes from the glare of Lieutenant Jim Peart's palm beacon. Peart was one of the few recent transfers to the *Enterprise* whose service record hadn't been marred by bad reviews or questionable evaluations. In fact, the wiry-but-tough young officer had quickly earned the trust of Security Chief Vale. On her recommendation, Riker had promoted him to deputy chief of security.

"Peart, take a team down to engineering," Riker said. "I'll check out the bridge with Heaton and Davila."

"Aye, sir," Peart said, then turned on his heel and swept his light across the rest of the search party. "Kuchuk, Cruzen, continue searching this deck," he said. "Tomoko, Goodnough, you're with me." The two fresh-faced female engineers followed Peart down the intersection toward the aft emergency hatch to the engine room.

Riker motioned to Heaton and Davila, who stayed close behind him, tricorders out and searching for survivors. Riker relied on his memory of the standard *K'Vort*-class cruiser interior layout as he worked his way toward the forward ladder. During his second year aboard the *Enterprise,* he'd participated briefly in the Klingon-Federation Officer Exchange Program. He had served as Captain Kargan's executive officer on the *K'Vort*-class *I.K.S. Pagh,* an experience that taught him as much about the Klingons' thinking as it did about their cuisine. One lesson he had vowed never to forget was that although *gagh* is eaten live, it is not swallowed live. The point is to kill the feisty worms between one's teeth and savor their salty blood as a delicacy. To ingest live *gagh* is to intentionally give oneself an intestinal parasite—a fact he'd learned only a week after his return to the *Enterprise,* when Dr. Pulaski diagnosed his stomach cramps as an unexpected souvenir of his tour of duty on the *Pagh.* Only in hindsight did he realize that was the reason his Klingon shipmates had laughed as they'd watched him unwittingly make a fool of himself swallowing a bowl of the live worms.

He'd had few opportunities to visit Klingon vessels since then, but every time he stepped aboard one of their ships he could still taste the bitter skin of the *gagh* and remember his revulsion as the worms wriggled down his throat. Today was no different. Despite its scouring by fire, the interior of the cruiser was as pungent as Riker expected it to be.

He climbed the access ladder to the command deck. Heaton and Davila kept pace behind him. The sound of their boots on the metal ladder rungs reverberated off the unadorned duranium bulkheads. Riker pulled himself over the top, then helped Heaton by holding her tool kit while she got back to her feet. While waiting for Davila to join them, he tried opening the door. It was jammed.

"Give me a hand," Riker said to Davila as the security guard cleared the ladder tube. Davila stepped over next to Riker and grabbed the right-side door. Riker wedged his fingers into the narrow crack between the doors and planted his foot to pull the left door open. "Pull," he said. The door's rough metal edges cut into Riker's fingers as he strained against it. His triceps burned from the effort. After a few seconds of wondering whether he'd have to phaser the door open, he heard the scrape of metal on metal as the door slid open.

The bridge was a tomb. The pilot and the weapons officers were slumped over their consoles. A gray-haired warrior lay on the deck in front of the aft disruptor controls. The captain listed to the left in her chair, her arm dangling so low that her talonlike fingernails scraped the metal deck grating. Only one red bridge light, the one directly above her seat, was still lit. The rest of the bridge was illuminated by the overlapping beams from the search party's palm lights.

Heaton gestured with her tricorder toward the Klingon captain. "She's alive." She rechecked her readings. "Barely."

Riker walked over to the dying Klingon woman. As he stepped in front of her, he realized that he knew her. Her name was Vekma. Fourteen years ago, she had been a junior officer aboard the *Pagh* during his brief tour of duty; now she was a captain. He added her name to the growing list of his former shipmates who had preceded him to a captaincy. "Captain Vekma," he said. "Can you hear me?"

She opened one eye. The capillaries around her pupil had hemorrhaged, turning the white of her eye blood-magenta. She struggled to focus. She coughed out half a mouthful of blood, which mingled with a column of saliva that dangled from her chin. After a moment he saw her look of recognition.

"Riker," she said in a rasping voice. He nodded. "Captain Logaar?" she said, asking about her fleet commander's fate.

He decided the less he said about the slain Klingon fleet captain, the better. He shook his head. "He didn't make it."

"Betrayed," she said, then groaned with pain.

"Yes," he said. "We don't know why they fired."

"Not them," she said, struggling to force out the words. "Picard. Denied me . . . death in battle. Cheated me."

Riker felt his face go hot with shame. It would have been easier to let her blame Picard, but he felt compelled to confess the truth. "It wasn't Picard," he said. "I towed your ship out of orbit."

"PetaQ!" she cried, hurling the Klingon expletive at Riker like a *d'k tahg.* "Robbed me of *Sto-Vo-Kor!"* Her dangling hand shot up and clutched his throat. On the edge of his vision he saw Davila reach for his phaser. He waved the security officer back as Vekma tightened her grip. "Damn you," she said. "A curse on your House!" She labored to draw one last lungful of air, then spit at him. He winced as the spittle struck his face. Her final breath gurgled out of her, and she went limp. Her hand relaxed its grip and fell away from his throat. He massaged his bruised neck muscles and gasped for air.

His combadge chirped as he stood and sleeved the sputum from his face. *"Peart to Riker,"* the deputy chief of security said over the com. *"All dead in engineering, sir."*

"Acknowledged. Riker out." He looked around the bridge and felt ashamed. He of all people should have known better than to deprive a Klingon ship and crew of a glorious end in combat. But in the heightened stress of the moment, he'd exercised his Starfleet training, obeyed the carefully nurtured instinct to pull an allied ship out of danger. He knew that if the Klingon fleet learned that the *Taj* had been treated this way, it would bring dishonor not only to Vekma, but to all those members of her crew who had died in battle over Tezwa. But now the deed was done; the *Taj* had been rescued, and its disgrace was now all but ensured.

Riker resigned himself to living with the knowledge that he'd probably just forfeited the honor of hundreds of valiant Klingon warriors. He tapped his combadge. "Riker to *Enterprise*," he said. "We've finished our sweep of the *Taj*." The bitter news stuck in his throat: "No survivors."

Chapter 10
U.S.S. Enterprise-E

THE PARADE OF WOUNDED had been nonstop since Troi had arrived in sickbay. Normally, her purview was the healing of emotional wounds and psychological trauma, not the mending of flesh. But in a dire crisis, she had enough emergency medical training to be called upon for help with triage.

She pressed her palm against a woman's open abdominal wound. The Vulcan engineer's copper-based green blood was warm and sticky. She had been impaled by a bulkhead fragment that had been turned into flying shrapnel by a ruptured electroplasma conduit. "I need some help here," Troi said, raising her voice to be heard above the anguished groans of the wounded. Sighing, Dr. Tropp stepped over to Troi. He removed the jagged chunk of metal from the Vulcan's torso, sprayed a temporary bandage over the gash, then abruptly left Troi to assess other patients, who waited, with varying degrees of equanimity, in the corridor.

Sickbay was packed from wall to wall. Every bed was filled with victims of the Tezwans' surprise artillery attack and casualties of Riker's rescue of her and the captain. There were cuts, burns, blunt-force traumas, broken bones. At times like this she was grateful for the rigorous training that Starfleet demanded of all its personnel, officers and enlisted crew alike. A less disciplined group of people might succumb to panic or paralyzing fear in such a crisis. Most of the *Enterprise* crew remained relatively calm; even the injured were, for the most part, able to control their emotional responses.

Sometimes, of course, there were exceptions. Part of Troi's value to a triage team was her ability to ferret out emotionally disturbed patients before they endangered themselves or others. If not for the remarkable self-control of the majority of the patients, she wouldn't have risked using her empathic senses so freely in a combat-triage center. Thankfully, she hadn't had any reason to sedate or restrain any patients today.

She credited much of the crew's stoicism to their having been tempered by bitter experience during the Dominion War. But seeing how matter-of-factly the crew responded to violence and injury worried her for different reasons. Had the crew become too jaded? In their effort to defend themselves from emotional trauma, had they suppressed their emotions to the point where they might lack empathy for the pain of others? Such pathologies might not be diagnosable until years after the war's end, but Troi was certain they would manifest eventually.

The only member of the crew about whom she was

genuinely worried was herself. From being marched at gunpoint out of the rage-poisoned Tezwan Assembly to standing on a blood-slicked floor crowded with burned and broken shipmates, the past few hours had inflicted a relentless emotional assault on her already troubled mind. She wanted to withdraw, even if for just a short while, to restore her equilibrium—but she knew that her quarters would offer little solace once Riker returned.

Though he could suppress the bitter turmoil that churned in his subconscious mind, she found his agony impossible to ignore. His anger and despair over the murder of his father haunted her even more acutely than it plagued him. Troi didn't want to add guilt to her fiancé's anguish by telling him that, to her, he was a living grief transmitter. So she kept her feelings hidden from the one person to whom she wished she could turn for comfort, in the hope that he could heal his heart soon enough to help her soothe her own.

The com chirped. *"Picard to Dr. Crusher."*

The red-haired chief medical officer looked up from her medical tricorder. "Crusher here."

"Commander Riker informs me there are no survivors aboard the Taj," Picard said. *"Do you have a casualty report yet?"*

"We've confirmed three dead in engineering," Crusher said. "We're looking at more than a hundred fifty wounded. I'll have a final list to Commander Riker within the hour."

"Understood. Picard out."

Crusher issued a list of medical instructions to a team of nurses and medical residents who followed close behind her, then stepped aside and placed a hand on Troi's arm. "Are you all right?" she said. "You look a little shell-shocked."

"I'm fine," Troi lied.

"We have everything under control," Crusher said. "Why don't you go get some rest?" Troi started to protest, but her best friend gave her a gentle push toward the door. "Go, we'll call if we need you." Before she could say no, Troi found herself standing in the corridor.

She looked back into sickbay at the crowd of patients, the surgical-emergency cases and the walking wounded, and wished there were more she could do to help them. But as the door closed, she knew that her role in their recoveries would begin tomorrow, when it would fall to her to heal the wounds that lay beyond the reach of the scalpel and the hypospray.

Chapter 11
Earth

AZERNAL WAS OF THE OPINION that Martok always looked angry, even when he was in a good mood. Tonight, however, the Klingon chancellor was the epitome of rage. He had roused Azernal and President Zife in the wee hours of the Paris morning to verbally eviscerate them from across the light-years, on a secure subspace channel. Azernal reduced the volume on his monitor, which showed Martok and Zife on opposite sides. Martok was glowing with fury under the red-tinted lights in the High Council chamber on Qo'noS, while Zife's blue face looked ghostly pale in the sterile glow of his own monitor.

"Six thousand warriors!" Martok said. *"Murdered in cold blood! I supported your mission for peace. Now it's your turn to stand with us—and help us take revenge!"*

Azernal was still reviewing the details of the tragedy. Reports were only now being relayed from the *Enterprise* back to Starfleet Command, which was maintaining an open and secure data channel to the president's office. He concluded, to his horror, that Bilok had seriously misjudged Prime Minister Kinchawn. The wily Zakdorn silently berated himself for not having trusted his first instincts; he had suspected from the outset that Kinchawn was dangerous, unstable, unreliable. Then he saw the casualty reports. Martok wasn't exaggerating. Azernal's jaw fell open as he saw that this one political misjudgment had metastasized into a fatal catastrophe for thousands of Klingon soldiers.

Zife, who sounded only semicoherent, spoke before Azernal could suggest any talking points with which to placate Martok. *"Revenge isn't really a policy the Federation supports,"* Zife blathered. As Azernal expected, the offhand remark further incensed the Klingon ex-general.

"My soldiers died escorting your flagship, and I will avenge them, with or without you!" Martok's tone changed from a roar to a growl. *"And I'll remember this the next time I'm asked to risk Klingon blood for the Federation."*

During Martok's furious harangue, Azernal transmitted a private text message to Zife. The president glanced at the message, then looked back at Martok. *"If the Klingon Empire chooses to retaliate against Tezwa, the Federation cannot participate. The Eminiar Amendment of our charter prohibits us from engaging in the wholesale destruction of worlds, even during wartime."*

"I don't want to destroy them," Martok said. *"I plan to conquer them! To plant my flag and make those* yItaghpu' *kneel before the Empire!"*

Azernal was relieved that, for once, Zife had phrased a statement exactly as he had written it for him. By provoking Martok into a denial, he'd gained a clearer picture of the Klingons' strategy. Unfortunately, Azernal realized Martok's plan would be a tragedy for the Klingons.

If Martok insisted on invading Tezwa no matter the cost, the end result would be massive casualties and the loss of so many ships that the Klingon Empire would be left all but defenseless in the Archanis sector.

The Federation, itself stretched too far in the wake of the Dominion War, would be unable to prop up a Klingon Empire so gravely weakened. Equally serious, a crippled Klingon Empire would be an ineffectual ally against such aggressive potential foes as the Romulan Star Empire, the Tholian Assembly, a regrouped Dominion, or the Borg.

Azernal, for his own part, had another reason to view Martok's response as the worst possible outcome. Had the Klingons chosen to vaporize Tezwa from space, Azernal would have genuinely lamented the appalling slaughter of innocents, but he also would have been relieved; such an assault would eradicate any evidence that the Federation had designed and manufactured the artillery that just butchered thousands of Klingon soldiers.

Instead, Martok had opted to launch a costly invasion and long-term occupation that would subjugate the planet under the trefoil aegis of the Klingon Empire—an outcome certain to expose the Federation's role in causing the conflict.

The moment the Klingons learned that their ally the United Federation of Planets had recruited and cultivated this bloodthirsty juggernaut on their border, it wouldn't matter that Zife and Azernal's intentions had been good. Tezwa had been designed as a deadly trap, into which a desperate and retreating Starfleet could have led a Dominion attack fleet to its doom. But that wasn't what the Klingons would see.

All they would see is a world without honor that massacred the pride of the Klingon fleet. And next to it they would see the so-called ally that gave Tezwa's treacherous *petaQpu* the weapons with which to commit these rash and bloody deeds.

Azernal keyed another text message to Zife, who scanned it quickly before answering Martok. *"Chancellor,"* Zife said, *"there may yet be diplomatic alternatives that we could—"*

"Diplomacy! They nearly destroyed your flagship! And all you want to do is talk?"

"If we can resolve this without further bloodshed," Zife said, *"we might—"*

"No," Martok said. *"This is a dangerous time for the Empire. We cannot be seen as weak."* Azernal knew what Martok really meant: that his position as chancellor was politically vulnerable, and that *he* could not afford to be seen as weak.

Azernal transmitted a trio of text messages to Zife, who looked flustered by the speed with which he was being inundated by information. Azernal reminded himself to be patient, that the president wasn't quite as quick to absorb new facts and ideas as he himself was—but then, few humanoid species were capable of operating on the same mental level as the Zakdorn.

"Chancellor," Zife said as soon as he caught up with Azernal's sub-rosa suggestions, *"if we're to aid you, it will take at least three days for our nearest five ships to*

reach Tezwa. Delay your attack until we can regroup and join you."

"Unacceptable," Martok said. *"Tezwa is preparing to launch its fleet. Better to attack while they're still in spacedock, before they can threaten our colonies."*

Azernal was running out of options for Zife to propose. He tried one last idea. *"Give us thirty-six hours,"* Zife said. *"By then, the* Enterprise *will be able to give you an analysis of Tezwa's weapons and defensive systems, to guide your attack."*

"We'll accept the Enterprise*'s report,"* Martok said. Then he quickly added: *"If it's ready in precisely four hours. Because that's when our invasion begins."* His proclamation was met by several seconds of shocked silence. *"If you have nothing more to add, Mr. President . . . ?"*

Azernal signaled Zife that he did not. Zife shook his head. *"No, Chancellor,"* Zife said. "Qapla', *Martok, son of Urthog."*

Martok grimaced, seemingly pained by the sound of a Klingon valediction issuing from the mouth of a spindly Bolian. *"Martok out."* The channel from Qo'noS closed. Zife and Azernal sat alone in their respective chateaus, quiet in the deepest hours of the night, staring at one another on their computer monitors.

Several agonized seconds passed without comment.

The harsh monitor-light deepened the dark half-circles beneath Zife's tired gray eyes. *"Best authority?"* he said.

The remark caught Azernal off-guard. "Sir?"

"You told me that you had it 'on the best authority' that Kinchawn wouldn't fire."

Azernal swallowed, then coughed a few times—not because he was nervous but to buy time to formulate an answer. He considered how reliable Bilok had been in the past, then ran through scenarios that might account for this sudden reversal of fortune. He quickly settled on the most likely answer. "I now think that the line of communication to my source on Tezwa was compromised, most likely within the last three weeks."

"That's as good an explanation as any," Zife said. *"But it doesn't benefit the thousands of Klingons or countless numbers of Tezwans who were killed today."*

"No, Mr. President, it doesn't. I'm sorry."

"We need to move on this, Koll. In four hours the Klingons will march into a disaster of epic proportions. In addition to my concern for their *potential losses, I'm worried that they'll inflict millions of civilian casualties."*

"Actually, sir," Azernal said with caution, "I estimate civilian casualties will be roughly forty-three percent of the total population—approximately two-point-one billion people."

Zife stared at him in shock for a moment, then closed his eyes, let out a pained sigh, and planted his face in his hands. When he looked up again at Azernal, his look was one of dread. *"And when they secure the artillery installations . . . ?"*

"They'll link them to us within a matter of hours. A few days from now, we'll be at war with the Klingon Empire."

Zife snorted. *"I suppose you have a wargame scenario for that, as well."*

"Yes, sir." He paused and wondered whether Zife really wanted to hear it. Then he decided that the president *had* to hear it. "The Federation suffers more than ninety billion civilian casualties. The Klingon Empire limits its civilian casualties to just under forty billion. The imperial armada defeats Starfleet in just under a year, but its own losses are near-total. The Federation fragments into unaligned systems. The Tholians conquer the Klingon Empire within four years, while the Romulan Star Empire annexes up to seventy-eight percent of former Federation worlds within a decade."

"Bolarus?" Zife said, his thoughts clearly turning homeward.

"More than likely it's destroyed by the Klingons. If it survives, the Tholians move to block the Romulans from seizing it. . . . They fail." Zife seemed to retreat into himself, sinking into his worst nightmare of a galactic doomsday scenario. Azernal snapped him back to the present. "Mr. President, we can't let the Klingons land on Tezwa."

Zife seemed punch-drunk. *"How do we stop them?"*

"That's where the *Enterprise* comes into play," Azernal said. "They're the only Starfleet vessel close enough to do what has to be done."

"And what, exactly, is that?"

"There's only one way to stop the Klingons from conquering Tezwa," Azernal said. "We have to conquer it first."

Chapter 12
U.S.S. Enterprise-E

PICARD MASSAGED HIS WRIST as he, Data, and La Forge studied the scanner information scrolling across the wall console in his ready room. It had been over an hour since an engineer in transporter room four had removed the Tezwan manacles from the captain's hands. The rough metal had left Picard's skin chafed and raw. He hadn't yet made time to go to sickbay—partly because he knew many members of his crew needed medical attention far more than he did, and also because he wasn't interested in another awkward nonconversation with Dr. Crusher.

"We've put together a fairly detailed picture of what hit us," La Forge said. He tapped a few commands into the system and called up a schematic of an enormous spherical shell, inside of which was a massive energy cannon. "It's a rapid-frequency nadion-pulse cannon, twice as powerful as anything I've ever seen." La Forge pointed to the bottom of the diagram. "Here's the power-transfer node." The chief engineer nodded to Data, who changed the image on the display to a topographical map of Tezwa. Webs of incandescent red lines radiated across the surface from six points, each sixty degrees' latitude apart.

"The guns are powered by six remote generators," Data said. He magnified a scan of a node that joined six separate power lines. "Based on detailed scans I made during our low-altitude flyover, I have concluded that the power-generating facilities also serve as fire-control centers."

Picard frowned. "Even against that much power, our shields should have lasted longer."

"I have a theory about that," La Forge said. He handed his padd to Picard, who skimmed it as the engineer spoke. "Based on feedback patterns we recorded as the shields collapsed, I'd say the cannons are using a rotating pulse frequency. Each shot is actually millions of separate pulses, each at a slightly different nutation."

Picard shot a quizzical look at both officers. "Which has what effect?"

"The rapid cycling of the pulse frequency," Data said, "coupled with the high power level, turns the shield into a resonant harmonic field. The resulting feedback overloads the shield emitters."

"Can we compensate for the effect?" Picard said. "Cancel it out, perhaps?"

"I'm afraid not, Captain," La Forge said. "We'd have to replace all our shield emitters—assuming Starfleet can design some that can take the heat."

The more Picard heard, the more suspicious he became. He'd read all the briefing materials on Tezwa, but not one item in any of those voluminous reports had led him to suspect the Tezwans possessed this level of armament. He turned toward the map of Tezwa. He narrowed his eyes as he scanned the image and tried to divine its secrets.

"This doesn't add up," he said. "None of their other technologies are anywhere near so sophisticated." He replaced the image with a local starmap. "Look how isolated they are. Why would they need such overpowering defenses?"

Data cocked his head slightly. "Perhaps for the same reason that Starfleet originally designed them," he said.

Picard turned and stared with a shocked expression at the android second officer. "These are Federation weapons?"

"That's the other bad news," La Forge said.

"The designs are very similar," Data said, answering Picard's question. "The rapid-frequency nadion-pulse cannon was first proposed in 2366, as a possible defensive countermeasure against the Borg. Two prototypes were built, but it was deemed too complex for rapid, widespread deployment."

Picard looked to La Forge for confirmation. "Geordi," the captain said, "have you compared the original prototypes to the weapons on Tezwa?" The engineer nodded grimly, his metallic eyes hidden in the shadow of his brow. "How similar are they?"

"Almost identical," La Forge said. "The main differences are the power supply and the safety systems." He gestured with a tilt of his head toward the schematic on the wall console. "If you ask me, I'd say they stole our designs and put those guns together in a big hurry."

"Is there any way the Tezwans could have developed this technology independently?" Picard said.

"Ten years ago, they didn't have any of the components of that defense system," La Forge said. "Five years ago, they were still making the transition to type-six antimatter reactors. It would take a miracle for them to make a jump like that."

Data wore a doubtful expression. "It is . . . unlikely."

Picard hoped La Forge and Data were wrong, but he knew from experience that when they agreed on technical matters such as this, they were very likely right. If that was the case today, then an already tragic failure of diplomacy had just escalated into a full-blown interstellar incident, complete with espionage against the Federation. Picard wondered whether this would cause President Zife to support the Klingons' march to war.

The com sounded, followed by Security Chief Vale's voice. *"Bridge to Captain Picard,"* she said.

Picard turned away from La Forge and Data, more for his own concentration than for any expectation of privacy. "Go ahead."

"You have an incoming transmission from Earth, on an encrypted channel," Vale said. There was a brief pause. *"It's the president,"* she added.

"I'll take it here in my ready room." He looked at Data and La Forge. "Gentlemen, if you'll excuse me." The two officers nodded and exited to the bridge.

Picard sat down at his desk, activated his monitor, and entered his security code. The stars-and-double-laurel emblem of the United Federation of Planets appeared. Seconds later, the blue-and-white crest was replaced by four faces. In the upper left-hand corner was President Zife, the Bolian chief executive of the Federation. To Zife's right was Admiral Kathryn Janeway, who had, of late, begun taking a greater role in shaping Starfleet's political agenda. In the lower left-hand corner was Picard's supervising officer Admiral Alynna Nechayev, and beside her was Admiral William Ross.

"Mr. President," Picard said.

"Captain Picard," Zife said.

"Admirals," Picard said.

Janeway, Nechayev, and Ross overlapped one another with their one-word replies of *"Captain."* Picard took a breath and adopted his most polite expression, because he fully expected the conversation to go downhill from there.

Chapter 13
Tezwa

KINCHAWN INCREASED THE VOLUME of his holographic signal interception. He wanted to be sure he heard every word clearly as he eavesdropped on another clandestine subspace communication between his deputy prime minister and the Federation president's top advisor. Bilok looked frazzled by the day's events. Azernal, on the other hand, was slightly red in the face, like a *naka* root that had been dipped in boiling water just long enough to acquire some color.

"You said he wouldn't fire," Azernal said. The Zakdorn's anger was unmasked, and Kinchawn preferred it that way. It was easier to goad a person into exposing their feelings than it was to intuit them, especially when that person was an alien.

"I can't explain it," Bilok said. *"He's gone mad."* Kinchawn smirked. It amused him to see Bilok so off balance.

"Well, I have worse news," Azernal said. *"Worse for*

you, in any event. Kinchawn was right—the Klingons are backing down."

Kinchawn leaned forward at this news.

"*You can't be serious,*" Bilok protested. "*How can they do nothing after such a betrayal?*"

"*The Klingons are in no better condition to fight a war right now than we are,*" Azernal said. "*So if I were you, I'd start looking for a way off that rock—because there won't be anybody coming to your rescue. You're on your own.*"

Bilok's crown feathers ruffled, betraying his alarm. "*But Kinchawn is—*"

"*In control,*" Azernal interrupted. "*There's nothing more we can do.*"

"*You can't just abandon us,*" Bilok said. "*We might be able to help you. Plans are in motion. We simply need—*"

"*More time?*" Azernal shook his head. "*Time's up. . . . The path of least resistance has been closed.*"

Bilok fell silent and seemed to weigh the Zakdorn's words for several long seconds. "*I understand,*" he said finally.

"*Good luck,*" Azernal said. Then he terminated his transmission. Bilok closed his subspace channel a moment later, leaving Kinchawn alone in the comfort of his office atop the *Ilanatava*. The prime minister stood and walked to his balcony. The nighttime cityscape of Keelee-Kee was abuzz. Air traffic of all kinds, from hovercars to transport shuttles, swarmed like glowing insects around the spires of the capital city.

Kinchawn doubted the Klingons would really back down so easily. He had expected at least one attempt at large-scale retaliation, an assault that he could pummel with his cannons. No doubt the civilian population would suffer a few million casualties, and those who survived would be terrified. But fear inspired patriotism, and patriotism guaranteed loyalty. Of course, he knew he could count on the people's quiet acquiescence even without a Klingon orbital bombardment to soften their cynicism; it would just make Tezwa's transition to a fully military government a more gradual process.

But the idea nagged at him: *Why wouldn't the Klingons strike back?* He considered the possibility that Azernal and his president had brokered a deal with the Klingons, made some kind of unspoken arrangement to keep the peace—all to prevent the Klingons from learning the truth. To hide the origin of the nadion-pulse cannons dotting the equatorial and tropical latitudes of a planet situated along a border they shared with the United Federation of Planets. To keep the Klingons from learning that it was the Federation president himself who arranged to have the guns put there, at a time when he expected his people to face the Klingons on the battlefield.

Certainly, a desire to avert a cataclysmic war was more than sufficient motivation to make the Federation get involved. But Kinchawn couldn't imagine what the Federation might offer as a sop to slake the Klingons' unquenchable thirst for war. What did the Federation have that would be enough to convince the Klingons to silence their cries for vengeance?

Weapons? The Klingons had more than enough armaments. Ships? Starfleet barely kept itself in operation these days; certainly it had no vessels to spare. Money? Last Kinchawn had heard, the Federation had no hard currency to trade, and its economy was esoteric to the point of being almost hypothetical. Territory? The Federation was struggling to hold itself together in the wake of the Dominion War, and the threat of one world's departure during the previous year had nearly triggered a political brushfire. Surrendering valuable worlds and shipping lanes was not likely to be a viable strategy for them.

Perhaps it was exactly as Azernal had told Bilok; maybe the Klingons had finally overextended their reach and now had chosen to cut their losses early. Kinchawn's only problem with this theory was that it would require taking Azernal at his word, a practice that in his experience was a precursor to betrayal.

That thought led him to a third possibility, one that seemed to be the most likely of all. He concluded that Azernal was lying to Bilok, and that a Klingon attack fleet was, in fact, en route to Tezwa at that very moment.

He returned to his desk and looked over the casualty projections his generals had forwarded to him. The estimates for his home city of Odina-Keh were grim, at best. If the Klingons mounted an even moderately competent assault, most of Odina-Keh's population would be killed in the first barrage. His wife, Sorokala, and his children, Lokowon and Rodoko, would not survive. He considered having them moved now to a shielded facility outside Arbosa-Lo, but he knew that the *trinae* would trumpet his family's flight and use it to spark a panic. Then he imagined the political leverage he would have in the aftermath of the attack, when no one would dare to question a prime minister whose own family lay counted among the slain.

Kinchawn vowed to mourn his kin with sorrow-songs. He knew he would be haunted by the memory of their faces long after their ashes had cooled and their names had been inscribed on his family's ancestral *tava*. But the prime minister had long since accepted that when it came time to pay the price for absolute power, he would not count the cost—however dear it proved to be.

Chapter 14
*U.S.S. Enterprise-*E

PICARD WAS SURPRISED by how smoothly the conversation with his superiors was going. He had expected to bear the brunt of all manner of recriminations, to be held up to the flames for not preventing the unfolding catastrophe on Tezwa. Instead, he was simply being burdened with the impossible task of fixing it.

"We've already reassigned the Amargosa, *the* Musashi *and the* Republic *to join you as soon as possible,"* Ross said. *"But it's up to the* Enterprise *to hold the line."*

"We'll do our best, Admiral—"

"I'm sure," Ross interjected.

"—but the *Enterprise* is no match for an entire Klingon invasion fleet," Picard finished.

"We're not asking you to fight the Klingons, Jean-Luc," Nechayev said. Picard found her tone patronizing. *"Just talk some sense into them."*

"Buy us time to find a diplomatic solution," Janeway said.

"I can't guarantee they'll listen," Picard said. The admirals' reactions implied they had hoped for a different answer. "Do we have any idea how large a force they're sending?"

Nechayev shook her head. *"Not a clue. Long-range sensors picked up twenty ships leaving Qo'noS, but there's no telling how many cloaked vessels regrouped at the Zurav Nebula. You could be facing two dozen—or two hundred."*

"How far do you want to take this?" Picard said. "What, precisely, should we do if either side refuses to stand down?" He didn't want to be seen as difficult or uncooperative, but the orders he was receiving were disturbingly vague. He was unsure whether that indicated Ross and the others lacked a coherent plan of action, or if they simply intended to deploy him and the *Enterprise* as rogue operators, ones whose actions could easily be later disavowed in the face of controversy.

A moment of uneasy silence followed Picard's question. President Zife cleared his throat, then spoke. *"Captain, I want you to neutralize the artillery on Tezwa and prevent the Klingon attack force from landing on its surface. Do whatever is necessary to accomplish those objectives. Use any means, any tactics, any force of arms required. Do I make myself clear?"*

Picard was taken aback by the president's order. In all his years in Starfleet, he had heard few executive directives that were so brazen in calling for results at any price. Even more distressing—assuming he had heard the president's order correctly—his crippled ship and beleaguered crew were being tasked with the tactical equivalent of seppuku.

It was an all but impossible mission—and exactly the sort of thing for which the *Enterprise* was known across the galaxy.

"Yes, Mr. President," Picard said, after a brief hesitation. But doubts still nagged at him. "Admiral Ross, one other matter concerns me."

"Go on," Ross said.

"Two of my senior officers have analyzed the artillery on the planet surface," Picard said. "We believe the guns may be of Starfleet design."

"The Tezwans are using Starfleet technology?" Janeway said. She seemed duly alarmed by the prospect. The president, on the other hand, remained silent but attentive to the conversation. Picard stayed focused on his conversation with Ross.

"As I said, Admiral, we believe the weapons may be based on Starfleet designs, but without a closer inspection we can't be sure who manufactured them." Picard was reluctant to press forward with this inquiry, but he felt it was his duty. "Admiral, was Starfleet Intelligence aware of the guns' presence on Tezwa before the *Enterprise* was ordered into orbit?"

Ross became indignant. *"Absolutely not,"* he said.

Nechayev jumped in to add her assurances. *"We vetted the intel on Tezwa ten ways to Sunday before we sent it to you,"* she said. *"If we'd known about those guns, you would've known about those guns."*

"Yes, of course," Picard said. "I'm sorry. I had to ask."

"Captain," Janeway said, *"I'll have my people look*

over your scans of the guns. We'll let you know the moment we find anything."

"Thank you, Admiral."

"You have less than four hours until the Klingons attack," Ross said. *"Whatever you're going to do, do it fast. . . . And good luck."* Ross reached forward to terminate the transmission, but stopped as the president added a final comment.

"Captain, I just want to say that we all know what a terrible risk you're about to take," Zife said. *"I wish I didn't have to put you and your crew in the middle of all this, but . . ."* Zife's voice tapered off, apparently taking his last few thoughts with it. Picard wondered what the man had been about to say. Was he going to explain why the Federation had chosen to meddle in the Klingons' political affairs? Was he going to reveal that Tezwa had some critical long-term value to Federation security? Zife regained his composure, straightened his posture, and looked up with a blank stare. *"Do whatever it takes,"* he said. *"Good fortune, Captain."* And with that, Zife ended his transmission, and the admirals did likewise.

Picard's monitor switched off, and his ready room was dark except for the distant, cold flicker of a small and icy planet that orbited on the farthest edge of Tezwa's star system, which was officially catalogued as Tezel-Oroko, for its primary star and failed-protostar gas-giant partner. He took a sip of his Earl Grey tea, and grimaced as he realized it had become tepid while he had been speaking with the Starfleet brass.

He set down the cold ceramic mug on his desktop and recalled the words of Earth's nineteenth-century Greenland explorer Fridtjof Nansen: "The difficult is what takes a little time; the impossible is what takes a little longer." As Picard grappled with the enormity of the task that lay ahead of him, however, he wasn't certain he had enough time even to attempt the difficult, never mind the impossible. Which, naturally, he took as an indication that he'd best get started.

He keyed the master com switch on his desk. "Picard to all senior personnel: Assemble in the observation lounge."

Chapter 15
An Undisclosed Location

DIETZ STOOD ALONE in the darkened room. His tall, stringy frame concealed his toughness. He shook his head and ran a hand over his spiky brush-cut hair while he watched the playback of President Zife's conference with Captain Picard and Admirals Ross, Nechayev, and Janeway.

Zife's order to Picard was naked in its desperation and glaring in its lack of detail. *"Do whatever is necessary to accomplish those objectives,"* Zife said again as Dietz replayed the recording.

The door hissed softly open behind him. His black uniform jacket made a stiff, synthetic creak as he turned and looked over his shoulder to see his supervisor L'Haan walk in. Even though the Vulcan woman appeared to be younger than he, he knew that she was at least a hundred years his senior. Her raven black hair was straight and shoulder-length, and the lines of her own all-black uniform flattered her lithe body. Except for her faintly greenish complexion and sharply pointed ears, Dietz had long been of the opinion that she reminded him of artists' depictions of the ancient Egyptian queen Cleopatra.

"What is their status?" she said, skipping any salutations or preamble. She stood beside him as he replayed the recording of Zife's order, then paused the playback.

"They're bungling it," Dietz said. "If we don't step in, we'll be at war with the Klingons by tomorrow."

"What is Azernal doing?" she said.

"Trading code phrases with his Tezwan *braccio destro*." Dietz called up a recording of Azernal's conversation with Bilok. He cued up a reference from the end of the conversation and played it. *"Time's up,"* the recorded Azernal said. *"The path of least resistance has been closed."*

"The great strategic mind at work," L'Haan deadpanned. "A child could parse his code phrases." It was an open secret among their peers that L'Haan considered the Zakdorn chief of staff to be overrated as a strategist. "How long until he and Bilok can set up a com channel that Kinchawn hasn't compromised?"

"Four hours, at least."

"Most unfortunate," L'Haan said. She leaned forward and switched Dietz's screen to a status report on the progress of the Klingon attack fleet. The perfectly coiffed ends of her silken hair grazed his arm, and imparted to the air a fleeting fragrance of lilac as she straightened her posture. Dietz knew she wasn't oblivious of his attraction to her; she simply was too disciplined to let it faze her. "If the Klingons conquer the planet, there will be no chance of rectifying Zife and Azernal's mistakes," she said. "If Picard and his crew fail, we'll have to embrace a permanent solution to the Tezwa problem."

Dietz's eyes widened involuntarily, but only for a moment. Wiping out the planet was an extreme response, but under the circumstances it might be the most prudent course. Logistically, its chief advantage was that all essential tactical assets were already deployed. Two years ago, one of their field operatives had programmed backdoor codes into the control systems for Tezwa's artillery system. With a minimum of effort, Dietz could remotely trigger a catastrophic reaction in the system's antimatter power cores that would destroy the guns—as well as the surface and entire population of the planet.

Starfleet had long ago surrendered its authority to order the destruction of planets, and the Federation had signed a treaty with several neighboring powers that officially banned the practice, even in wartime. Seven years ago, however, prior to the official start of the Dominion War, the joint Romulan-Cardassian attempt to vaporize the Founders' homeworld, though unsuccessful, had proved that neither of those governments had any intention of abiding by such agreements.

The Federation had openly condemned the attack, but Dietz and his compatriots had grasped the cold, hard truth: Unless the Federation was willing to take such brutal actions to guarantee its own survival, it would eventually become little more than a footnote in the history of a culture that had such icy resolve. That was something which Dietz could not let happen.

"I'd need about twenty minutes to start the sequence," Dietz said.

"Very well," L'Haan said, folding her hands behind her back. "Monitor the *Enterprise*'s progress. If the Klingons land troops on the planet, initiate the protocol."

"And if Picard contains the situation?"

L'Haan pondered that contingency. She unfolded her hands. "In that unlikely event, wait for new orders."

"Understood," he said. "What about black ops, or sleepers?"

"No," she replied, shaking her head. He was half-hypnotized watching her hair sway with the side-to-side motion. "Do not activate any field assets until we define our objectives."

"Understood," he said.

L'Haan turned away and walked toward the door. As it closed behind her, Dietz began making preparations for the top-secret implementation of the protocol once known as General Order 24.

Chapter 16
U.S.S. Enterprise-E

THEY'RE TAKING THIS rather well, Picard mused ironically.

The captain surveyed the reactions of his senior officers to Starfleet's latest orders. Looks of incredulous dismay were volleyed from one officer to the next, down the length of the table. In the hush that had fallen like a curtain, Picard could hear the tiny squeak of every slowly pivoted chair, and the grimly resigned sigh of Dr. Crusher, who sat to his left at the far end of the table.

The rectangular monitor on the observation lounge wall was divided into quadrants. One outlined the Tezwans' artillery system; another showed the current damage-and-repair status of the *Enterprise;* the third tracked the position, estimated size, and approximate arrival time of the Klingon attack fleet; the last tracked the status of Tezwa's newly acquired fleet of two dozen war ships, which were even now powering up for rapid deployment into orbit over the planet.

"I'm open to suggestions," Picard said.

La Forge leaned forward to look past Data, who sat to Picard's immediate right. "Well, we still don't have weapons or shields," the engineer said. "So I'd suggest not getting ourselves shot at—by the Klingons or the Tezwans."

"I'll second that," Vale said.

Picard looked at Troi, who sat at the far end of the table, opposite Crusher. "Counselor? Any advice on diplomatic options?"

"I'm afraid not, Captain," she said. "Judging from the level of hostility I sensed between the rival political factions on Tezwa, I'd say they're on the verge of a *coup d'état*. Negotiating with them while Kinchawn remains in power seems unlikely, and possibly counterproductive."

"What about the Klingons?" Picard said.

"I have to believe that if anyone could have stopped them from launching the attack, it would've been Worf," Troi said. "Now that they're en route, I think we should assume the worst."

Picard hunched forward, rested his hands on the desktop, and folded his fingers together. "Number One? Thoughts?" Riker looked exhausted. Picard hadn't picked up on that earlier, in the dim lighting of the bridge. He wondered whether he should have insisted his first officer take a proper leave of absence following the murder of Kyle Riker on Delta Sigma IV.

"We know diplomacy's out," Riker said. "And even at our best, going into battle against these odds would be suicide. . . . The way I see it, we have exactly two options left: subterfuge, and sabotage."

"My thoughts exactly," Picard said.

"Our first step has to be neutralizing Tezwa's artillery," Riker said. "Can we hit them with long-range photon torpedoes?"

"No," Vale said, turning slightly to address her remarks as much to the captain as to the first officer. "Tezwa's defense system would shred them before they reach the atmosphere."

"And if any did reach their targets, they wouldn't penetrate the guns' shields," La Forge said. "Any attack powerful enough to knock out the shields would cause collateral damage on a global scale."

Riker picked up his padd and checked an item in Data and La Forge's analysis of the Tezwan guns. "Your report says the guns are controlled by six firebases located around the planet."

"That is correct," Data said. "Those facilities also supply the power for the planet's defensive systems."

"Can we disable just those six firebases?" Riker said.

"Their shields are even tougher," Vale said.

"True," Data said. "However, unlike the guns, they are configured to repel only orbital and aerial attacks."

La Forge half-swiveled his chair toward Data. "That's right," the chief engineer said. Picard was convinced he could see a gleam in the man's synthetic, silvery eyes. "The shields don't extend low enough to stop ground assaults," La Forge continued. "We can't *beam* through them, but we could *free-fall* through the shields, and approach the bases on the ground."

Vale looked concerned as she posed a question to Data. "How many people would be in one of those firebases?"

The android thought for a moment. "Given the unusual degree of similarity between the Tezwans' artillery and the prototypes designed by Starfleet, I would estimate each firebase is run by approximately forty-five personnel. The guns themselves would have only a handful of technicians, to perform routine and emergency maintenance."

"So we're looking at two hundred seventy hostile personnel in the firebases," Vale said. She shook her head. "I don't know. Even if we had enough people to launch an attack like that, the Tezwans would blow us outta the sky before we reached the ground."

"A large-scale attack might not be necessary," Data said. "After all, our goal is to engage in sabotage—not a war of attrition."

"Absolutely," Riker said. "We have to think in terms of a covert operation, small-unit tactics." He looked to La Forge and Data. "If we're going to sabotage Tezwa's defenses, where do we hit them? What's the system's most vulnerable point?"

"Thought you'd never ask," La Forge said. He picked up his padd, punched in a short string of commands, and aimed it at the wall monitor. The schematic of the Tezwan artillery system enlarged to fill the entire screen. "The guns were made for power, and they've got it in spades." He highlighted an isolated component of the guns. "What they *don't* have are good backups for their prefire-chamber capacitors."

Crusher half-raised her hand. "Could we pretend for a moment that I have no idea what you just said?"

Vale jumped in to field the question. "The prefire chamber is a key component in a directed-energy weapon," she said. "Before the weapon fires, it builds up a specific amount of charge in the prefire chamber. When it has enough power stored, it collapses a restraining field and releases the energy in a single, massive burst to the emitter array, which focuses the pulse and modulates its frequency."

Crusher nodded. "And what happens if this prefire chamber doesn't have a good backup?"

"The weapon has no ability to compensate for an overload," Vale said. "If enough energy floods the chamber too quickly—"

"Boom," La Forge said, mimicking an explosion by spreading apart his hands and fingers.

Picard feared the consequences of such an attack. "What risk would that pose to the civilian population?" he said.

"None," La Forge said. "The results would be implosive, not explosive. And once the guns implode, the feedback pulses would destroy the firebases the same way. We can take out the entire system without risking collateral damage to the environment."

"But the maintenance personnel inside the guns?" Picard said, weighing all the costs against his conscience.

"Once we control the firebases, we can override the gun crews' access codes and lock them out of the system," Data said. "When we are ready to initiate the system collapse, they can be given enough warning to evacuate before the guns implode."

"What's the minimum safe distance for retreat?" Riker said.

"Thirty meters, maybe less," La Forge said. "As I said,

the effects'll be implosive. Once you're out of the facilities, you're pretty much clear."

Picard nodded approvingly. "Very good," he said. "But you'll still be facing heavy resistance in the firebases."

"The statistics are misleading," Data said. "Of the forty-five personnel we expect to encounter at each facility, only twelve are likely to be armed security personnel. At any given time, only four of those guards are likely to be on duty."

"Also," La Forge interjected, "once we capture the bases' operation centers, we can isolate the remaining personnel behind locked doors—for their safety *and* ours."

Picard's brow wrinkled with skepticism. "And the firebase personnel would have a fair chance to escape?"

"Yes, sir," Data said. "We could set the systems to release the lockdowns on a time delay, enabling us to leave the bases without a direct confrontation."

Riker stroked his bearded chin for a moment before he spoke. "What if the firebase personnel signal a warning to their headquarters? We could end up facing a lot of angry reinforcements."

"I already have my people putting together subspace signal jammers," La Forge said. "They're short-range, and they'll only have enough juice to run for a couple hours, but they'll do the trick. The firebases will still have internal, hard-wired communications, but external coms'll be down for the count."

Vale's lips tightened into a worried frown. "How long will it take to deploy these jammers once we're on the ground?"

"Flip of a switch," La Forge said with a confident shrug. "Set 'em and forget 'em."

"Well done, Mr. La Forge," Picard said. "Unfortunately, the artillery is only one part of the problem. The Tezwans also have a fleet of their own. Even without the support of the planet's guns, they'll still try to engage the Klingons."

"Well, we're already taking control of the firebases," La Forge said. "We could use the Tezwans' own artillery to stop their fleet—*before* we destroy the guns."

The idea of slaughter on such a scale appalled Picard. "You're not suggesting we destroy twenty-four starships?"

"No. We'll just disable them."

"He's right," Vale said. "We can reduce the guns' power settings, and tweak their frequencies to cripple the Tezwan ships. Worst-case scenario, they'd still have emergency batteries for life-support."

Crusher looked unconvinced. "What if they don't?" she said.

"They're in orbit above their homeworld," Vale said. "They can use their escape pods and go home."

Riker looked at Vale. "How's our intel on the Danteri ships they're using?"

"Pretty good," Vale said. "The *Excalibur* and the *Trident* have been updating Starfleet's records with new technical data. We should be able to knock out the Tezwan ships without causing any serious casualties."

Picard nodded. "All right," he said. "But if we remove all the Tezwans' defenses, we'll be leaving them exposed to a massacre by the Klingons. How should we go about halting the Klingon invasion force?"

A subtle smirk tugged at the corners of Riker's mouth. "This would be a long shot," he said.

"Naturally," Picard said.

"When I served aboard the *I.K.S. Pagh,*" Riker said, "I noted that they used security prefix codes much like ours. Each ship had a unique code sequence that its captain could change at will. But they also had an override code—a code the crew didn't know, and which could be changed only by Klingon High Command."

"An override code?" La Forge said. "As in, we'd take remote control of every ship in their attack fleet?"

"Exactly," Riker said.

"It is an interesting proposition," Data said. "However, it raises three important questions. First, how do we obtain the code? Second, how do we push a signal containing the codes through the Klingons' shields? And last, how do we time the disabling of the Klingon fleet so as not to leave it at the mercy of the Tezwans, or vice versa?"

"We'll transmit the code signals on a super-low-frequency subspace channel," Riker said. "They developed it for use when their ships are cloaked. If we can get the override codes, the SLF channel specs should be bundled with them." Picard masked his alarm at the notion of stealing the SLF data, one of the Klingon Empire's most closely guarded military secrets.

"The timing *is* tricky," Vale said. "The key is to disable both forces before the Klingons make orbit. If either side gets even one shot off, this whole party'll be for nothing."

Riker nodded. "Agreed. What's the Klingons' ETA?"

"Best guess?" Vale said. She checked her padd. "Three hours, thirty-eight minutes."

"I think we're forgetting an important detail," Troi said. "The Klingons are not going to excuse Kinchawn's sneak attack just because the Tezwan fleet is disabled or their artillery's been destroyed. Unless the Tezwans can placate the Klingons without insulting their honor, our intervention will only delay the invasion by a matter of hours."

Picard knew Troi was right, but he also realized she was raising an issue they could not address. "Unfortunately, Counselor, the Tezwans alone must bear the burden of making amends with the Klingons," he said. "Our mission is to stop the invasion. We can only hope that once we've done our part, the Tezwans will seize the opportunity to do theirs." He looked toward Riker. "Will, destroy the firebases. Take whatever resources or personnel you need, and go as soon as possible." Picard pushed away from the table. "If there's nothing else—"

Crusher spoke up. "Captain, we still haven't said how we're going to get the Klingons' override codes."

Picard had been able to tell from Riker's poker face that the first officer had known the answer to that question when he'd suggested stealing the codes. And though Picard was loath to admit it, he concurred that it was their best—and only—hope of stopping a brutal and tragic conflict. He looked Crusher in the eye and told her only what she needed to know.

"Leave that to me," he said.

Chapter 17
Qo'noS

IN THE STILLNESS of the night, Captain Picard's voice was grave. *"Millions of lives depend on your answer, Mr. Ambassador."*

Worf sat alone in his private residence, weighing his oath of duty to the Federation and his loyalty to his former captain against his pledge to his kinsman, Chancellor Martok.

Years ago Picard had stood with Worf as his *cha'DIch* when the Klingon High Council, then presided over by K'mpec, stripped him of his honor. And it had been Picard who had protected him from a possible Starfleet court-martial after he'd slain Duras to avenge his own murdered mate, K'Ehleyr. Indeed, Worf's debts of honor to his former commanding officer were almost too numerous to recall.

But Martok was his kinsman. Worf had helped him escape a Dominion prisoner-of-war camp; in return, Martok had invited Worf to serve aboard his ship, the *I.K.S.*

Rotarran, during the Dominion War. Side by side they'd fought many harrowing battles for the glory of the Empire, and in the flames of the aftermath they had forged a bond that only warriors who had bled together could truly understand. It was Martok who had ushered Worf into his House and helped restore his honor, Martok who had stood with him on the day he married Jadzia. And after Worf's beloved wife was slain, it was Martok who had risked everything to help him win a great battle in her name, guaranteeing her noble spirit a place in *Sto-Vo-Kor.*

But now, in the deepest hours of the night, Picard was asking Worf to violate his oath of service as the Federation's ambassador to Qo'noS, betray the patriarch of his adopted House, and sabotage the soldiers of the Empire. To become a spy.

The burden of the decision was heartbreaking.

"What you ask . . ." he began, then halted. He looked away from the monitor and struggled to collect his thoughts. His mouth was dry with hesitation. His thick, upswept eyebrows knitted together in tense concentration. He looked back at Picard's image on the screen. "Is there no other way?"

"I wouldn't ask if there were," Picard said.

Worf thought for a moment. "If I am detected, it could be construed as an act of war against the Empire," he said.

"Not if you act on your own authority," Picard said. *"In the absence of an executive order, the president can disavow any knowledge of your actions. Legally, the Federation would be protected."*

"And I would be executed," Worf said.

"You've risked your life and honor to defend the Federation before, Mr. Ambassador," Picard said. *"The circumstances may have changed, but the stakes are no different. . . . The needs of the many—"*

"Outweigh the needs of the few—"

"Or the one," Picard finished. Worf recalled that Picard was aware he had mind-melded with former Starfleet officer and famed Vulcan diplomat Spock roughly three years earlier. Some years prior to that, Picard himself had mind-melded with Spock during a covert mission to Romulus. Worf had long wondered whether Spock's mind-meld had left any lingering psychic traces; the almost reflexive way Worf had volleyed the old Vulcan homily with his former captain confirmed that suspicion.

The Klingon ambassador brooded. Picard's logic was sound, at least on its face. As a younger man, Worf might not have been swayed by appeals to the greater good, but experience—and yes, perhaps, maybe even Spock's mind-meld—had imparted to him a small measure of wisdom, and a sense of a larger universe.

But the true origin of his reluctance was not concern for the political fortunes of the Federation. The truth gnawed at him like a burning knife twisting through his stomach. After decades of struggling to balance the scales of honor and justice, after suffering humiliation and injustice for the good of a Klingon Empire that had turned its back on him, he had finally in the last few years been able to come *home.*

Here he could stand in the High Council chamber as both a respected envoy of the Federation and a Klingon warrior. He could walk unescorted through the torrid, bustling streets of the First City and be hailed on every smoky corner as the warrior who slew Gowron and could have seized the Empire for himself, but gave it back to a man of the people. He could be welcomed into the mess hall of any warship in the imperial fleet and join the grizzled veterans as they guzzled tankards of *warnog,* gorged themselves on jawfuls of *gagh,* and passed the hours filling the ship with roaring battle-songs.

To betray Martok by stealing the fleet's master command codes and giving them to Picard—no matter how noble the purpose, no matter how many Klingon warriors' lives would be spared from a wasteful end—was to risk being expelled forever from the world and people he'd struggled all his life to know firsthand. He was being asked to risk not just his life and honor, but his history and his heritage—his past, his present, and his future.

"How much time do we have?" Worf said.

"Just over three hours."

"I understand," Worf said with a quick nod. "I will contact you as soon as I am ready to transmit the codes."

"Thank you, Mr. Ambassador."

"Captain," Worf said. His next words stuck in his throat. He was not fond of sentiment, but he had learned the hard way not to wait to tell people things they deserved to hear. "Whatever happens . . . I want you to know that it is, and always has been, my greatest honor to serve with you."

Picard's expression brightened with what Worf recognized was pride. *"The feeling is mutual,"* Picard said. "Qapla', *Worf."*

"Qapla', Captain." Picard ended the transmission, and

the screen of Worf's monitor reverted to the blue-and-white emblem of the Federation.

"Worf to Mr. Wu."

Even in the middle of the night, his senior attaché, Giancarlo Wu, replied immediately. *"This is Wu."*

"I will be officially unavailable until further notice. Please make the necessary arrangements."

"Very good, sir."

"Worf out."

He walked with fast, purposeful steps into his bedroom and took from his closet a large, heavy robe with a deep hood. As he put it on, he felt his pulse quicken.

Yesterday I longed to return to a career of action, he recalled. Slipping a phaser into his shoulder satchel, he steeled himself to do exactly that.

Chapter 18
U.S.S. Enterprise-E

RIKER LEANED AGAINST the frame of the window, which arched inward over his head toward the ceiling. He had dimmed the lights so as not to have to look through his reflection. Beyond the transparent barrier, the stars were sharp and bright, devoid of the flicker that people who lived their lives planetside took for granted. Soft, bluesy jazz-piano music fell like a misting rain of sound from the speakers hidden in the ceiling.

The door swished open. Troi walked in, silhouetted by the cold, bright light spilling in from the corridor. She stopped after taking only a few steps inside. The door closed behind her, and the room melted back into darkness and starlight shadows. She paused to look around. "Will?" she said. She sounded concerned. He hadn't meant to alarm her, but he realized that, under the circumstances, asking her to meet "right away" in their quarters might have given her cause to worry.

"Over here," he said.

She took a cautious step in his direction. "Are you okay?"

"I'm fine," he said. "I just wasn't in the mood for light." He heard her footsteps as she moved toward him. He held out his left arm toward her. "How're you doing?"

She sidled up to him and nestled under his arm. "I've been better," she said. He hugged her gently to him. She wrapped her slender arms around his waist and tilted her head upward. "What are we listening to?"

"Junior Mance," he said. "One of the great Chicago masters."

"Chicago?" She rested her head against his chest. "I thought you preferred New Orleans jazz."

"I *play* New Orleans style," he said. "But it's not all I like. Geordi actually recommended this to me a few weeks ago." Riker listened for a few moments as one of Mance's elaborate and brilliantly constructed piano solos evoked the intermingled joys and sorrows of a bygone century. "I downloaded some holodeck re-creations of shows Mance played in New York, in the early twenty-first century. . . . He was amazing."

"It is beautiful," Troi said. "Sophisticated. . . . Elegant."

He hugged her a little bit closer and gave her a gentle kiss on her forehead. "Reminds me of you."

She looked up and smiled at him. "Charmer," she said. "Shouldn't you be planning the away mission?"

"It's already planned," he said. "Geordi's getting the gear ready, and Data's handling the logistics."

"So what are you doing in here?"

He touched her hair, memorized its silken texture as her dark tresses enveloped his fingers. "Just wanted to spend a few minutes with you before I go," he said. He tried to keep his thoughts rooted in the present; he focused on the softness of Troi's hair, the gleeful surges of Mance's blues-inspired jazz-piano melodies, the untainted beauty of the stars. Anything to shield his *Imzadi* from his lingering fear that he might not come back from this hastily conceived commando assault against the Tezwans' heavily fortified fire-control centers.

But he could tell from the way she tightened her arms around him that she could sense everything he was trying to hide, from his anxiety about the mission at hand to the pain he was working so hard to put behind him. If anyone were to ask him why he'd risked the ship to rescue Troi and Captain Picard from the Tezwans, he would tell them it was to prevent the enemy from gaining the additional advantage of hostages. But he suspected that Troi sensed the truth: After having his father torn from him, he simply had not been able to bear the thought of losing his fiancée and his captain, as well.

The com chirped. *"Data to Commander Riker."*

"Riker here."

"Commander La Forge and I are ready to proceed, sir."

"Acknowledged," Riker said. "Assemble the strike teams in the shuttle hangar. I'll meet you there in five minutes."

"Aye, sir. Data out."

Riker lifted a wayward lock of Troi's hair from her eye, tucked it back where it belonged, and let his hand caress her cheek. "I have to go."

"I know," she said. "Be careful." She pulled him down into a passionate kiss, fueled as much by love as by fear.

She pressed her tear-streaked cheek against his bearded face. Her voice quavered. "Come home," she whispered.

"You know I will," he said. He kissed her again and considered saying something that began, *If I don't make it back . . .* , or, *I just want you to know . . .* , then decided against it. *Better to leave on an optimistic note,* he decided. "See you in a few hours," he said.

Summoning his nerve, he freed himself from her arms. He walked to the door, which slid open. The bright light in the corridor made him wince. He looked back into his quarters. His eyes were already adjusting to the light, and he could barely discern Troi's petite shape in front of the window. "Leave a light on for me," he said. Then, before he could change his mind, he stepped away and let the door close behind him.

Chapter 19
Qo'noS

WORF WALKED QUICKLY and used his hand to keep his *targ*-skin satchel concealed beneath his hooded robe. The streets of the Klingon capital were all but empty in the predawn gloom, but distant traffic and a slight wind blended into soft white noise. A sudden, brief downpour had just ceased, leaving the city streaked with wet reflections. Tugging his hood low across his brow, he crossed the boulevard with haste, rounded the corner, and strode across a wide plaza toward the Federation Embassy.

The embassy resided in one of the city's newer buildings. The structure was enormous, the color of rust, and shaped like a squat, inverted pyramid. Its four corners, more than two hundred meters overhead, were supported by four towering pillars. At street level the building was surrounded by a ten-meter-high perimeter wall above and behind which was a forcefield powerful enough to stop nearly any conventional attack, from phasers to photon grenades to speeding vehicles on suicide runs.

Runoff stormwater cascaded from the embassy's roof and washed down the gradual incline from the building's perimeter into the plaza, where it pooled ankle-deep. Worf sloshed across the plaza and approached the front gate of the embassy.

He entered an eight-digit code that opened the outer door of the security lock. As he stepped inside the tiny, harshly lit vestibule, the reinforced blast door closed behind him, cutting off all sound from the street. The only sounds in the vestibule were the low-frequency hum of the scanning machines and Worf's own breathing. As he had done countless times before, he put his hand into the slot and lowered his face toward the retinal scanner. He heard the hum of the machine working as it verified his DNA and confirmed the signal from his identity chip.

"Please authenticate your identity," the machine said in a pleasing feminine voice.

"Worf, son of Mogh, ambassador to Qo'noS," he said.

"Welcome, Mr. Ambassador," the voice said. The security lock's inner door slid open, and Worf walked through it into the embassy. Standing in the corridor on either side of the door was a pair of Starfleet security officers. Both were outfitted with torso armor and helmets and carried heavy phaser rifles. "Good morning, Mr. Ambassador," they said in unison as Worf walked past. He grunted, nodded curtly, and kept moving.

Half a minute later he was in the turbolift and descending quickly to the lowest level of the embassy. This was a "secure level," where, technically, even he did not have full clearance.

Once there, he hotwired the turbolift's controls, and

engaged the manual override. Guiding the turbolift car downward through a combination of careful attention to audible clues and an acute sense of changes in the vibrations beneath his feet, he lowered it until it reached the *real* lowest level of the embassy—the one that wasn't on the blueprints, and which he wouldn't know of except for his family's old friend Lorgh, a longtime agent of Klingon Imperial Intelligence. He heard the door mechanisms catch and engage. He disabled the security lock. Pushing his fingers into the crack between the doors, he pried them apart with an agonized grunt that grew into a roar.

The doors separated to reveal a narrow corridor whose dim lighting was the color of human blood. At the far end, opposite the turbolift, was a single door. In front of that door stood an Andorian in an all-black uniform. Worf's first step out of the turbolift had barely touched the floor before the man aimed a Starfleet-issue type-3 phaser rifle and challenged him: "Mr. Ambassador, please step back into the turbolift."

Worf halted and eyed the tense young Andorian. "This is a matter of Federation security," Worf said. "Lower your weapon."

"Sir, you have five seconds to get back in the turbolift."

Worf clenched his fists. "You are making a grave mistake."

"I'm sorry, sir, but I can't let you proceed."

"I need to speak to Commander Zeitsev. *Now.*"

Judging by the shocked expression on the Andorian's face, he clearly was surprised to learn that Worf knew the identity of Starfleet's *real* chief of intelligence operations on Qo'noS. Worf concluded this young man would be a terrible poker player. "But you . . ." he stammered. "You're not supposed to . . ."

"To what?" Worf said. "Know who he is? Know what kind of equipment he has behind that door?" Worf took a step forward and was amused to see the man with the rifle take an instinctive step backward. "I need to see him now. Billions of lives depend on it."

For a moment, the Andorian's resolve seemed to waver. Then he shook his head. "No, sir," the Andorian said. "I can't. You need to—"

Worf pressed his thumb onto the tiny push-switch concealed in his right hand. It emitted a low-power subspace signal that triggered his phaser, which he had fastened snugly along the bottom of his satchel so that its discharge would strike someone standing directly in front of his left hip. The shimmering golden beam burst through the side of the satchel and floored the unsuspecting Andorian in a single shot.

"Very nice," a man said over the com speakers. His voice reverberated in the confines of the metallic-surfaced corridor. *"Well done, Mr. Ambassador."*

"Thank you," Worf said. "Open the door."

"Of course," the voice said. *"Come in."*

Worf heard the clacking of the far door's security bolts being released. He walked away from the turbolift, stepped over the stunned Andorian, and pressed the control pad next to the door, which opened with a low hydraulic hiss.

The room on the other side was illuminated by a blue flicker. He stepped inside and looked around. To his right was a wall-sized rectangular viewscreen. Its display had been subdivided into thirty-two images of equal size and identical proportions to one another and the master screen itself. The images included Klingon and Federation newsfeeds, and what Worf surmised were illegal taps on internal Klingon security systems. Images of Klingon politicians whom Worf recognized blinked in and out, replaced by surveillance-camera images of people he didn't know, places whose significance was unclear, and random scrolls of alphanumeric information in several languages. He thought for a moment that he might have glimpsed his own residence, but it went by too quickly for him to be certain.

Silhouetted in front of this mercurial wall of images, with his back to Worf, was Commander Vasily Zeitsev. He stood and tapped commands into a Starfleet-type com panel that was mounted on a lectern's angled top surface. He spoke without turning to look at his visitor. "Good morning, Ambassador."

"Commander Zeitsev," Worf said.

Worf waited for Zeitsev to ask why he'd come looking for him. But the intelligence chief continued his work, his slight frame defined by his military-perfect posture and solid-black uniform. After several seconds, it became clear to Worf that Zeitsev was forcing him to extend himself verbally if he wanted the encounter to progress. It was the conversational equivalent of judo or the *Mok'bara,* in which the aggressor was the one more likely to be off balance. Worf understood that in most tactical situations, it was more advantageous to defend a strong position than to attack one. But with the Klingon fleet rapidly nearing Tezwa, he had no time for roundabout strategies. A direct approach was his only option.

"I need your help," Worf said.

"I hardly think so," Zeitsev said. "You seem perfectly capable of causing an interstellar incident all by yourself."

Worf took a breath and focused his thoughts. He would not let the arrogant spymaster goad him into a foolish outburst. "I need information about the Klingon High Command's internal computer network."

"You'll have to be a bit more specific," Zeitsev said.

"How many terminals have access to their Fleet Command Center?"

Zeitsev paused in his work. He half-turned and peeked over his shoulder at Worf. After a moment, he resumed working. "Several dozen at least. How much access do you need?"

"Top-level," Worf said. "Fleet command codes."

Zeitsev punched a single key on his panel, and the entire wall of images went dark. A row of harsh overhead lights snapped on as he spun and marched toward Worf, who held his ground. Zeitsev looked older than his fifty-odd years, and his chiseled features were creased and pallid. His eyes, however, were almost as intense as those of a Klingon. He planted himself toe-to-toe with Worf, who towered over him. His voice was hard and sharp.

"What, precisely, are you up to, Mr. Ambassador?"

A smirk tugged at the corner of Worf's mouth as he felt the conversational advantage shifting in his favor. "That," he said, "is classified."

Zeitsev glared at him, then chortled.

"Of course it is," he said, darkly amused. "It always

is." His mouth turned down, into a frown. "There's a Klingon fleet heading toward Tezwa. Your former ship, the *Enterprise*, is there now." Worf grimaced defensively as Zeitsev continued talking. "They don't stand much of a chance, going it alone against an entire fleet. . . . Do they, Mr. Ambassador?"

Worf glowered at the smug little man. "No," he said at last. "They do not."

"But if Picard had some means of disabling the fleet . . ."

"It would be a decisive advantage."

Zeitsev nodded. He turned and walked back to his lectern. "The Imperial Command headquarters is a fortress," he said. "We don't have time to get you in there." He keyed a string of commands into the panel. "The Great Hall, on the other hand . . . you can get in there anytime you want."

The wall screen snapped on to show a floor-plan schematic of the Great Hall. A dozen points on the blueprint were marked by blinking red Klingon trefoils. "These twelve terminals are the only ones in the building with access to the Fleet Command Center," Zeitsev said. "Naturally, they're all in the private offices of the senior councillors." He looked at Worf, then added: "And in the chancellor's office, of course."

"Of course," Worf said.

Zeitsev turned off the wall display. "I just want to make clear, Mr. Ambassador, that neither I nor any of my people can be involved in any act of overt espionage on Qo'noS."

"I understand," Worf said.

"Good," Zeitsev said. He nodded toward the door. "You can let yourself out now."

Worf exhaled an angry breath, then turned to leave. Zeitsev called after him. "And Ambassador . . . ?" Worf turned back toward the gruff-voiced intelligence officer. "Don't forget to pick up the package in your office."

Worf didn't understand at first. "Package . . . ?"

Zeitsev turned away, deactivated the overhead lights, and resumed scanning dozens of screens of information. Worf realized that Zeitsev was likely using him as a pawn in some kind of covert campaign of one-upmanship against Imperial Intelligence. But with time running out for the *Enterprise* and the Klingon troops racing toward their doom on Tezwa, that was a risk Worf accepted as necessary. He walked out the door and stepped over the still-incapacitated Andorian, leaving Zeitsev alone with his hidden agendas and his wall of flickering blue secrets.

Chapter 20
U.S.S. Enterprise-E—
Shuttle Hangar

CHRISTINE VALE FELT a cold shiver travel down her spine as Riker began the tactical briefing. It wasn't that his presentation was so inspiring; it was that the Tezwans' sneak attack had damaged the *Enterprise*'s environmental systems, and in order to maintain full support in critical areas, compartments such as shuttle hangars and cargo bays had to make do with reduced ventilation and minimal thermal support.

She and most of the other strike-team personnel huddled together or wrapped their arms around themselves for warmth. An exception was Data, who, as usual, was unfazed by a situation that everyone around him found wholly irritating.

Riker stood in front of the group and pointed out their objectives on a large, slowly turning globe of Tezwa generated by a portable holographic emitter. "We're going to separate into six teams," he said. "Each team will consist of a leader, two engineers with demolition kits, and one security officer." He paced back and forth once as he continued. "The mission profile is just as hard as it sounds: Free-fall insertion; jam the bases' external communications; enter the bases; take control of their operations centers; isolate their personnel; disable the Tezwan fleet on Captain Picard's command; sabotage the reactors, on five-minute delays; exit the bases; and leave the Tezwan troops a three-minute escape window."

He tapped a key on his padd, and six red points of light appeared on the holographic sphere. "These are the six firebases we have to destroy," he continued. "The first is near the planet's arctic circle, on the Solasook Peninsula. Data, that one's yours. You'll be taking Obrecht, Heaton, and Parminder."

Data nodded his acknowledgment to Riker. The two engineers, Obrecht and Heaton, gestured politely to Data, ostensibly to identify themselves. *They must be new,* Vale realized. *They don't know that Data memorizes every crew member's name and face the day they come aboard.* She was pleased to note that Security Officer Parminder, a petite and strikingly attractive woman with raven black hair, a medium-brown complexion, and a gentle London accent, did not see any need to remind Data of her identity.

The holographic globe rotated slightly, then paused.

"The second firebase," Riker said, "is in the southern hemisphere, beneath the Kolidos Desert. Peart, you'll take Scholz, Morello, and T'Sona."

"Aye, sir," Peart said.

Vale clenched her jaw to keep her teeth from chattering. She felt her skin turning to gooseflesh, starting with her legs and spreading upward. She noticed that, like Data, the first officer didn't seem to mind the cold. *Probably his Alaska upbringing,* she decided.

"Vale, this one's yours," Riker said as he advanced the globe another one-sixth turn. "Firebase three straddles the equator. The catch is that it's also nine-point-six kilometers underwater." He gestured to four pressure suits that were set apart from the rest of the equipment. "We've modified your team's gear for underwater operations. Just to confirm: Sakrysta, Spitale, Fillion—you've all passed deep-dive training, right?" The three officers all murmured their assent. "Okay, good," Riker said. "Let's move on."

Underwater, Vale groused to herself. *Great, just great.*

"Target four is in the northern hemisphere, inside Mount Ranakar," Riker continued. "The only vulnerable point is the entrance at the summit, but there's no safe landing zone up there. Geordi, you and your team will have to land on the plateau just beneath the summit, scale the western face, and take the base in less than two hours." Riker pointed at three personnel in succession. "T'Eama, Wathiongo, Braddock—you'll be pulling Mr. La Forge up the mountain by his bootstraps," he said, flashing a broad grin.

"That's a long climb, Commander," Braddock said. "Can't we just use gravity boots?"

"No," La Forge said, jumping in. "The tachyon spill from that base would make them inoperative."

Braddock seemed to deflate. "Oh," he said. "Right. Sorry."

T'Eama raised her hand politely. "How far will we have to climb to reach the summit?"

"Roughly two hundred meters," Riker said.

"Only two hundred meters?" La Forge joked. "Want us to build you anything while we're there?"

Riker played along, apparently aware that he was asking everyone to accomplish absurdly difficult objectives with little planning, few resources, and no margin for error. "No," he said. "Just scale a mountain, overpower a garrison ten times your size, and blow up the firebase."

"Right," La Forge said. "Got it."

Wathiongo and Braddock chuckled nervously. Their Vulcan teammate T'Eama cast a disdainful look at the two human men, then returned her attention to Riker's briefing.

The first officer turned to Lieutenant Taurik, the assistant chief engineer. Taurik was slender and sometimes projected a bookish persona, but Vale knew better than to underestimate the man. He had proved himself to be cool and competent under fire, and his ingenuity and courage had helped save La Forge's life a few months ago, during a violent brush with a team of Satarran covert operatives.

"Firebase five is in the Linoka Forest, which covers more than half a continent in the southern hemisphere. You'll be taking Rao, Mobe, and McEwan." Taurik responded with a curt nod, and Riker moved on. "The last firebase is in the Mokana Basin, about a hundred kilometers south of the equator. Tierney, Barnes, Razka—you're with me on this one."

Vale envied Riker's choice of security officer. Razka was one of the most experienced personnel in her department. Reviewing his records after his transfer to the *Enterprise* last month, Vale had been surprised to learn the Saurian was 148 years old. The reptilian male had spent nearly his entire life as a Starfleet noncommissioned officer; he'd fought the Klingons in the twenty-third century, battled the Tzenkethi and the Cardassians in the middle decades of the twenty-fourth century, and over the past decade had faced both the Borg and the Jem'Hadar in combat. In addition, he was likely to feel very much at home in the sultry jungle environment on Tezwa.

"Timing will be critical on this mission," Riker said. "From initial insertion, to coordinating our attacks, to destroying the firebases, we have two hours and fifteen minutes, and we have to stay in synch. If we fail to capture all the bases, the free ones can take over control of the others' guns." He looked at Vale. "Lieutenant, do you have anything to add?"

Vale stepped forward, then turned to face the group. "One thing working to our advantage is Tezwa's lighter gravity," she said. "It's about eighty percent of what we're used to on most Federation starships. Geordi, that should help your team when you're climbing that cliff face. For the rest of you, if you get into a hand-to-hand combat situation, remember that even though the Tezwans are tall, they'll probably weigh a lot less than you do."

Security Officer Braddock raised his hand. Vale pointed to him. "Lieutenant," the young man said, "is it safe to assume the Tezwans will be shooting to kill?"

"Yes," Vale said. "But standard rules of engagement still apply. Our weapons stay on heavy stun."

"But sir, they outnumber us ten to one, or more," Braddock said. "If they're using lethal force—"

"Brute force won't get this job done," Vale said. "We need to rely on stealth, diversions, and traps. And remember, we're looking to destroy equipment and facilities—not people. Keep casualties to a minimum. That's an order."

"Yes, sir," Braddock said, clearly disgruntled about going into action with most of his options unavailable.

Spitale was the next to lift her hand. "Lieutenant, if we're using subspace signal jammers, how will we get our orders from Captain Picard? Or stay in contact with each other?"

Taurik piped up with the answer. "We encoded a harmonic subcarrier into the jamming pulse that will let us communicate with one another and the *Enterprise* on a special frequency. It will also protect our tricorders."

Spitale nodded at the Vulcan engineer. "Okay," she said, and let the matter drop.

Picard's voice echoed from the com speakers high above on the hangar ceiling. *"Bridge to Commander Riker. We're ready to proceed."*

"Acknowledged," Riker said. "We'll let you know as soon as we're ready to deploy. Riker out." The first officer regarded the strike teams with a resolute expression. "Any more questions before we board the *Taj?*"

For the sake of morale, Vale decided not to ask him if it was too late to request a transfer.

A few seconds later, no further questions having been raised, Riker ended the briefing. "Suit up. Team leaders, check your team's suits. Security personnel, check your team leaders' suits. Make sure the implanted transponders are working. They'll help you find each other if you get separated and keep you from hitting each other with friendly fire."

The group moved in an orderly fashion to don their gear and begin the premission check of their weapons and equipment. Vale led her trio of specialists to their pressure suits, which had been modified with extra air supplies. In addition, grafted onto the matte black outer skins of the suits were webs of jury-rigged coils that she recognized from the *Starfleet Survival Guide* as an improvised structural-integrity field system.

Spitale held her suit at arm's length and eyed it suspiciously. "Will these work at ten kilometers?"

Lieutenant Fillion looked at the athletic young blonde and shrugged. "You're the engineer," he said. "You tell me."

"Relax," Vale said, pulling off her uniform jacket. "It'll work. It's a marvel of modern engineering."

"Wow, a marvel," Fillion said, sounding unconvinced. "Imagine what we could do with *two* hours' notice."

Vale had to give the man credit: He'd developed a healthy cynicism for the logistical prowess of Starfleet. "Just suit up," she said, shimmying out of her trousers and grabbing her pressure suit. "If you don't like it, you can exchange it."

"For what?" he said.

"A court-martial," Vale said.

As Fillion scrambled out of his uniform and into his pressure suit, Vale concealed her amusement: Never in a million years would she have thought she would need to resort to the threat of a court-martial to get a man out of his clothes.

Chapter 21
U.S.S. Enterprise-E—Bridge

KELL PERIM PRACTICED a series of high-impulse maneuvers as she acclimated her fingers to the helm controls of the *I.K.S. Taj*. The Klingon ship had sustained serious damage during the Tezwan sneak attack, but the *Enterprise* engineering staff, using Klingon starship-repair schematics from the Dominion War, had quickly restored the cruiser's impulse power and warp engines and outfitted the *Taj* with hardware that let Perim remote-pilot the ghost ship from the safety of the *Enterprise* bridge.

With Riker, Data, and Vale all absent from the ship, the young Trill lieutenant was the acting first officer. She could have assigned the beta-shift conn officer to pilot the *Taj* on this, its final mission; after all, Lieutenant Magner was a good starship pilot—very good, in fact. But from the moment Perim had piloted the Klingon warship through a simple evasive pattern, just to test the remote-command system, she'd found herself unwilling to relinquish the controls.

Perim had never piloted a Klingon vessel before. Even though the sensation was dulled by the long-distance nature of the experience, she could tell, even from the cold telemetry readouts, that the dark starship had a deadly grace unlike anything else she'd ever flown. True to the destiny of violence it had borne since the moment its keel had been laid, the *Taj* cut through space like a warrior's blade. It responded like a lover to Perim's touch, turning and yawing and accelerating at her slightest whim. It was, in a word, magnificent.

Her orders were to pilot the *Taj* into orbit over Tezwa, and, at the last moment before the planet-based artillery destroyed the Klingon cruiser, adjust its heading and velocity so that its debris would scatter across the widest possible area of the upper atmosphere. At the same time, Ensign Le Roy at ops would beam the strike teams off of the *Taj* and into orbit. The general idea was that the ship's debris, as it fell into the atmosphere, would mask the strike teams' descent. However, if Perim's controlled sacrifice of the *Taj* was off by even a tenth of a degree, she might kill all six strike teams instantly.

Adding to her anxiety was the fact that one of the teams was being led by Deputy Chief of Security Jim Peart, with whom she had, only two nights ago, shared a romantic dinner that had promised to lead to more dates, and more dinners, and who knew what else—assuming he didn't go and get himself killed pulling another of his trademark crazy-brave stunts. And also assuming she didn't accidentally leave him trapped in a lethal maelstrom of burning starship wreckage.

"Strike teams standing by," Riker said over the com.

"Routing the Taj's *transporter controls to the ops station."*

"Acknowledged," Picard said.

"Transporter control verified," Le Roy said. "Coordinates preset for low-orbit destinations."

"Thank you, Ensign," Picard said. "Helm. Ready?"

"Aye, Captain," Perim said, even though her hands had begun to tremble.

"Lieutenant Wriede?" the captain said.

The willowy, dark-haired tactical officer looked dissatisfied. "The *Taj*'s weapons are offline," he said. "Shields at sixteen percent."

"Do the best you can," Picard said, then turned his attention back to the main viewer. "Ensign Le Roy, patch in the *Taj*'s viewscreen. Let's see what she sees."

"Aye, sir," Le Roy said as she keyed in the command. The only change was a barely noticeable shift in the starfield.

"Helm, take her in," Picard said, pointing at the screen.

Perim activated the *Taj*'s warp engines. The stars on the main viewer stretched away from Tezwa, presently a single point at screen-center that rapidly grew larger and brighter.

"Ensign Le Roy," Picard said. "Energize transporters on my mark."

Perim watched the rapidly changing data on her console. A bitter pang of regret began to take hold of her heart as she realized the proud Klingon vessel was only moments away from destruction. "Ten seconds to orbit," she said. The shimmering orb of Tezwa enlarged to dominate the viewscreen.

"Prepare to engage impulse engines," Picard said. He

walked forward and stopped between Le Roy and Perim at the front of the bridge. Behind him, officers at noncritical stations stopped what they were doing and turned to watch the end of the *Taj*.

Perim's index finger hovered above the warp-power cutoff. "Dropping to impulse in three . . . two . . . one." She pressed the key. The stars retreated to static points, and the curving horizon of the planet rolled until it stretched across the bottom edge of the screen frame.

"Evasive pattern Sierra-two," Picard said. "Half-impulse." Perim had finished the maneuver before the captain had finished giving the order. The warship was grace incarnate as it raced toward oblivion.

"The planet's artillery is locking on," Wriede said without looking up from his tactical display. "All guns charging."

"All power to shields," Picard said. Perim could almost sense the heat from atmospheric friction as thermal effects flared across the main viewer. Anguish tightened her throat.

"They've got a lock!" Wriede shouted.

"Helm," Picard said, "ten degrees yaw, give them a good target." He glanced at Le Roy. "Energize!"

"They're firing!" Wriede said as Le Roy started the transport sequence.

"Steady," Picard said.

Perim saw the barrage of artillery blasts converge toward the viewscreen. Out of the corner of her eye, she saw Le Roy finish the transport sequence with a deft slide of her hands across the ops console.

The artillery blasts hit home. The main viewer whited out with static, then blinked back to a serene starfield.

"The *Taj* has been destroyed," Wriede confirmed.

Perim blinked back her tears as she and Le Roy rose and stood at attention next to their consoles. *I was its pilot for less than an hour, and it's like losing an old friend,* she brooded. *I always fall too hard, too far, too fast.* She thought of Jim Peart and the danger he now faced as he led his strike team toward Tezwa. *One date and I was thinking about us having a future,* she reflected. *Now he'll probably come home in pieces. Some future.* She sighed. *Better just not to get involved.*

After a moment of quiet mourning for the ship they'd sacrificed, Picard broke the silence. "The strike teams?" he said, looking at Le Roy.

"Transport went perfectly," the short-coiffed blonde replied. "They should be entering the atmosphere now."

"Debris scatter?" Picard asked.

"Ninety-eight percent of optimal," Wriede said.

Picard nodded, his jaw tight. "Well done, everyone," he said. He moved back to his chair and sat down. "Lieutenant Perim," he said. She turned to face him. "I believe you're in the wrong seat."

After a moment of confusion, she realized what he was saying and stood up. She felt terribly self-conscious for a few seconds, then walked to what she couldn't help but think of as Riker's chair. As Lieutenant Magner took over for her at the helm, she sat down next to Picard. "Sorry, sir," she said.

"It's all right," he said. "Just get us ready to face the Klingon fleet."

For a few minutes she busied herself requesting damage reports, ordering battle drills, and shifting the damage-control teams' repair priorities. She was about to ask Dr. Crusher for an update on which personnel had been cleared to return to duty when Picard leaned over and spoke to her in a low voice.

"Are you all right, Lieutenant?"

The question caught her off guard. "Yes, sir."

"You've seemed upset since the strike teams deployed."

She stared at her feet for a moment before she looked up and answered him. "It's the *Taj,* sir," she said. "It's just that . . . she was a fine ship."

"Yes, she was," Picard said. "But if her sacrifice serves a greater good, her loss won't have been in vain."

Perim had nothing else to say, so she just nodded. She knew the captain was right, and that the Klingon cruiser's seemingly senseless end had made possible their one hope of stopping an invasion that would cost many millions of innocent lives. But even knowing why it had been necessary, she couldn't deny her sorrow, or her guilt for being the one whose hands sent a ship so noble and beautiful to its lonely demise.

Chapter 22
Tezwa Orbit

TRANSPORTING INTO ZERO g had been brutally disorienting, and materializing so close to the explosion of the *I.K.S. Taj* had placed Riker and his strike team in the midst of a shock wave that left him feeling like he'd been kicked inside out.

As soon as he regained tactile sensation, he activated his orbital skydiving suit's low-power deflector field. A few seconds later, a storm of blast-scattered particles rushed past him. A sizable chunk of the cruiser's bulkhead tumbled by, a bit too close for the first officer's liking, on its way to a fiery end in the atmosphere.

The other strike teams had materialized far enough away that Riker couldn't see most of them. One small group of specks, which he surmised was Taurik's team, was on its way planetside. They trailed behind a glowing shower of debris from the crewless Klingon battle cruiser, which he'd convinced Picard to sacrifice as a decoy to cover the beam-in of the strike personnel.

He looked around for his team. On his left and right, respectively, were engineers Tierney and Barnes. Razka had materialized in front of him, and was already angling himself toward the planet for his descent. Riker gestured to Tierney and Barnes, who signaled back that they were ready to make the dive. With a forward slash with his forearm, he keyed his suit's thrusters and rocketed toward the nightside of Tezwa.

The planet was aglow with two kinds of light. The major population centers resembled webs of steady, artificial-looking illumination that radiated out from several points in the highlands and traced wide paths along the coastlines. But the more remote regions of the planet were still ablaze with the aftermath of the Klingon counterattack. Vast rural areas had been turned into what Riker could only guess were now killing fields of plasma fire and jet black glass. Wreaths of smoke and pyroclastic ash had already begun to smother the planet in a bleak and deadly shroud.

A chunk of the *Taj* painted a reddish streak of flame across the upper atmosphere as it fell toward the inferno below. Seconds later, several more slabs of the Klingon ship's outer hull ignited as they struck the rarefied air. Riker adjusted his descent to follow the wreckage's trajectory, then transmitted the new coordinates to his strike team.

He felt the temperature inside his suit begin to rise as he plummeted toward the smoldering darkness below. As the planet's gravity pulled him downward with a merciless hand, he caught sight of another fragment of the *Taj* as it erupted into a short-lived cloud of sparks and then disintegrated.

Riker offered a silent but heartfelt salute to Captain Vekma and her crew as the last shards of their vessel faded into dust and billowed across the nightscape. He remembered the crush of her hand around his throat and the metallic odor of blood on her breath as she had cursed him for cheating her and her crew of honored deaths in battle. He doubted that Vekma or her crew would approve of the cause for which their ship had ultimately been sacrificed . . . but he hoped it would bring them honor in *Sto-Vo-Kor* all the same.

Chapter 23

Tezwa—Solasook Peninsula, 0200 Hours Local Time

DATA LED BRAVO TEAM through the dark canopy of storm clouds. He fell like a missile, his arms tight against his torso, his legs pressed together and feet extended. He checked the holographic display projected on his suit's faceplate. Obrecht and Heaton were ninety-three-point-six meters behind him and gaining at a rate of point-two meters per minute, well within safety parameters. The android second officer calculated that he could safely withstand a landing at more than twice the planned velocity, but he knew that his human compatriots could not.

The telemetry indicated that they were nearing chute-deployment altitude, but there was no sign of a break in the cloud cover. The wind resistance was sharply rising and the temperature was steadily dropping to well below freezing. The numbers added up to a grim result: He and his team were descending into a blizzard.

He signaled his team to deploy their parachutes as they pierced the upper level of precipitation. He keyed his chute release. The carbon-nanofiber canopy erupted above him, unfurled with a roar, and slowed his descent with a violent snap.

Wild flurries of snow and sleet swirled around him, driven forward by a relentless wind. He couldn't see the rest of his team, but based on the information he was receiving from their transponder signals, he knew that they had all activated their parachutes and were maintaining formation within fifty meters of him. From inside the heart of this winter storm, the view in every direction was identical. He focused his attention on the readouts from the suit's built-in sensors, and on reacting to the brutal wind that was forcing him into an accelerating spiral as he neared the ground.

The altimeter rapidly dwindled toward zero. Data accessed his skills database and set himself in the textbook-perfect posture for a high-speed landing on a possibly hard and uneven surface. His feet broke through a top layer of icy crust and sank into deep, soft snow. Adjusting his stance in less than two-tenths of a second, he used the natural cushion to his advantage and came to a stop standing upright, buried up to his waist. He unclasped the breakaway harness for his parachute, which fluttered to the ground behind him.

He turned and pulled his chute toward him, hand over hand, rolling it into a tight coil. When it was reduced to a compact bundle, he stuffed it beneath the snow cover. Using the control pad on the arm of his suit, he activated its camouflage circuit and selected the adaptive gray-and-white arctic pattern.

He keyed his suit's secure internal com. "Data to Bravo Team," he said. "Sound off, please."

"Obrecht, here."

"Heaton, here."

"Parminder, here."

"Lock on to my signal and regroup," Data said.

Data waited for the rest of his team to rejoin him. One by one they emerged from the white curtain of the storm, vague shadows at first, then crisp outlines. Heaton reached him first, followed by Parminder and Obrecht. As they closed to within arm's reach, he noticed that part of what made them so difficult to see was that they had also engaged their camouflage.

"Status," Data said.

"Good to go," Parminder said.

He made a twirling gesture with his finger to Obrecht, who turned his back to him. Data opened a side pocket of the engineer's backpack and removed a tricorder. He scanned in the general direction of the firebase and adjusted the device's settings until he had a solid fix on the target's location. He turned toward the target, noted the topography of the terrain ahead, and judged it passable. He started the hard trudge forward through the knee-deep snow. "Follow me," he said.

Chapter 24
Tezwa—Nokalana Sea, 1000 Hours Local Time

FROM SPACE, the vast expanse of ocean had looked tranquil. Now, as Christine Vale and Delta Team plummeted toward it, and the coastlines of continents vanished beyond the edge of an increasingly close and level horizon, she saw white-crested storm waves rolling across an angry sea.

"Delta Team," she said into her helmet mic. "Close it up and stand by to open and drop on my marks."

She monitored her squad's relative positions. The timing of this jump would leave little room for error, and she couldn't guarantee their safety unless they all maintained precisely the same altitude and rate of descent. This was going to be what the old-timers used to call a HALO jump—high altitude, low opening. They would wait until they had dropped low enough to evade the Tezwan's defense scanners, open their chutes only long enough to slow their fall to just less than the maximum impact that their suits' structural integrity fields could absorb, then release their breakaway harnesses and drop into the ocean at more than two hundred kilometers per hour.

All in a day's work, Vale mused. *If you're insane.*

She noticed that Fillion was lagging nearly a full second behind the rest of the team. "Fillion, tighten up."

"If I get any tighter, I'll implode," Fillion said.

"If you don't catch up, you'll be dead."

"Aye, aye, sir," came his flip reply. *"Commencing emergency butt-clench."*

"Spare us the details," Vale said. She was beginning to wonder whether bringing Fillion on this mission would prove to be a mistake. He was smart, cool under fire, and was one of the few security officers on the *Enterprise* who was qualified to make this kind of high-risk deep-sea dive from orbit. But his infallible talent for making a smart remark in response to any order—a key reason he washed out of Starfleet Special Ops and ended up on the *Enterprise*—was grating on her nerves. She feared that if the Tezwans didn't kill him, she might have to.

Seeing that Fillion was back in position, she checked the holographic heads-up display on her helmet faceplate. "Get ready," she said. "Roll in five . . . four . . . three . . . two . . . one . . . roll!" Pulling her body into an almost fetal curl, she tucked her knees toward her chest. She quickly confirmed that the rest of her team had finished the maneuver. "Open chutes in four . . . three . . . two . . . one . . . GO!"

Her team's parachutes raced upward in unison, amorphous silver blurs reaching toward the ashen sky. As they unfurled, her own canopy expanded. A jolt of deceleration trauma shot through her back and shoulders.

The churning ocean took on more distinct and increasingly ominous details as she continued to fall. As her rate of descent slowed to just under one hundred kilometers per hour, she activated her suit's improvised structural-integrity field.

"Fields on, stand by to drop," she said. The altimeter dropped to eighty meters, then seventy. She started her countdown. "In three . . . two . . . one . . . drop!" She and her team unclasped their breakaway harnesses and plummeted, feet-first, into the lead-colored water. It was almost like striking a solid surface. The impact jammed her knees and pelvic joints upward with a dull, grinding pain. Spasms shot up either side of her spine. She choked back a grunt of agony and reminded herself that if not for Tezwa's lighter-than-Earth gravity, she'd probably be dead right now.

The pain abated. Clarity returned, and she magnified her helmet display. Fillion and Sakrysta were clumsily fishing their diving fins from their chest packs, while Spitale had already equipped her gear and was swimming toward her with easy, languid kicks. Vale retrieved her fins from her own pack and carefully slipped the flexible attachments over her boots. By the time she secured her fins in place, Spitale had moved to a flanking position on her right, while Fillion and Sakrysta swam quickly to regroup with them. Diffuse gray daylight from above danced in wave-distorted ripples across the divers.

The warbled voice of the ocean seemed to come from every direction. It was a low, constant roar punctuated by long, keening notes and tiny bubbles of noise that popped from the deep, then were swallowed by the endless depths. An enormous school of metallic-hued fish passed with a low *whoosh* beneath Vale and her team. The fish seemed to sparkle in the refracted flicker from the surface, cast in sharp contrast against the impenetrable darkness that yawned beneath them.

Vale opened a flap of her chest pack and took out her tricorder. The device's familiar, bright bluish glow lit her up like a spotlight as she checked their position and established a bearing to the target. She set the device to stay locked on to the submerged Tezwan firebase and relay its readings to her team's helmet displays. A moment later, all three of her personnel waved to confirm they had received the transmission. Vale gave the signal to activate their gravity belts, which would help pull them down despite the planet's lighter gravity and their high buoyancy in its dense, richly saline ocean.

The team swam downward, past aquatic life-forms of all types and sizes; undulating eels snaked between them while enormous tentacled mollusks and self-illuminating, semiliquid transparent blobs hovered on the periphery of their vision. Several minutes later, the scant light from the surface rapidly melted away. The team was enveloped in pure, cold darkness.

Soon after the light faded, the sounds of the sea retreated as well. In the claustrophobia-inducing shadow, Vale was acutely aware of the rush of her own breathing, which roared loud inside her helmet—the hopeful gasps of intake, the low gusts of exhalation, one after another, steady and hypnotic.

A soft, synthetic tone inside her helmet notified her that she and her team had just reached a depth of four kilometers. She hadn't really needed the alert. With little else to focus on in the unbroken black void, her eyes had remained fixed on two readouts on her faceplate: her bearing and her depth. But even if her heads-up display hadn't provided her with a constant meter of her downward progress, the increasing sensation of pressure would have been a more than sufficient reminder.

Nearly forty minutes after the beginning of their dive, a second chime announced the eighth kilometer of their descent. Vale activated her suit's tachyon filter, which could render even the most lightless environment into one with at least twilight-level, monochromatic-blue illumination. In the distance below, she could now discern the first edges and outlined shapes of the undersea base. The structure slowly grew brighter and more distinct as she swam deeper. "Spitale," Vale said. "Activate the signal jammer and drop it ahead of us."

As the compact jamming unit sank toward the ocean floor, Vale strained to locate the exposed pressure hatch that she intended to use as the point of entry to the base. Unable to find it, she wondered if perhaps she had gotten turned around during the dive and was looking at the structure from the wrong side. A quick survey of its other key features confirmed that she was looking at it from the correct angle. Her confusion was dispelled a moment later as she realized that an unfamiliar shape was blocking the pressure hatch.

It was a submarine, docked and anchored—and obstructing the base's only viable point of entry.

Fillion's voice crackled softly over the secure channel. *"Lieutenant? Is that thing supposed to be there?"*

Vale stared grimly at the imposing submersible vessel. "No," she said. "It isn't."

A brief moment, tinged with dread, passed in silence.

Sakrysta, a normally quiet Kriosian woman—whom, Vale recalled with some embarrassment, she had mistaken for a Trill when they first met—said what no one else wanted to. *"So, um . . . what now?"*

Vale continued to aim her intense stare at the submarine. "I'm thinking," she said calmly. "I'm thinking."

Chapter 25

Tezwa—Mount Ranakar, 1400 Hours Local Time

LA FORGE SAW THE ACCIDENT COMING, but there was nothing he could do to stop it.

The entry into the atmosphere had gone smoothly, as had the free fall. But after Piper Team had opened their parachutes and dropped below the cloud cover, they discovered that their landing zone was completely concealed by a thick gray blanket of fog. Though it would help conceal their midafternoon arrival from unwanted observers, it presented an unexpected hazard because their heads-up displays were suffering heavy interference from the hidden base's energy field. Of the four of them, only La Forge—with his full-spectrum synthetic vision—was able to see the ground beneath its misty shroud.

He'd been able to coach T'Eama and security officer Braddock toward safe touchdowns, but Wathiongo, who had appeared to be on a safe line of approach, became caught in an unexpected wind shear that pushed him toward the jagged outcroppings of rock which dotted the middle of the cliff face. Before La Forge could warn him, the engineer's parachute snagged on the rocks and came apart with a brittle rip.

T'Eama and Braddock weren't able to see what was happening behind the thick curtain of vapor. La Forge alone witnessed, with growing distress, Wathiongo's unprotected fall toward the ground. The man ricocheted off the cliff face and vanished into the forest canopy several dozen meters below. Distant snaps and cracks of breaking branches heralded the man's plummet toward the ground. Then the sounds of his fall ceased.

La Forge guided himself toward a clearing in the trees, on his left. His feet skimmed the leafy branches that reached up, like supplicative arms, from the forest canopy. A sudden gust of wind at his back caused him to miss the clearing by a few meters. He instinctively pulled his limbs inward as he crashed through the upper foliage layer and rammed a path through the heavier boughs below. The furious series of impacts jabbed him with sharp tips of broken edges and pummeled him with one blunt impact after another. He felt the welts and bruises multiplying beneath his protective gear.

His descent slowed with one hard jolt, then another, before he was yanked to a halt and left dangling, four meters above the ground, in the barren lower limbs of a tight cluster of trees.

Placing his trust in the laws of physics and the accuracy of Vale's premission report, he unlocked the breakaway clasp and dropped free of his snared parachute. In Tezwa's lighter gravity, he fell just a bit slower than he was used to, and he landed with a slightly less jarring impact than his muscle memory expected. It was almost like the sensation of falling in a dream, when one knows it's a dream and there's really no danger. *Of course, it depends on how far you fall,* he reminded himself, and he thought of poor Wathiongo. He keyed his secure com. "La Forge to Wathiongo, please respond."

No answer came. He activated the transmitter again. "La Forge to Piper Team. Sound off."

"T'Eama, acknowledging."

"Braddock here."

"Lock on to Wathiongo and regroup," La Forge said. Following the signal from Wathiongo's suit transponder, which registered as holographically generated bearing-and-elevation coordinates on the lower right-hand corner of La Forge's faceplate, the chief engineer powered up his suit's camouflage system and selected the gray-brown highland pattern. The forest floor was thick with scrub brush, thorny brambles, and dead vegetation. It all contributed to what La Forge considered to be an uncomfortably loud rustle that haunted his every step.

He pushed ahead toward Wathiongo. After a few minutes he saw Braddock and T'Eama converging from separate directions. Both of them seemed to be having difficulty finding their way through the fog. "T'Eama, Braddock," La Forge said. "I can see you both. Can you see each other?"

"Negative," T'Eama said.

"Not a thing," Braddock said.

"Braddock, you should be able to see Wathiongo soon."

"Still not . . . hang on, sir," Braddock said. The burly security officer pushed his way into a tall cluster of

bushes, then crouched out of sight. *"Found him, sir. He's alive."*

La Forge quickened his pace and joined Braddock at the same time T'Eama reached him. Moving into the bushes, they kneeled on either side of their fallen comrade. The signal jammer he had carried now lay on the ground a meter away from him. Braddock had removed Wathiongo's helmet and was affixing a cortical stimulator to the fallen man's temples.

La Forge removed his own helmet. "Report," he said.

Braddock took off his own headgear. "More broken bones than I can count," he said, setting down his helmet. "Serious internal injuries, skull fractures, concussion. I gave him ten cc's of telorathal to slow the bleeding and keep him stable." *Good thing Vale requires her people to take first-aid training,* La Forge realized. Braddock turned on the cortical stimulator. It hummed with quiet, regular pulses. "This should keep his brain functioning." He picked up his tricorder from the ground next to Wathiongo and scanned him. "We might be able to keep him alive like this for a few hours, but if we don't get him to a sickbay by then, he's dead."

"I presume he is not stable enough to be moved," T'Eama said as she doffed her helmet. Her hair, cropped in a short bob, was less rigidly styled than that of some Vulcans.

"Definitely not," Braddock said.

"Commander," she said. "May I suggest we camouflage Ensign Wathiongo's location and attempt to carry on without him?"

"We don't have much choice," La Forge said. "Braddock, do you know much about demolitions?"

"More than a little," Braddock said with an ironic nod.

"All right," La Forge said. "Fix him up, best you can. T'Eama, set up the signal jammer. When you're both done, salvage his critical gear. Then we'll move out."

T'Eama and Braddock set to work. La Forge looked up at the forbidding cliff they were about to scale. It was a nearly two-hundred-meter vertical ascent up a jagged face composed of what his old climbing instructor had called "jingle rock." The name was derived from the pseudo-musical sound it made when it collapsed under your feet and struck up a percussive melody while falling on anyone unlucky enough to be down below.

La Forge recalled making a joke about this mission an hour ago, during the briefing. But now Wathiongo was down and dying, and one look up made it clear that scaling this treacherous cliff would be no laughing matter.

Chapter 26
Tezwa—Linoka Forest, 1810 Hours Local Time

ENSIGN FIONA MCEWAN made a pinpoint-perfect landing. The nimble young redhead hit the ground and stepped clear as she released her parachute canopy. The fluttering swirl of fabric sank to the ground like settling dust.

Looking around, she saw the Linoka Forest was not what she had expected. It was dry and dead, bereft of foliage, little more than a wasteland. Barren tree trunks, acid-bleached to the color of bone, jutted from the charcoal-colored ground. The sunset blazed bloodred behind inky streaks of smoke and was almost indistinguishable from the sinister glow of fire that lined the horizon beneath it. Flakes of ash wafted through the air like snowflakes, borne aloft on hot gusts of wind generated by the inferno that raged only a few short kilometers away.

Collateral damage from the Klingon counterattack, McEwan realized. *I'd hate to see the populated areas right now.*

She made a quick head count of the rest of Echo

Team. Lieutenant Taurik, the leader, had already hidden his parachute and was rounding up the engineers, Mobe and Rao. McEwan rolled up her parachute, tucked it between two large rocks, then rejoined the rest of the group. She noticed that she was the only one who had activated her suit's olive-drab camouflage. *Probably because there's no forest,* she chided herself.

Taurik checked his tricorder, then turned and pointed with an extended arm. "The target is that way, sixteen-point-four kilometers," he said. "Move out, double-quick time." Taurik jogged away, and the rest of the team followed close behind him.

McEwan suspected she knew the answer to her next question, but hoped she was wrong. "Sir," she said, her voice quaking with each running step, "should we be running *into* the fire?"

"Our suits are designed to protect us from the thermal effects of atmospheric reentry, Ensign," Taurik said. "They should protect us for ninety-one minutes. The flames will conceal our approach to the entrance of the firebase."

Less than one kilometer ahead, the wildfire danced with malevolent glee. It was a red-orange giant, reaching from the ground to high above the swiftly igniting dead forest, each second multiplying its appetite and its fury.

And we're running straight into it. Like just about every other sentient being in the quadrant, McEwan had heard that Vulcans were renowned for their sound, logical judgment. As she followed Taurik into the heart of the inferno, she could only hope that he wasn't an exception to the rule.

Chapter 27

Tezwa—Kolidos Desert,
0615 Hours Local Time

PEART PEEKED HIS HEAD UP over the crest of the sand dune. He squinted into the rising sun. Silhouetted in the fiery golden dawn, four armed hovercraft—each carrying a dozen Tezwan soldiers—glided toward him. Dropping back behind the dune, he looked at the other members of Sierra Team.

"Four more," he said. "Less than a kilometer away."

"Damn," Scholz said. "What're they all doing out here?"

Peart shrugged. "Maneuvers? Training exercises? Who knows." He felt the others waiting for his next order. The Tezwans were closing in on his position from four directions. Sierra Team's adaptive desert camouflage might have helped them evade detection had their arrival not been so visible. But neither the time nor the location of the strike had been flexible; it was simply Sierra Team's misfortune to have been assigned a daylight landing in a location that was swarming with Tezwan soldiers.

"Dig in," Peart said. "T'Sona, bury Morello. I'll cover

150

Scholz." The strike team split into pairs and began digging frantically with their hands, burrowing through the loose sand with furious scooping motions.

The thrumming engines of the Tezwan hovercraft grew louder. Scholz hunkered down into his hastily dug trench, and Peart pushed the excavated sand back in on top of the tall engineer. Scholz's long, rudder-nosed face projected incredulity as he watched Peart. "And this will accomplish what?" he asked.

"It'll buy us time," Peart said as he covered Scholz's faceplate, fully concealing the man from view.

Peart moved with awkward, sliding steps toward T'Sona, who had just finished covering Morello. The petite Vulcan woman worked quickly and didn't say a word as she and Peart gouged a narrow trench in the shifting sand just below the peak of the dune. As soon as Peart deemed it wide enough, he rolled into it and pulled T'Sona in beside him. Spinning sand devils, whipped up by the approaching hover-vehicles, spun across the top of the dune as the two Starfleet officers scrambled to pull the sides of their foxhole in on themselves. Disturbed sand washed over them in waves as the Tezwan hovercraft passed overhead.

Peart lay absolutely still, his limbs entangled with T'Sona's, her faceplate flush against his own. He heard the thumps of feet landing on the dune, and the muffled hum of antigrav engines cruising past.

So far, so good, he decided. *Now all I need is a plan.*

Chapter 28
Tezwa—Mokana Basin,
2220 Hours Local Time

FLYING YELLOW BUGS with fat abdomens and terrifyingly large stingers swarmed around Riker's head, filling the sultry night air with an angry buzz. He waved them away as he slogged forward, each step a struggle to dislodge his boots from the deep, clinging mud. The hollow gulps of his feet pulling free of the wet earth were, in turn, drowned out by the steady chorus of screeches, squawks, and croaks that reverberated through the primeval wilderness.

Tierney and Barnes stayed close behind him, their own trudging clomps through the mud producing a regular cadence of guttural sucking sounds. Several paces ahead, Razka was clearing the path. He had brought a replicated machete, and was using the broad, angular blade to hack through the dense vines and thick undergrowth that blocked their path.

The heat by itself was suffocating, and it was made worse by the oppressive stench that polluted every breath Riker tried to draw. The cloying perfume of blossoming flowers was mixed with the sickly sweet odor of decaying flesh and the rancid stink of rotting vegetation. The air was steamy with humidity, like the vapor rising off a vast cauldron of fetid stew. It all conspired to leech perspiration from every pore on Riker's body. His hair was matted with sweat, which trickled in fat beads across his temples and dispersed into his beard.

The bugs and the heat and the stench would all have been inconsequential had Alpha Team not been forced to shed so much of its gear simply to traverse the jungle. The path was so thickly overgrown that within a few steps every protruding piece of equipment—from air tanks to helmet valves to items on their belts—had become hopelessly entangled in the vines and snaking burrweeds. The only solution had been to doff all but their most essential weapons and supplies. After setting up the signal jammer, they traveled light and fast, trusting the night and their adaptive, dark green camouflage to protect them. That meant no helmets, no overloaded backpacks, no self-contained air supplies—and, for Razka, no boots. He had assured Riker that he moved faster without them. Watching the Saurian blaze their trail, Riker realized Razka hadn't been boasting.

A staccato burst of animal shrieks on Riker's left was answered moments later by a long series of whooping caws, from higher above in the rain-forest canopy. An insect landed on the back of his neck. He swatted it away, but not before it bit him. The wound burned. It felt like a lit flame being held against his skin. He let out a small, sharp gasp of pain.

Razka stopped pushing forward and turned around, concerned. "Commander? Are you all right?"

"I'm fine," Riker said, massaging the area around the bite. The burning sensation became less severe, but clearly was going to persist for a while. "Keep going," he added.

Razka resumed hacking a channel through the vermin-infested foliage. Every slash of his blade provoked eruptions of insects and birds, and all manner of crawling and slithering life-forms scattered away between his bare, taloned feet as he pushed forward, methodical and relentless.

Riker noticed the air was growing warmer. Then he heard distant rumbles of thunder, harbingers of a tropical storm rolling in. Through the swaying boughs overhead, he caught glimpses of reddish lightning flashing in the north. He counted off the seconds until he heard more thunder, and estimated that the storm front was roughly ten kilometers away. A few minutes later, he caught another fork of lightning slicing across the night sky, and he counted off the delay once again. It was shorter this time. The storm was getting closer, and quickly.

Ahead, he heard a splash. He pushed through a hanging tangle of leafy vines and saw Razka waist-deep in a murky bog. The weathered Saurian had a tricorder in his scaly hand, held at arm's length while he scanned the swampy terrain ahead. He looked back at Riker. "Most of it's less than one-point-five meters deep," he said. "If we're careful, it should be a slightly easier path."

Riker eyed the swamp suspiciously. "You sure it's safe?"

"No," Razka said. "But neither is the jungle."

"Point taken," Riker said. He stepped toward the swamp. The bank was coated in slime, and he slipped forward, arms windmilling. Rather than risk pitching headfirst into the muck, he sprung forward and jumped feet-first into the muddy water. He landed a couple meters to the right of Razka and promptly sank up to his neck. A choking swallow of filthy water splashed into his gasping mouth. He spat it out and coughed. He treaded water for a moment, then worked his way back toward the shallows. He glared at Razka. "I thought you said it was less than one and a half meters."

"You have to know where to jump, sir," Razka said.

Riker frowned, then looked back at Tierney and Barnes, who had stopped at the swamp's edge. "Watch that first step," Riker said. Razka coached the two engineers into the putrid water, then resumed leading the team toward the target.

Riker hated sloshing through chest-deep filth, but he was grateful to be free of the suffocating closeness of the jungle. Overhead, the stars were blotted out by the sudden arrival of clouds, which were tinged pink with the glow of far-off fires burning out of control. Lightning flashed, and cut through the sky in long forks that arced into the jungle on all sides.

Riker felt something sinewy brush against his leg, beneath the opaque water. Then it was gone. He stopped moving. "We've got company," he said, looking down and trying to detect any sign of what had touched him. The rest of the team came to a halt. Razka drew his machete from the long scabbard slung across his back. Tierney and Barnes looked around nervously.

A pair of tentacles shot up from the water. In a blur they snaked around Barnes's throat and right arm. He was yanked into the air and backward, then down into the feculent murk. Tierney and Riker scrambled to aim their phaser rifles, but neither got a shot off before Barnes disappeared from view.

In one graceful action, Razka sheathed his machete and dived into the darkness below.

Riker and Tierney stood motionless, surrounded by the almost mechanical chirrups of insects and the rasping croaks of swamp creatures. An ululating birdcall echoed far away, then went silent. A cannonade of thunder tore across the sky and sent palpable tremors through the air and water.

The swamp monster exploded from beneath the swamp and rent the night with a tumultuous roar. Ten of its dozen tentacles flailed wildly around Riker and Tierney, slapping the water into a dark froth. One of the two tentacles that had snared Barnes had been severed near the beast's central mass, but the other was still locked around the young ensign's throat. Razka clung to a spiny protuberance next to the creature's fearsome, fang-filled mouth and resisted its manic, thrashing efforts to fling him aside.

Razka severed the base of the tentacle that continued to strangle Barnes. The animal unleashed a bloodcurdling howl. Riker aimed his rifle and fired a long burst into the creature's yowling maw. Half a second later, Tierney opened fire and added her phaser blast to his.

The creature recoiled, pulling all its appendages inward—then wrapped six of them around Razka, who flattened his machete against his chest. Riker and Tierney hit the beast in its center mass with two more long blasts. Then the Saurian's blade reflected a flash of lightning as it sliced through the suckered tentacles that had ensnared him.

With a stentorian groan, the monster sank beneath Razka's feet and retreated to its watery lair. Razka crouched chin-deep in the water as he backed slowly toward the rest of the strike team. Tierney helped Barnes back to his feet. Riker kept his rifle leveled against his shoulder and ready to fire until Razka sheathed his blade and said, "It's gone."

Shouldering his weapon, Riker called to Tierney, who was scanning Barnes with a tricorder. "How is he?"

"He smells bad, and he won't be talking much for a few days, but I think he'll be okay," Tierney said. Barnes looked at Riker and pointed over his own shoulder.

"Something's wrong with your shoulder?" Riker said. Barnes shook his head, then turned so Riker could see his back. "You lost your demolition kit," Riker realized. Barnes nodded with a grim frown. Riker exhaled a frustrated sigh. "Tierney, can we do this with just one kit?"

"I don't think so," the slender engineer said. "We can probably disable the firebase with one kit, but we need two to cause the feedback pulse that'll destroy the guns."

"Sir," Razka added, "if we don't destroy the guns, the Tezwans will be able to fire them manually. The *Enterprise* and the Klingons will be defenseless."

Riker pondered his options, then realized he didn't really have any. "How long until we reach the base?"

"Less than an hour," Razka said. "Provided we don't have any more close encounters with the local fauna."

"Tierney, you have as long as it takes us to get there to think of a way to do this with one kit."

"Aye, sir," she said.

Just then, to Riker's complete lack of surprise, the sky broke open and drenched the night in slashes of torrid rain.

Chapter 29
Earth

WHILE THE CITY OF PARIS slept beneath a placid dome of stars, President Zife paced anxiously, wearing a path into the off-white carpet of his elegant but minimalist office. He was dressed casually, in loose gray robes and soft, comfortable black shoes. He had always loved the panoramic view from here. Since his first day as president, this room's grandeur had made him feel important, made him finally believe that he was the elected leader of one of the most important political entities in the galaxy.

Now it felt like a gilded prison, lined with the artifacts of his imminent disgrace. Here, the desk at which he'd reviewed his chief of staff's ingenious plan to lay a trap for the Dominion. There, the pen with which he'd signed the classified executive order that set the plan in motion. Surrounding him on all sides, one of many worlds whose trust he had betrayed and whose wrath he felt lurking in a future that was all too swiftly taking shape on Tezwa.

The door chime sounded. "Mr. President," his secretary Yina said, "Mr. Azernal is here."

"Send him in," Zife said.

The door opened, quiet as a whisper, then closed behind Azernal. The crimson-garbed man plodded in with heavy steps, his shoulders hunched beneath an invisible burden. "I came as soon as I could, Mr. President," he said. Zife turned his back on him, finding the paunchy Zakdorn's pale reflection on the window far easier to tolerate than the man himself.

"How long until the Klingons reach Tezwa?" Zife said. He'd lost all sense of time since Chancellor Martok had delivered his declaration of war. Alone with his guilty conscience, it felt as if hours had slipped from his grasp, as if his every motion, his every thought were mired in hardening amber.

"Just over two hours, sir," Azernal said.

Zife could hardly believe it. Less than two hours had passed since Martok had roused him with an unbroken string of vulgar invectives. Barely an hour since he had shifted the burden of this unfolding quagmire onto the proverbial broad shoulders of the *Enterprise* and her crew. If the passage of the past two hours was a reliable indicator, then this would be the longest, darkest night of Zife's presidency.

"What's the *Enterprise*'s status?" Zife said.

"Picard's last report says that strike teams have been deployed to the planet surface," Azernal said. "Their orders are to destroy the artillery system using commando tactics."

Zife nodded, silently impressed by the bravado of Picard and his crew. Ordered to conquer a planet with little more than their fists, they'd jumped headfirst into the fray. "What's his plan for stopping the Klingon fleet?"

"Unknown," Azernal said. "His report said steps had been taken, but no details were provided."

"Best guess?"

Azernal pondered that for a few seconds. "Considering the unusually close bond between him and his former shipmate Worf, I'd suspect the captain has enlisted the ambassador's aid in some manner."

Zife wondered if Picard was negotiating directly with Martok. His brow wrinkled at the implausibility of such a notion, but he couldn't rule it out. "You think Picard is working a diplomatic angle?"

Azernal hesitated again, and averted his eyes from Zife as he spoke. "I think it would be in your best interest if I didn't speculate, Mr. President."

Zife didn't like the sound of that, but he knew that he'd dislike the sound of a blunter explanation even more, so he let the subject drop. He turned away from the placid nightscape of Paris and sat at his desk. "Computer," he said. "Alterian chowder." The replicator built into the desktop emitted a pleasing purr as it fabricated a spoon, and a white bowl filled with green soup. Zife preferred homemade chowder prepared with fresh *sahha* root and extra *hllok* leaf, but the tamer, replicated variety would suffice in a pinch. As soon as he lifted the first spicy spoonful to his lips, he found that he wasn't hungry, after all. He dumped the spoonful back into the bowl and let the spoon slip from his fingers. It plunked into the soup. Zife pushed the bowl away.

"We should redeploy the fleet," he said in a grim monotone.

"With all due respect, Mr. President," Azernal said, "I think that might be a bit premature."

"Premature?" Zife stared at the Zakdorn as though he were trying to burn a hole through the man. "How many hours before the Klingons discover the truth? How many days until they declare war? How long should we wait? Until their fleet lays waste to Trill? Or Deneva? Or Earth?"

"Moving our fleet now would betray our foreknowledge of the crisis," Azernal said. "My wargames account for the great majority of variables, but no advance scenario can predict all the random events that might occur. It's possible that the Klingon attack will destroy the evidence of our role in arming the Tezwans."

"Possible," Zife said. "But not likely."

"No," Azernal said. "It's not likely at all. But if the worst comes to pass, a delay of one day will be of little long-term strategic importance. However, if circumstances unfold in our favor, a hasty act motivated by fear could reverse the gains that fortune yields to us. . . . Patience, Mr. President."

Zife found it difficult to concentrate. Visions of disaster mingled in his thoughts with imagined accusations and his own feeble excuses. He labored to draw breath against the horrible weight pressing in on his chest. His voice was pitched with remorse. "We had so many chances, Koll," he said. "We could have stopped Kinchawn's military buildup by fast-tracking Tezwa into the Federation. . . ."

Azernal sounded uncomfortable. "Mr. President, I really think we—"

"We could have intervened to stop them from buying ships from the Danteri," Zife continued. "Or I could have met with Martok, explained the matter as one leader to another, and brokered a solution."

"Mr. President," Azernal said sharply. "Please calm down, sir. This isn't—"

"We must learn from our mistakes, Koll," Zife said.

"Sir, regret is a luxury we can't afford." The heavyset chief of staff rested his meaty hands against the far edge of Zife's polished black desk and leaned forward. "What's done is done, and steps have been taken to make things right."

"Make things *right?*" Zife almost laughed at the willful self-deception Azernal was asking him to commit. "We lied to our allies and led them into an ambush. We armed a madman and did nothing to contain his ambition until it was too late. And what is our answer now? How do we redress our sins?"

Lifting a padd from his desk, Zife sprang to his feet. He waved the small handheld device at Azernal. "Doublespeak! Commando tactics! Espionage! Why not call them what they really are, Koll? Why not admit we've sanctioned theft, lies, and murder?" He flung the padd at Azernal. The Zakdorn dodged the projectile, which clattered across the floor as Zife continued to rant. "Why not confess that we've made our officers into criminals to save ourselves?"

Azernal's voice was laced with cool anger. "We aren't saving *ourselves,* Mr. President. We're saving the Federation. We're preventing a power struggle that would engulf the quadrant and squander half a trillion lives." His voice grew louder and harsher. "So—with all due respect, sir—spare me your guilt, your moralizing, and your holier-than-thou rage. The people didn't elect you to be their conscience, they elected you to be their leader. To make the hard choices, to give the orders, and, when necessary, to *take the blame!*"

The verbal barrage overwhelmed Zife. The Bolian stood there, stunned by the ferocity of Azernal's tirade. He waited several awkward moments for Azernal to recant, but the irate Zakdorn, though he seemed to have regained his composure, offered no apology. Zife's knees wobbled. He planted his left hand on the arm of his chair to steady himself, then sat down.

"You're right," Zife said. "All the regret in the galaxy won't undo what I've done. . . . We can only go forward now."

"Yes, sir," Azernal said. "It's the only way."

"We should prepare for the inevitable, then," Zife said. "If Picard fails, what options do we have left?"

"We can avert a war with the Klingons," Azernal said, "or we can win a war with the Klingons."

"I'd prefer to avert the war," Zife said.

"As would I," Azernal said. "We'd have to convince the Klingons that someone other than us put the guns on

Tezwa. . . . A common enemy who would want to see our alliance shattered."

"Such as the Tholians," Zife said.

"Exactly," Azernal said.

"How do we point the finger at the Tholians when all the evidence points to us?"

"Simple," Azernal said. "We plant *new* evidence."

Zife's eyes narrowed. "You aren't serious."

Azernal looked insulted. "Why not?" the Zakdorn said. He paced in front of Zife's desk and mumbled to himself, shaping his plan in a stream-of-consciousness ramble, as he had done countless times during the Dominion War. "We frame the Tholians, then rattle some sabers with the Klingons. The Tholians deny everything, of course, which only makes them look more guilty."

A look of inspired mischief flitted across his face as he continued. "Then, just as the Klingons gear up for revenge, we cast doubt on our own frame-up job! We say we think *someone else* might be trying to goad us into a war with the Tholians, to lower our defenses in other sectors."

He nodded rapidly, his brow creased with intense thought. "We plant a few more clues to make it look like the Romulans framed the Tholians, tell the Klingons the Federation Council won't go to war without hard evidence of who did what, then we bury the whole thing in diplomatic investigations," he said. "Six months from now, we're back to status quo." He chuckled. "Simple, really. Don't know why I didn't think of it before."

Zife knew he was being maneuvered into another of Azernal's convoluted schemes, and that the solution couldn't possibly be so simple as he'd made it sound. But if another lie on his conscience was the price of sparing billions of lives from the horrors of war, it was a burden he was willing to bear.

Chapter 30
Tezwa—Keelee-Kee

IT WAS THE FIRST *Gatni* war council Bilok had called in more than a decade, and convening it in the middle of the night only made it feel like what everyone present knew it was: a conspiracy.

In addition to himself, Neelo, Dasana, and Elazol, four of the *Gatni* Party's senior ministers, had assembled in a remote and neglected research archive, in the Assembly Forum basement.

Itani, the minister of health, was a firebrand; at least once per day she could be trusted to unleash an apocalyptic vocal conflagration on the Assembly floor. In contrast, Edica, the minister of labor, spoke about as much as the granite statues that towered over the main entrance to the Forum—yet she managed to draft more pages of legislation than any other five ministers combined.

Unoro, the minister of justice, was regarded as a master dealmaker—which probably explained why he was the only *Gatni* other than Bilok who still occupied a senior seat in the Assembly. He'd undoubtedly fared better than Tawnakel, who still fumed over being forced to resign as minister of state; after being third in line of succession, being minister of the arts rankled.

Bilok had personally mentored all four of them, which was the only reason he trusted them enough to invite them here this evening. There was too much at stake to risk a larger gathering, which could easily fall prey to turncoats who would betray Bilok and his political brothers and sisters to Kinchawn's ruthless *Lacaam* Coalition.

"Our first priority," Bilok said in an urgent but hushed voice, "is to get me a new secure line of communication to the Federation. I've been informed that Kinchawn has placed a signal intercept on all transmissions from my home and office."

"Before we do anything," Unoro said, "we need to know more about your dealings with the Federation." Most of the other ministers murmured in agreement. Bilok expected they would be quite angry with him, but that couldn't be helped now.

"What I'm about to tell you must never leave this room," he said. "The future of our world and the Alpha Quadrant hinges on it." The other ministers nodded.

"Seven years ago," he continued, "shortly after Kinchawn rose to power, he made a deal with the Federation. They needed a neutral planet on which to build a massive artillery system. It was designed as a trap for the forces of the Dominion, with whom they were at war. You saw today what those guns can do.

"In exchange for helping them build their secret weapons, Kinchawn and the *Lacaam* Coalition received material aid meant to improve the standard of living for our people. Instead, Kinchawn sold those goods on the black market, through the Orion Syndicate. The money that he raised then bankrolled the *Lacaam'i* candidates' slander campaigns against us—and his new fleet.

"Four years ago, I was contacted by Koll Azcrnal, the senior advisor to the Federation president. He had come to believe that Kinchawn was unstable, and feared he might strike a bargain with the Dominion—betraying the Federation and its allies if and when they came looking to spring their trap. My charge was to ensure that Kinchawn didn't break his pact with the Federation. But—as you also saw today—I failed."

"A dangerous game you've committed us to," Itani said.

"I'd hardly call it a game," Tawnakel said. "Kinchawn's been signing pacts and making executive decisions without consulting the Assembly. I'd call that a dictatorship—and you *knew* about it, Bilok. But you said nothing."

"I apologize," Bilok said. "But it was necessary. I had to take a long-term view of the matter."

Neelo let out a derisive snort. "Did your 'long-term view' include Kinchawn dragging us to war? Or did it end just before millions of innocent people were killed in a tragedy you could have prevented?"

"Exposing Kinchawn would not have been a simple matter," Bilok said. "Its consequences would have stretched far beyond our world." He moved slowly around the room, addressing each of the ministers, delivering his points fast and hard, like knife jabs. "I expose Kinchawn, the Assembly erupts. Kinchawn moves to protect himself and suppresses dissent by force.

"Meanwhile, the Klingons accuse the Federation of violating the Khitomer Accords by putting heavy weapons so close to their shared border.

"We wage a civil war here on Tezwa, while the Klingons and the Federation fight a war of attrition all around us. In all likelihood they fight to a stalemate, then both collapse.

"Without the two great powers on either side of us, our once-neutral corner of space becomes a target of opportunity. One week the Tholians invade; the next, the Romulans become our masters.

"Or, I can choose to keep my own counsel and bide my time," Bilok said, returning to his original position at the head of the group. "I can win the trust of the Federation, and set the stage for Kinchawn's removal by convincing them that the *Gatni* Party can provide a more reliable, less militant ally."

Dasana wore a skeptical frown. "I concede that alienating the Federation serves no positive end, nor does sparking a war between them and the Klingons," she said. "But why seek out their alliance? Why not remain neutral?"

Several of the other ministers grumbled similar sentiments while Bilok formulated a reply.

"I've considered that question at length," the deputy prime minister said. "I've weighed the potential gains against the risks. And each time, I have concluded that we stand to gain more by becoming part of the Federation than we do by remaining outside of it."

Elazol looked unconvinced. "Such as?"

"A mutual-defense pact with hundreds of other worlds," Bilok said. "Massive improvements to physical infrastructure, including housing, transportation, and communications. Better medicine. Superior wildlife conservation. Better educational facilities. Access to advanced manufacturing techniques. I'd continue, but I think you get the point."

"Of course, you also become embroiled in their conflicts," Unoro said. "And they do seem to have a lot of them, for a people who preach the value of peace. Wars against the Cardassians, the Borg, the Dominion—and those are only in the past two decades."

"We're digressing," Bilok said. "The issue of Federation membership is a debate for another time. Right now we need to focus on the two most immediate threats to our security: the Klingons, and the prime minister himself."

"Well, we certainly have the means to repel the Klingons," Dasana said.

Elazol shook his head. "Just what we need—more violence."

"Minister Elazol is right," Bilok said. "We cannot defuse this crisis by escalating the war. We must not give in to fear—and we must not let Kinchawn use those guns again."

Itani's neck feathers ruffled with high dudgeon. "Are you suggesting we let those barbarians invade our world without a fight?"

"Of course not," Bilok said. "I'm saying we need to give them a better reason *not* to invade."

"Such as Kinchawn's head on a spear," Tawnakel quipped.

"You jest," Bilok said. "But you're right. Kinchawn created this mess. He alone gave the order to fire the artillery. We need to convince the Klingons that he can be held *individually* responsible for this atrocity, so that the rest of us don't need to be held collectively accountable."

"And we need to do it before the Klingons vaporize us," Neelo added.

"Preferably, we would act within the law," Bilok said. "An open vote of no confidence, followed by his arrest on thousands of charges of murder, for the Klingon soldiers he killed, and countless charges of negligence, for the millions of our people who were slain by the Klingons' counterattack."

"Neither of those charges addresses his subversion of the Assembly's authority," Unoro said. "He deserves to be charged with high treason."

"And so do I," Bilok retorted. "But there's no way to bring such a charge without exposing the Federation's complicity, and that brings us back to the very tragedy we're seeking to avert."

"Oh, I see," Unoro said. "So, in the name of political expediency, we've decided to run roughshod over justice?"

"Our goals are to remove Kinchawn and make amends with the Klingons," Bilok said. "Justice has nothing to do with it."

"Deposing him in an open vote will be nearly impossible," Neelo said. "Especially this soon after the battle."

"I know," Bilok said. "But we need to appease the Klingons before it's too late. If we have to resort to extralegal means to do so, that is a choice I can accept."

Itani looked horrified. "You're not advocating that we . . ." She apparently couldn't say the word. "But that's madness! What happened to principles? To ethics? To the rule of law?"

A voice like a groaning floorboard answered her. "Kinchawn abolished them long ago," Edica said, breaking her stony silence at last. "Just say the word, Bilok . . . and I'll assassinate that treacherous piece of filth myself."

Chapter 31
Qo'noS

DAYBREAK WAS HOURS AWAY, but the corridors of the Great Hall in the First City susurrated with the ominous undertones of a government preparing for war.

Worf noticed that security at the inner gate was tighter than usual. He was certain that the heightened state of alert was in force because of the impending invasion of Tezwa. The two guards who scanned him required that he empty the pockets and folds of his robes. They sifted brusquely through his effects. They eyed his identification card with suspicion, even though he knew the men recognized him from his many previous visits.

The taller of the two soldiers pointed to the diplomatic pouch slung at Worf's side. "Open it," the guard said.

"I will not," Worf said. Behind his shoulder he heard the other guard scrambling to lift his rifle. Worf maintained eye contact with the soldier in front of him. "It is a diplomatic pouch. Its contents are protected under the Khitomer Accords."

The first warrior backed away and raised his own weapon. Eyes were beginning to turn toward the conflict at the gate.

"Open it," the guard said again.

A guttural voice interrupted the confrontation. "The diplomatic privilege will be honored," said an older, gray-maned warrior, whom Worf recognized as General Goluk. The grizzled veteran pushed through the crowd of onlookers. He placed his hand on top of the guard's weapon and firmly lowered its barrel away from Worf. "He will not be searched. That is the law." He looked at Worf. "Apologies, Ambassador Worf, son of Mogh, House of Martok." Worf understood that the excessively formal greeting was Goluk's subtle way of rebuking the two overzealous guards.

Worf plucked his identification card from the hand of the guard behind him, then turned back to his benefactor and fellow member of the Order of the *Bat'leth.* "Apology accepted, General Goluk," Worf said. "I have urgent business with the chancellor."

"Of course, Mr. Ambassador," Goluk said. He turned and marched into the midst of the throng that stood between Worf and the private turbolift to the High Council chamber. "Move!" he bellowed, and his voice resounded off the distant arches of the ceiling, whose shape reminded Worf of a carbonized skeleton covered by a swath of blackened skin. The crowd parted, and Goluk marched through the gap and across the cavernous hall in long strides. Worf followed close behind him.

The turbolift ride to the top of the majestic structure was quiet. Worf had not had many dealings with General

Goluk, but he found him to be more agreeable than most members of the Klingon elite with whom he'd dealt since assuming his diplomatic post at the Federation Embassy—mostly because Goluk hated small talk.

The turbolift door opened to reveal a shadowy corridor. Its sparse lighting was a soothing dark crimson hue, like the standard duty lighting aboard a Klingon warship. Councillors' attachés and military advisors choked the corridor, moving from room to room, or scurrying toward the High Council chamber. A trio of young women, garbed in the robes of apprentice lawyers—and all from noble Houses, judging by the ancient family crests embroidered on their ceremonial white stoles—pushed past Worf as he stepped off the turbolift.

He heard the turbolift door hiss closed. Looking back, he saw that Goluk was no longer accompanying him.

He walked quickly and dodged through the slalom of bodies toward Martok's private chambers. Worf hadn't seen such manic goings-on in the Great Hall since the encounter with the Elabrej two years ago. It made sense, of course, that Martok would have summoned an emergency session of the High Council and marshaled every resource at his disposal. Unfortunately for Worf, the mass of people now crowding the Great Hall was going to make it difficult for him to accomplish his mission with any kind of discretion.

He arrived at the entrance to Martok's chambers. The huge double doors were cut from black granite and reinforced with duranium edge banding. The outer faces of the doors were engraved with a single, enormous gilded outline of the imperial trefoil inside a circle. Two warriors stood guard, one in front of each door. One kept his disruptor rifle slung low but clearly primed for action; the other stood in a classic ready position, feet apart, his *bat'leth* gripped in both hands and held horizontally, cutting edge down, in front of his waist.

The two guards pressed together to block Worf's path as he stepped toward the doors. "I have business with the chancellor," he said. The guards did not answer him. "Let me pass."

"He's not here," said the guard with the *bat'leth*.

"Council's in session," the other guard said.

Martok's voice resounded from the far end of the corridor behind Worf. "Mr. Ambassador!" Worf turned to see Martok stomping toward him with his usual bravado.

"Chancellor," Worf said. "I require a moment of your time."

"A moment is all I have," Martok said.

Worf stepped aside to let him pass. The two guards also moved out of Martok's path. At the chancellor's approach, the doors to his chambers swung inward. "Come in," Martok said to Worf as he marched past the ambassador, into his inner sanctum. Worf shot withering stares at the two guards, who made a point of avoiding eye contact with him. He followed Martok inside. The massive doors silently closed behind him.

Martok's chambers were well appointed, but not opulent. The amalgamation of ancient weapons, modest comforts, and one of the newest House crests in the Empire reflected the chancellor's rise from common-born soldier to imperial head of state.

The floor, walls, and ceiling were rough, gray stone.

The walls on either side of the main door were draped with six enormous war banners. The colorful flags—which were replete with rips, burned edges, bloodstains, and the dust of battlefields light-years away—were testaments to Martok's distinguished decades of service.

Eight broad, hard armchairs surrounded a low, octagonal stone table, which sat atop a huge Kryonian tigerskin rug in the middle of the room, between four wide pillars. On the pillars, two meters above the floor, were black iron sconces, inside of which danced licks of bright orange flame.

At the far end of the room was a broad desk. Its shape was irregular—organic, like an amoeba. The desktop was composed of immaculately polished petrified wood, and was utterly bare and pristine. At the desk was a high-backed, hardwood seat that Martok simply called a chair, but which Worf thought looked more like a throne. The wall behind the desk was dominated by a huge, multipanel window shaped like the Klingon trefoil.

To the left was a door that led to the chancellor's private wardrobe. On the right was the room's single extravagance: a well-stocked liquor cabinet, including onyx bloodwine goblets and polished-steel steins for ale and *warnog*.

Martok moved past his desk. "I have to get back soon," the chancellor said as he opened the door to his wardrobe and stepped inside. "What do you need?"

Worf stopped in front of the desk. "I am concerned that your invasion of Tezwa violates the Khitomer Accords," he said.

"Nonsense," Martok growled from the antechamber.

"The accords specifically permit us to defend ourselves from attack."

"And if Tezwa attacks Qi'Vol, you will be within your rights to retaliate," Worf said. Arguing, even insincerely, on behalf of the Tezwans sickened him, but for now he needed to think like a diplomat instead of like a warrior. "But to invade a planet that might be able to claim it was acting in self-defense—"

"You can't be serious." Martok stepped out of his wardrobe, attired in a different ceremonial robe. Worf recognized the vestments as the ones traditionally worn when making formal declarations of war. "Self-defense? They launched a sneak attack! They murdered six thousand Klingon warriors!"

"The Tezwans will say they had no right to be there," Worf said. "They will insist that the very presence of your ships above their world was an act of aggression—from which they defended themselves." Defending the cowardly *petaQpu'* made Worf furious, but his mask of calm dignity didn't waver. Martok dismissed Worf's arguments with an angry wave of his arm.

"Ridiculous," Martok said. "They permitted us entry for negotiation. Safe conduct was promised."

Worf had no rebuttal; Martok was right. Interstellar law was clear on the matter of safe conduct. Worf changed tactics.

"Regardless," he said, "the Federation is alarmed by the ramifications of such a precedent. We must ask the High Council to consider our petition for limitations on the Empire's actions in this matter." Worf was treading on dangerous ground; by speaking with the voice of the

Federation, he could ensure that his request would have to be officially reviewed by the High Council, in accordance with imperial law. That would get Martok out of his chambers for a few minutes, giving Worf the time he needed. But if his plan backfired, this overstepping of his authority could result in his own arrest by the Federation.

Martok clearly did not like what he was hearing. "What kind of limitations?"

"First, the planet and its star system must remain neutral," Worf said. "Rather than an invasion followed by an occupation, we ask that the Empire restrict its mission to pacification, then withdraw its military forces."

"It's too late to negotiate these terms," Martok said. "The order's been given. Tezwa will be invaded."

"If the Klingon flag is raised on Tezwa, we will demand parity," Worf said. "The Federation will claim sovereignty over two unpopulated star systems on our shared border—Mahtaan and Hrabosk."

Martok considered that idea, then harrumphed. "That's more reasonable," he said. After a moment, the idea seemed to grow on him. "Very well, then. Parity. I'll offer your proposal to the council." The chancellor adjusted the front of his robe. "If there's nothing else . . . ?" Martok gestured toward the door.

Worf stood his ground. "I would prefer to wait here for the council's answer."

Martok grunted, then marched toward the door. "Suit yourself," he bellowed as the doors swung open before him. "I expect it will be a short debate," Martok said. The doors closed behind him with a heavy bump.

As the magnetic locks engaged, Worf opened his diplomatic pouch and reached inside. The "package" Zeitsev had somehow delivered to Worf's office with hardly any advance notice of his intentions—or so it seemed—had contained several devices tailored to facilitate his mission. He knew Zeitsev was well connected, but this had surpassed all expectations. Some of the tools in the kit were ones that Worf had heard of being used by Starfleet Intelligence; a few he had thought were still at the prototype stage. Two he had never realized existed at all, until tonight. He hoped most of them would be unnecessary.

Martok had no computer hardware in his office, despite Zeitsev's insistence that this was one of the few direct links to the Fleet Command Center. Worf had been here only twice before, and on neither occasion had he seen Martok use a computer. The chancellor despised replicators, and preferred to conduct state business face-to-face whenever possible.

Worf palmed a tiny scanner and pulled it from the pouch. He kept it tucked clandestinely inside his palm while he checked the room for security devices. He detected four. He keyed the device's signal jammer, confirmed the security devices were offline, and set the tool on the desk.

Reaching back into his pouch, he removed a tricorder. He did three sweeps of the room before he registered the matte-surfaced holographic emitter crystal embedded into the ceiling above Martok's desk. *That makes sense,* Worf thought. *He hates clutter.* He moved behind the desk and seated himself in Martok's chair. His fingertips traced the undersides of the armrests, searching for a concealed switch. There wasn't one. *It must be voice-activated,* Worf concluded.

"Computer, activate holographic interface."

Nothing happened. *It has to be* his *voice,* he realized.

Digging inside the pouch, he found the small dermal patch he sought. He pressed it to his throat, just above his trachea, then fished its remote control from under the holomask emitter. He cycled through the remote's preset options, and selected Martok's voice pattern, which he'd recorded just minutes ago.

It unnerved him to hear Martok's voice roaring out of his mouth. "Computer," he barked. "Activate holographic interface."

"Submit for retinal-pattern verification," the deep, masculine computer said.

Worf had feared this might be the case. Imperial Command was justifiably paranoid when it came to information security. If he had been able to gain physical access to the primary headquarters, he might have been able to access the system with little more than a stolen password or a decryption algorithm on his tricorder. But for remote terminals such as these, Imperial Intelligence had no doubt insisted upon biometric security protocols, to prevent unauthorized access.

Worf saw little point in attempting to bypass the system. If he made a mistake, it would almost certainly trigger an alarm. And although Zeitsev had been able to provide Worf with a bundle of high-tech gadgets, none of them contained Martok's security code.

With less than two hours remaining to the invasion of Tezwa, Worf had three options.

He could attempt to infiltrate the Fleet Command Center and steal the master command codes from its computer by direct access. The odds against his survival were staggering. The odds of his success were infinitesimal. This was not so much a plan as a death wish, a futile road to be taken when all others had clearly failed. Worf was still far from that course of action.

He could set up surveillance equipment in Martok's office, wait for the chancellor to access the system, then record Martok's password. Its merits were that it was simple and presented minimal risk. Its most serious flaw was that there was no guarantee Martok would need to access the Fleet Command network in the next two hours. Equally troubling was the fact that Worf might have to resort to violence against his own kinsman in order to copy his retinal patterns, to fool the system's biometric-identification system.

The thought of so directly betraying Martok galled Worf. Infiltrating the Fleet Command Center might have provided him with numerous access codes to choose from; he could have accomplished his mission without necessarily compromising the chancellor himself. If he broke into the system using Martok's codes and biometric profile, the ensuing disgrace might place the chancellor's political future—as well as his life—in jeopardy.

There was one last possibility, but it would mean crossing the line into outright criminality; he would have to commit to an agenda of espionage, extortion, and perhaps even murder.

The magnetic locks of the main door released with a soft, muffled click.

"Computer, terminate connection." The holographic trefoil blinked off as he removed the dermal voice patch from his throat with one hand and scooped up his signal jammer with the other. He stepped over to the liquor cabinet and thrust his hands into his pockets to hide the gadgets. He deactivated the jammer as the doors opened and Martok returned.

"Good news, Mr. Ambassador," Martok said with a *gagh*-eating grin. "The council accepts your request for parity."

"Excellent," Worf said.

Martok eyed him strangely. "Planning on raiding my stash of bloodwine?"

"I was just leaving." As he passed by Martok he paused and added, "Perhaps next time."

Martok gave him a hard, friendly slap on the back. "Count on it," he said. "Come back later, we'll celebrate. This is going to be a glorious day for the Empire!"

Or not, Worf mused glumly as he left Martok's chambers and set out to commit a great evil in the service of a greater good.

Chapter 32
Earth Orbit—McKinley Station

McKinley Station was exactly as Koll Azernal had last seen it three years ago—cold, sterile, and depressing. Little more than a ring of prefabricated industrial modules, it embodied all the least-glamorous aspects of Starfleet. It was drab, utilitarian, and uniform to a degree that Azernal suspected even the Borg might envy. The facility's one redeeming feature was its stunning low-orbit view of Earth, but even that was only visible half the time, unless one walked constantly around the station's outer ring to keep up with its semihourly rotation.

Looking down from a currently unoccupied docking port, Azernal admired the delicate webs of lights adorning the Eurasian continent. The crisp edge of daybreak was creeping across the curve of the planet. Dawn was rising on Moscow and Tehran; in a few short hours it would rouse Rome, then Paris.

Another thing Azernal disliked about McKinley Station was its acoustics. Sounds of all kinds could bounce their way around the outer ring and come back, full circle, to their point of origin; voices carried like curses in a cathedral. Which is why he heard Quafina's footsteps a full minute before he saw him.

Nelino Quafina was, by his species' standards, a fairly handsome individual. His glistening scales were a splendidly uniform shade of silvery gray, and his eyes were large, even for an Antedean. His cranial fins were large and well shaped, and ever so slightly darker than the rest of his scales. He walked in long, graceful strides, his webbed feet padding softly across the smooth metal deck. His flowing garments, tailored in five different shades of metallic blue, gave his towering frame an almost imperial bearing, in Azernal's opinion.

Viewing the species objectively, Azernal couldn't understand why so many humanoids found the icthyoid visage of Antedeans aesthetically displeasing. He surmised that recent history played a role; there were more than a few individuals in the Federation who, for some inexplicable reason, still bore a grudge over the trivial fact that an Antedean assassin, disguised as one of his planet's delegates, had tried to blow up the Pacifica conference fourteen years ago.

Quafina stopped next to Azernal and joined him in admiring the view. "You called," he said. His voice sounded hollow, a peculiar effect of the Antedeans' efforts to mimic humanoid speech. Their larynges evolved to produce vibrations in a fluid medium, by drawing liquid or air inward. Consequently, Quafina, like most Antedeans when removed from their natural aquatic environment, always sounded like he was swallowing his words.

Azernal opened the door to the airlock. "Step inside."

Quafina looked into the cramped pressure compartment, then fixed his expressionless eyes on Azernal. "You first."

"Your faith is touching," the Zakdorn said as he stepped into the airlock. Quafina followed him in a moment later, and stooped sharply to fit inside. Azernal shut the door. The setting was now intimate to the point of being claustrophobic, but at least it was private.

"We have to stop meeting like this," Quafina said.

Azernal ignored the quip. "We need more shipments to Tezwa," he said.

"Unofficial, I presume?"

"Of course," Azernal said.

"More of the same?"

"Not exactly," Azernal said. "We need to mask the source of our earlier shipments."

Quafina made a few short clicking noises. "In what way?"

"We need to make it look like they came from the Tholians."

Quafina made a few more clicking sounds, slower and deeper this time. "Difficult," he said. "I can do it, but it will take time to prepare and arrange."

"How long?"

"At least a few weeks," Quafina said.

"That might be too late," Azernal said.

"It could be done faster using official resources," Quafina said, his tone accusatory.

"Absolutely not," Azernal said. "Strictly off the books. I can't have Starfleet Intelligence putting their hands all over this. Use whatever channels worked last time."

"Then it will take a few weeks," Quafina said. "Unless you can get me access to a time machine."

"And bring Temporal Investigations into it? No, thank you."

"Then we're done."

Azernal bristled at Quafina's openly confrontational tone, but said nothing as the Antedean opened the inner airlock door. Quafina ducked his head and exited, then moved quickly away down the gradually curving corridor.

Trade secrets being the lifeblood of the intelligence profession, Azernal knew better than to pry into Quafina's methods. Honestly, it was better if he didn't know all the details. He still had no clue how the wily Antedean had smuggled to Tezwa the vast quantities of contraband technology needed to build the nadion-pulse cannons, or how, under constant scrutiny as the Federation's secretary of military intelligence, he'd kept his activities hidden from his subordinates.

What mattered was Quafina got results without getting noticed, and that's all Azernal really needed to know.

Chapter 33
An Undisclosed Location

"IF KINCHAWN DOESN'T LAND US in a war with the Klingons, this lumbering hothead will."

Dietz remained silent while he stood next to L'Haan, who humored Zeitsev's rant via secure subspace com. *"I'm not sure what he's planning to do,"* Zeitsev continued. *"Whatever it is, it probably won't be very subtle."*

L'Haan responded in her usual cool, rational manner. "How do you suspect Ambassador Worf learned of your identity?"

"An excellent question," Zeitsev said. *"His connection to the chancellor and alliances through the Order of the Bat'leth may be part of it. He's better integrated into Klingon society than any previous Federation ambassador since Curzon Dax."*

"With alliances come enemies," L'Haan said. "Regardless, his involvement changes matters. As does his contact with you."

"I know," Zeitsev said. *"Protocol's being followed."*

"Good," L'Haan said. "We will continue to monitor Ambassador Worf from here."

Zeitsev nodded once. *"Zeitsev out."* He terminated the transmission, and the screen went dark.

Dietz waited for her to say something. He loved the sound of her voice, always so calm and measured, her enunciation all but flawless. Eye contact with her was usually too intimidating, so he often found himself watching her lips, admiring their symmetry and uniformity of texture.

Her lips parted then, and she spoke, breaking the spell.

"What became of Azernal's transmission to Quafina?"

Dietz looked up into her intense, brown eyes, then just as quickly looked away to his computer terminal. "They just left McKinley Station, about five minutes apart."

"Do we have a record of their meeting?"

"Negative," Dietz said, sorry to disappoint her. "We didn't have time to tap into the station's internal sensors." With a few deft strokes Dietz called up Quafina's full dossier on a secondary monitor. He highlighted a note he'd flagged earlier. "I predict there's an eighty-three percent chance Quafina's being tapped to participate in a cover-up on Tezwa."

"Actually," L'Haan said, "the likelihood is eighty-nine-point-six-one percent."

Dietz controlled his breathing and tried to keep his pulse from rising, but he still felt a flush of warmth in his face as shame colored his cheeks. L'Haan, if she noticed his embarrassment, didn't acknowledge it. He hated making such easily avoidable errors in front of her.

"We won't know Quafina's agenda for another hour or

so," he said, his composure somewhat regained. "Should I continue to prepare for a Klingon invasion?"

"Yes," L'Haan said. "Even with Worf's involvement on Qo'noS, Picard and his crew are still likely to fail. We should be ready to take appropriate steps."

"Perhaps we should wait until we see what Azernal and Quafina are doing," he suggested. "What if they have their own contingency plan? We might be able to avoid taking a drastic step that would draw unnecessary attention."

L'Haan regarded him with a dubious, sidelong glance from beneath an arched left brow. He felt as though he stood accused in her gaze. He considered defending his statement, then decided against it. Dietz and L'Haan had debated policy in the past, and, not surprisingly, had found their opinions quite similar. He wasn't squeamish about destroying the planet; he simply disliked such heavy-handed methods. Like most of those in the organization, he preferred subtler tactics—precision and secrecy, rather than naked demonstrations of force.

"Continue your preparations," she said. "If they become unnecessary, I will rescind the order."

"Yes, sir."

"One more thing," L'Haan said. "Wake the Orion Sleeper."

Chapter 34
Tezwa—Solasook Peninsula, 0256 Hours Local Time

"I CAN'T SEE a damn thing down here."

"Keep scanning," Data replied, watching Obrecht from an icy ridge above the suspected location of the firebase's entrance.

"Aye, sir," Obrecht said, making it sound like a complaint. Beside him, Heaton continued sweeping the area with her own tricorder, trying to lock on to the elusive, scan-shielded door.

Data considered Obrecht's protest a slight exaggeration, but he was willing to concede that the blizzard had impaired visibility to a dangerous level. The fact that the arctic polar region was also gripped in an extended period of night further complicated matters, and led him to wonder whether their arctic camouflage was necessary. If not for his suit faceplate's light-intensifying filter, he would not be able to see the two engineers at all in the darkness.

The fierce gales of the storm provided a low, constant yowl of noise beneath their encrypted transmissions.

Parminder emerged from the gray of the storm, next to Data. *"Jammer's set."* She looked up anxiously at the starless sky. *"How long until the Klingon fleet arrives?"*

"Approximately one hour, nineteen minutes, twenty seconds," Data said, referencing his internal chronometer. "That is only an estimate, however."

"Commander," Heaton said, wiping the falling snow from her tricorder display for the eleventh time in two minutes. *"I think I have a reading on the base entrance."* She pointed at the steep, icy slope in front of her. *"Under there,"* she continued. *"It's buried. Pretty deep, too."*

Data activated his own tricorder, and Heaton transmitted her scan results to him. He checked the readings, and confirmed the most probable location of the base's entrance was currently concealed beneath more than four meters of packed ice and snow.

"I could melt it off with my rifle," Parminder said.

"No," Data said. "The energy discharge would alert the troops inside the base."

"Guess they don't get out much," Obrecht said. He looked around with a dismayed expression at the whirlwind snowfall. *"Can't say I blame them."*

"Well, we can't exactly wait around for spring thaw," Parminder said. *"Assuming spring ever comes up here."*

"Sir," Heaton said. *"I have something else."* She pointed past the firebase entrance, up a long and gradual slope. *"Ninety-eight-point-one meters on relative bearing oh-one-four. Five-point two meters below the surface, in the permafrost."*

Data synchronized his tricorder with hers and reviewed the readings. He compared the sketchy sensor profile against the copy of the Starfleet prototype-firebase schematic. Down below, Heaton continued to study her own tricorder screen. "Your analysis, Lieutenant?"

"I'd say it's the subspace signal buffer," she said.

"I concur," he said. "Good work." Data had been positive that the readings were from the buffer, but he had learned by observing Commander Riker that part of helping train junior officers was encouraging them to use their skills and trust their conclusions. "Let us regroup there," he said, rising to his feet and walking down the gradual incline to his right. Parminder followed close behind him.

Obrecht and Heaton had a head start climbing the slope, and remained barely visible as shadows between drifting curtains of storm-driven snow. The pair did not become clearly visible until Data and Parminder approached to within three meters. Both engineers were intently reviewing their tricorder screens. *"Definitely the buffer, sir,"* Obrecht said.

Data turned to face Parminder. "Can you cut down to the permafrost without hitting the device?"

The petite, dark-haired woman nodded. *"Yes, sir."*

"Please begin," Data said, stepping out of her way. Heaton and Obrecht followed his lead, and gave Parminder a wide berth.

The slender security officer adjusted the settings of her phaser rifle, planted her feet to steady herself against the hammering blasts of wind, and began melting through the snow and ice with short, controlled bursts. In just under two minutes she had cleared from the hard-packed snow a wide crater nearly twice as deep as Data was tall, with a small patch of bare, frozen-solid earth at its nadir.

Parminder halted her efforts and looked at Data. *"Below here, the risk of hitting the buffer is higher,"* she said.

"Understood," he said. "The device is approximately one-point-six meters below the surface. Select a wider beam dispersal. Thaw the ground without cutting through it. We will excavate the buffer manually."

"Aye, sir," Parminder said, and reset her rifle. She bathed the ground in a warm-orange glow of energy, shifting the beam's center point in a slow, even rotation around the buffer's reported position. Snowflakes hurled by wind into the beam's path were transmuted into swiftly dispersed wisps of steam.

Obrecht and Heaton continued to scan the area with their tricorders while Parminder worked.

"Lieutenant Heaton," Data said. "Do you detect any change in the readings from the buffer?"

"Negative, sir," Heaton said. *"All readings steady."*

Data chose not to point out the redundancy of her reply.

"Average soil temperature around the buffer has increased to sixteen degrees centigrade," Obrecht reported.

"Cease fire," Data said. Parminder released the trigger of her rifle and stepped back from the now-warmed patch of ground. Snowflakes melted as they touched down. "We need to excavate the buffer immediately," he said.

Data and the three officers got down on their hands and knees and surrounded the thawed area. They clawed through the top layer of newly made mud and began scooping away the loose, clumpy dirt below it with their gloved hands. A latticework of weed roots made it difficult to tear through the soil, which was cooling rapidly beneath their hands.

Several minutes of manic digging later, the subspace signal buffer lay exposed before them. Data noted that its components were not merely modeled on Starfleet designs—they were genuine Federation-manufactured parts. "I will remain here," he said. He pointed to the elevations on either side of the firebase entrance. "Lieutenant Obrecht, take up position on that rise. Lieutenant Heaton, take position on the opposite elevation. Then wait for my orders." The two engineers acknowledged the commands and hurried down the slope into the raging night.

Data began disconnecting optronic cables from the signal buffer and patching them into his tricorder. "Ensign Parminder, conceal one explosive charge in front of the main entrance to the firebase. Angle its effect to project away from the entrance."

Parminder looked confused. *"Sir?"*

"When the charge is set, camouflage yourself on the slope above the entrance and wait for my orders."

"Aye, sir," she said, and followed Heaton and Obrecht back toward the firebase entrance.

Data removed his helmet and opened the access flap behind his left ear. He retrieved a spare optronic cable from his equipment pack and patched one end into his positronic matrix. The other end he connected to his tricorder, which was now linked into the firebase's communications system. Using his tricorder as a capacitor and software resource, he initiated a rather complicated dialogue with the firebase's main computer. Whoever had installed this system had lacked the sophistication to identify or remove its preprogrammed "back-door codes." Data considered that to be a good indicator that, even if this base's technology had come from the Federation, Starfleet had not been involved in its installation.

It took him eleven-point-eight seconds to assume master control of the base's primary and backup computers. He could only hope that the Tezwan soldiers inside the base would prove to be as gullible as their pirated technology.

Chapter 35

Tezwa—Kolidos Desert, 0658 Hours Local Time

FORTY-THREE MINUTES had elapsed while Sierra Team hid under the sand. Cramps had started to knot together in Peart's calves while he lay entombed with Vulcan security officer T'Sona, who seemed to accept the predicament with a poise that Peart found quite irritating.

Two things had worked in Sierra Team's favor so far.

The first was that the Tezwans, despite their overwhelming advantage in numbers, had shown a marked reluctance to search the area on foot, preferring to remain overhead in their hovercraft. Based on the footfalls Peart heard tromping by—in what seemed like a particularly sloppy search pattern—he estimated there were fewer than twelve infantrymen deployed. That left the bulk of the enemy personnel—nearly one hundred ninety troops—cruising around overhead.

The second thing Sierra Team had going for them was dumb luck. In Peart's opinion, that was the best advantage of all.

Before he heard the throb of a hovercraft slowly edging closer, he felt the pulse of its engine through the ground, telegraphing its approach like a swelling heartbeat.

He tensed as the hovercraft passed directly over their position. The loose sand that covered him and T'Sona quivered and shifted, settled under them, flowed around them like water. Peart keyed his com. "Scholz, Morello. Whatever happens, stay down. T'Sona—follow my lead."

Making use of the planet's lighter gravity, Peart leaped up, erupting like a geyser from beneath the sand to grab the rear edge of the hovercraft. T'Sona froze for a moment, apparently not having expected this to be his tactic of choice. Springing into action, her superior Vulcan strength enabled her to make the slightly longer jump needed to join Peart on the still-moving hovercraft.

As Peart pulled himself up and over the craft's safety railing, the dozen Tezwan soldiers sitting inside simply stared in shock for nearly a full second. He and T'Sona vaulted over the railing. The Tezwans collided with one another while trying to get out of their seats and arm their weapons all at once.

The gangly one closest to the rear of the hovercraft had almost succeeded in aiming his rifle at the two Starfleet officers when Peart punched him in the chest. Hollow bones cracked loudly, audible even over the craft's engines. The fragile-looking, feather-headed Tezwan rifleman sailed backward, toppling most of his squad behind him and pinning their weapons beneath a jumble of flailing limbs.

Before any of them could scramble free, T'Sona drew her rifle from its back-mounted holster and stunned the entire group with one wide-beamed blast. Jumping over the pile of unconscious bodies, Peart snapped off one shot to stun the hovercraft pilot, then pulled the man from his seat and took his place.

In every direction he looked, other hovercraft crews were looking up from their search patterns. He and T'Sona had just used up their quotient of surprise.

Peart grabbed the vehicle's steering yoke and felt the trigger for the vehicle's forward-mounted dual pulse cannons. He squeezed it and held it down as he rotated the hovercraft in a smooth arc to starboard. Electric-blue pulses split the quiet desert morning with a high-pitched shriek. Peart strafed the closely grouped squadron of anti-grav vehicles, which erupted in sparking explosions, belches of flame, and billowing plumes of smoke. Several craft rolled sideways, tossing their crews across the sand. A few pitched nose-first into the ground and rolled into the valleys between the dunes. Trailing the cannon bolts were wide-dispersal phaser stun-blasts fired by T'Sona.

Five seconds later, eleven hovercraft had been reduced to twisted, smoldering wreckage. Then a fusillade of screaming blue flashes slammed into Peart's hijacked vehicle. The cockpit controls spat up a fountain of sparks as the craft rolled to port. Free-falling from the seat, he tucked and rolled.

Tumbling up to a ready position, he increased his phaser rifle to maximum power. T'Sona was crouched on the ground next to him, huddled beneath the listing but still airborne crippled hovercraft, which was spewing out a very convenient smoke screen. Peart squinted in the direction of the four Tezwan-controlled hovercraft that had downed their stolen vehicle and were now rapidly drawing closer. In a few seconds, the four vehicles would be in optimal range of his rifle—and he and T'Sona would be sitting ducks for their pulse cannons.

He didn't feel like waiting that long.

Setting his rifle to rapid-pulse mode, he sprinted away from the wrecked craft and ran flat-out, directly across the four vehicles' field of fire. Keeping his trigger down, he bull's-eyed one craft's engines. As it pitched to the ground and catapulted its crew into the arms of the desert, the other three hovercraft returned fire at Peart. Dodging and spinning in random directions, he found himself surrounded by the angry whine of energy pulses that filled the dry desert air with the scent of ozone.

Then he heard the screech of T'Sona's weapon firing at full power, and the satisfying crack and clap of explosions that took down two more hovercraft. He heard a lone antigrav engine on his right. Turning, he reduced his rifle to heavy stun. The pilot of the last airborne hovercraft looked like he couldn't decide whether Peart or T'Sona presented the greater threat, and as a result his forward cannons had ended up aimed at neither of them. Fortunately for the pilot, the twelve soldiers behind him had all taken aim at whichever Starfleet officer happened to be on their side of the vehicle, and Peart was now looking down the barrel of six enemy weapons.

Two sets of rapid-fire phaser blasts lit up the soldiers from behind. Peart and T'Sona dived and rolled up to shooting stances, picking off the Tezwans who were lucky enough to duck the first barrage. Peart wasn't really certain whether he or T'Sona fired the shot that stunned the pilot. Overlapping stun-blasts blanketed the

Tezwans already on the ground, ensuring none of them would be going anywhere for a while.

The shooting ceased. The hovercraft slowly floated down and settled with a soft bump on the sandy ground. Peart looked over at Scholz and Morello, both of whom were sitting upright, their lower bodies still concealed in the sand, their rifles propped up vertically against their shoulders.

"Why didn't you tell me you know how to fight?" Peart said. "We coulda used you guys out here."

Morello shrugged. "We didn't want to get in your way."

Peart couldn't fault the man's logic. "Okay, you have a point," he said, climbing into his second stolen vehicle of the day. "Come get these clowns outta my hovercraft."

Chapter 36
Tezwa—Nokalana Sea, 1116 Hours Local Time

KEEP LOOKING, Christine Vale commanded herself. *It's got to be here somewhere. You just have to find it.*

Vale had never been fond of underwater operations. Working underwater was a lot like working in space. All the consequences were reversed, of course—crushing pressure versus vacuum, freezing instead of instantly boiling, implosion rather than explosion, flooding as opposed to venting—but they were still just as deadly, and the environment just as unforgiving. One other thing they had in common was the awkwardness of movement. Each milieu was alien to human physiology in its own way, and Vale, left to her own devices, would avoid them both.

But here she was, now with less than an hour—give or take a few minutes—until the start of the Klingon invasion, looking for the firebase's waste-exhaust port, which refused to be found.

The meter-wide venting aperture was almost certain to be located on the ocean floor, within less than a fifty-meter radius of the entrance tower. Unfortunately, that meant Vale now had to search an area of nearly eight square kilometers, one meter at a time, while swimming in circles. Her tricorder also wasn't proving to be of much use. *The port must be camouflaged,* she reasoned.

Spitale's voice crackled over the com. *"Spitale to Vale,"* she said. *"Ready to go here."*

"Acknowledged," Vale said. Spitale had been burdened with the team's second-hardest assignment: deducing a structural weak spot in the entrance tower's outer shell that, if ruptured, would cause rapid flooding of the entire base but also leave the Tezwans a path of escape to the docked submarine. It was a testament to the young woman's intelligence that within a matter of minutes she had found an exterior hatch used by maintenance robots and determined it to be this base's Achilles' heel.

The ocean floor was rocky and barren, permanently sequestered from daylight. No vegetation grew down here. Vale's only company as she swam in lonely, ever-widening circles around the base were roaming crustaceans, skittish bottom-feeders, and a single luminescent aquatic predator that had wearied of shadowing her after its third zap from her phaser, which the *Enterprise*'s team of weapons experts had specially modified for underwater use.

Another transmission scratched over the speaker in her helmet. *"Sakrysta to Vale."*

"Go ahead," Vale said, hoping nothing had gone wrong. Sakrysta and Fillion's mission was to sabotage the submarine's weapons and primary propulsion. Once Delta Team started their assault, they couldn't let the submarine crew shoot at them or move out of jamming range to alert the planet's military.

"We're in position," Sakrysta said.

"Glad to hear it," Vale said. "I'm still—" She was about to apologize for her delay in finding the elusive waste vent when a chugging surge resounded through the depths. Turning to look behind her, she saw a jet of air bubbles and discolored fluid surging up, seemingly out of solid rock. She locked her tricorder onto the frothing plume, which dwindled and vanished a few moments later. She keyed her com. "Stand by."

Following the tricorder's target lock, she found herself floating above an expertly disguised metallic iris. Its outer surface was composed of natural composites from the surrounding sea bed, but the durable metal inside defied her tricorder's attempts to scan it. On a hunch, she chipped away a small chunk of the outer coating, then fired a low-power phaser burst at the exposed metal underneath. The phaser beam reflected off the metal like a flashlight beam off a mirror. The tricorder still couldn't read the metal, but it detected a momentary surge of several types of rare particles.

Chimerium, Vale realized. *The only place to get this stuff is Sarindar. And only the Federation has the right to export it from the Nalori Republic. Starfleet might not have put this stuff here, but we definitely built it.*

She increased the power of her phaser and swiftly burned a hole through the ocean floor right next to the phaser-proof iris, cutting at a sharp angle into the shaft beneath. She was gambling that because chimerium was so rare and difficult to work with, whoever built this facility would not have used it for something so mundane as a waste-exhaust shaft. Her hunch proved correct, and her phaser beam easily sliced a short, twenty-centimeter-wide channel directly into the exhaust shaft.

She holstered her rifle and carefully removed two ultritium charges from her chest pack. "Vale to Delta Team," she said, keying her com. "I'm in position. Everybody confirm."

"Spitale, ready."

"Sakrysta, set."

"Fillion, good to go."

"Acknowledged," Vale said. "Sakrysta and Fillion, you're first. Go!"

The two explosions sounded much closer than Vale knew they were, and she recalled that water was superior to air as a medium for propagating sound waves.

"Spitale," Vale said, "go!" Moments later, another rumble of watery thunder shook the ocean depths. She armed the fuses on her ultritium charges and released them into the shaft. She turned and swam away from the exhaust port as quickly as she was able. Moments later the cacophonous boom roared behind her, sending up a fiery rush of gas that dislodged the chimerium iris, which then sank into the ocean floor as the shaft imploded beneath it.

"Vale to Delta Team, sound off."

"Sakrysta here."

"Fillion here."

"Spitale here."

So far so good, Vale congratulated herself. "Sakrysta, rig the airlock with a light charge," she said, swimming with broad, strong strokes and kicks back to the now-flooding base. "As soon as the base personnel are out, blow the airlock so they don't come back—but don't compromise the sub itself."

"Aye, sir," Sakrysta said. *"I'm on it."*

Vale checked her chronometer. If the Klingon fleet was punctual, the invasion would begin in fifty-two minutes. Her best guess was that it would take at least thirty minutes to flood the entire base and cut off the airlock access. That would leave twenty-two minutes to blast their way in, find the target points, plant the charges, help disable the Tezwan fleet, and reach minimum safe distance from which to blow up the base.

She rolled her eyes in mute protest. *Piece of cake.*

Chapter 37
Tezwa—Mount Ranakar, 1525 Hours Local Time

LA FORGE DANGLED by four fingertips from the cliff face. He tried to ignore the rock-strewn ground, thirty-odd meters below his feet. Fumbling for his gauss gun, he was acutely aware of a steady downdraft that was thinning the fog. That was good news for T'Eama and Braddock, who would now be able to see far enough ahead to better plan their climb. Clearer conditions, however, would also increase the team's risk of being spotted.

The trio climbed more or less side by side—Braddock on the left, T'Eama in the center, La Forge on the right—linked by belaying lines connected to climbing harnesses. They had shed their bulky dropsuits in favor of lightweight, camouflage climbing gear. Even in Tezwa's reduced gravity, every gram of encumbrance mattered. Even more critical, however, were flexibility and mobility. To navigate the perilous vertical ascent would demand agility, caution, and strength.

Steadying his gauss gun, La Forge aimed for the underside of what looked like a fairly solid rock shelf fifteen meters above him. He fired and shot a slender, electromagnetically propelled piton through the ledge. Trailing behind the piton was a microthin line of duranium cable. His fingertips began to ache under the stress of supporting his weight. He thumbed the cable retractor. A few seconds later the line went taut as the piton—now expanded into a miniature grappling hook—caught and held fast on the other side of the ledge.

Holding on to his gauss pistol, he used his free hand to play out some slack in his belaying line, then switched the cable retractor to its stronger setting. Locking both hands around the compact device, he shot upward as it towed him toward the ledge. As he neared the underside of the outcropping, he stopped the retractor and searched for a toehold. Spying one to his right, he wedged the front spikes of his crampons into it and locked his gloved hands around a tiny lip on the side of the rock shelf over his head. He keyed the gauss pistol's hook release. The grappling hook folded neatly back into its shell and retracted into the pistol, which he holstered.

Ignoring the burning pain in his triceps and chest, La Forge struggled to lift himself up onto the narrow ledge. Below him he heard the gentle *fwup* of Braddock's gauss-pistol shot, followed by the crack of its slug punching through stone. La Forge laid his right forearm across the ledge and released his foothold as he prepared to steady his aim for the next shot.

A brittle jangling of broken rock was his only warning.

Braddock's target surface had collapsed under his weight, and now was falling down toward him. T'Eama gripped the cliff wall in front of her and braced herself. The belaying line that linked her to Braddock snapped taut. He swung beneath her like the weight at the end of a pendulum. The tumbling rocks, of course, fell straight, and missed him as he swung clear.

La Forge was ready to exhale a relieved sigh when T'Eama's handhold crumbled under her fingers. Now she and Braddock both were plummeting, and depending on La Forge to be their anchor. Realizing he had no time to snap off another shot with his gauss pistol, he locked his arms around his meager chunk of real estate and braced for the inevitable.

Their combined weight wrenched him downward. Jagged edges along the ledge bit into his arms and ribs. His spine felt like it was being stretched in some medieval torture device.

Where his ledge met the cliff, a hairline fracture formed. Dust escaping from the crack stung his sinuses. He glanced down. T'Eama and Braddock scrambled to find purchase on the cliff. Clawing with her slender fingers, T'Eama found a narrow sliver of flat ledge. She latched on to it and pulled herself up. Now she was supporting Braddock's weight, and the knifing pain in La Forge's shoulder and lower back subsided.

By the time La Forge had driven a new piton into the cliff, affixed a carabiner to it, and transferred the slack from his harness, Braddock had found a new path up the cliff and resumed his ascent. T'Eama kept pace beside him, and both of the junior officers showed greater caution in securing their lines before releasing their handholds. It took them nearly five minutes to recover their lost ground, and another five to climb until they were once again level with La Forge.

"You two okay?" La Forge said while the pair fastened new pitons of their own into the rock face.

"Yes, sir," T'Eama said, checking her carabiner lock.

"Shook up, but yeah," Braddock said, securing his line.

"We have to pick up the pace," La Forge said. "We're less than halfway up, and the Klingons'll be here in forty minutes."

"Sir," Braddock said. "Even if we reach the top in time, how are we supposed to get inside the base?"

"Just climb," La Forge said. "Let me worry about the plan."

"Yes, sir," Braddock said, and began looking for his next avenue of ascent.

La Forge stared up the next hundred-plus meters of barren rock and was grateful that one of the privileges of command was keeping one's own counsel—because he had absolutely no idea what he was going to do when they reached the top of the cliff.

Chapter 38
Tezwa—Mokana Basin, 2328 Hours Local Time

FROM BENEATH THE MUDDY SWAMPWATER, Razka saw the lone Tezwan sentry glowing like a ripe piece of fruit in the sun. The young man's body was bright with heat radiation, warmer than most humanoids the Saurian security officer had encountered.

Undulating and twisting through the thick vines that choked the swamp bed, Razka swam slowly closer to the patch of dry ground where the guard paced through his lonely midnight vigil. The storm that had doused the strike team earlier had ended as quickly as it had begun, leaving a musky humidity in the air and thick mud covering the ground.

Biding his time, Razka observed the sentry's pattern. The man never lingered at either end of his short patch of clear soil. He carried his rifle with its stock tucked against his left shoulder, barrel down, ready for combat. Judging by his twitchy response to every random noise that trilled from the tropical darkness, he wasn't at ease in this wild place.

Behind the soldier was a field maintenance station for the firebase's powerful shield emitters. The station was well camouflaged, to most humanoids' unaided eyes. But to Razka the blocky, four-meter cubic structure shone like a bonfire. When the guard, bright as he was to Razka's thermal vision, passed in front of it, he was all but a silhouette by comparison.

The sentinel stopped at the farthest end from Razka, scanned the night with unseeing eyes, then walked back toward him, one squishing step after another. Razka plucked a pebble from the swamp bed and gently extended his leathery, scaled hand out of the water. With a quiet flick of his fingers, he sent the rock soaring into the brush beside the maintenance station. The tiny stone landed with a rustle and a clatter.

The guard spun toward the sound and aimed his rifle at nothing. Razka exploded from the water behind him.

The long-limbed Tezwan was faster than he expected, and turned almost completely around before Razka could strike.

The agile Saurian batted aside the barrel of the guard's rifle, sending its burst of sizzling blue energy into the jungle canopy. Continuing his fluid forward motion, Razka rolled his left arm around the guard's rifle and slipped inside the Tezwan's inner perimeter of defense. He slammed the palm of his right hand up into the sentry's chin.

The guard's feet lifted from the ground as Razka's blow sent him sprawling backward, limp as an overcooked *loka* leaf. His rifle remained locked in Razka's arm as he thudded, empty-handed and unconscious, against the maintenance station.

Razka removed the power cell from the Tezwan's weapon, tossed it aside, then checked the sentry's pulse. Satisfied the man was alive and would recover, he keyed his com.

"Razka to Alpha Team," he said, clearing the camouflage from the maintenance controls. "I'm here. What's your status?"

"We're just outside the shield perimeter," Riker said. The first officer sounded like he was out of breath. *"Pretty heavy activity out here."*

"Acknowledged," Razka said. "Stand by." He checked his chronometer. Alpha Team was on schedule, with a comfortable forty-five-minute window of opportunity before the Klingon fleet was expected to arrive. He accessed the maintenance station's manual override circuits and began modifying the shield emitter's field geometry. *Lucky for us these weren't concealed properly,* Razka mused. *Looks like someone didn't follow all the directions when they put this place together.*

He finished programming his changes to the shield emitters' field geometry, set it for a five-minute delay, and slipped back beneath the murky water for his return to the strike team's standby position. He rejoined them in the heavy foliage north of the firebase's protected zone just in time to see his work come to fruition. With a shimmer like heat distortion, the defensive shield—normally a convex shape above the base—inverted and enveloped the Tezwan patrol gathered outside the base entrance.

Some dropped instantly. A few of them twitched first,

then collapsed. Exactly ten seconds after the shield in-version occurred, it reversed itself. The night reverted to normal, albeit a little bit quieter than before.

Razka noted with pleasure that when he was debriefed later by Lieutenant Vale, he would be able to tell her without prevarication that the Tezwans hadn't seen it coming, and they hadn't felt a thing.

He activated his tricorder and confirmed that the shock pulse had also disabled the remote security devices out-side the base entrance. "All clear," he said to Riker.

"Okay," Riker said. "Let's move up."

Razka was disquieted by the fatigue he heard in Riker's voice. The first officer was moving a bit less confidently than he had just an hour before; his body language had changed, as if he were concealing an infir-mity. Blinking his thermal iris into place, Razka saw that Riker's body temperature was higher than normal. Of particular concern was the glowing-hot pinpoint wound on the back of Riker's neck.

Not wanting to alarm Tierney or Barnes, he moved closer to Riker and kept his voice down. "Sir," he said. "Are you sure you're all right?"

"Yes," Riker said, a bit too defensive for Razka's com-fort. "I'm fine. Why?"

"Your neck, sir," Razka said. "You're injured."

"It's just a bug bite," Riker said.

"Sir, may I suggest—"

"Razka, take point," Riker said, raising his voice in what Razka deduced was an effort to mask his pain and sound more like himself. "Clear a path to the operations center."

"Aye, sir." Razka knew that as long as Riker remained

coherent, no good would come of arguing with him. In more than a century of service to Starfleet, Razka had never been guilty of insubordination. Until the first officer's ailment became incapacitating, he was still in command.

Using a combination of brute force and high-tech tools, the cunning Saurian bypassed the security panel for the firebase's door. The portal slid open to reveal a short staircase leading down into a narrow, dark corridor. Though his thermal vision revealed no sign of Tezwan troops in the corridor, his olfactory receptors caught their distinctive scent. *Three, possibly four,* he reasoned as he distinguished the intermingled odors. *Probably in concealed positions. A second line of defense. Overlapping fields of fire, if they're smart.* He sniffed the air from the corridor again. *Definitely four of them. A veritable death trap.*

He looked back at Riker and the two engineers. "Wait here," he whispered with an evil grin. "I'll be right back."

Chapter 39

Tezwa—Linoka Forest, 1931 Hours Local Time

IT'S LIKE RUNNING a marathon on the sun, McEwan fumed.

For nearly an hour and a half, Echo Team had been sprinting in circles, rushing headlong through walls of flame that burned white-hot and stretched thirty meters into the night sky, which was obscured by the mountain of mushrooming black smoke.

Lieutenant Taurik had been correct when he told them their suits would protect them from the heat of the fire. What he had failed to mention was that their tricorders were not quite so resilient. His own tricorder had been reduced to worthless, sparking junk in less than twenty minutes, leaving them to find their way for the past hour without its guidance.

Glad my rifle sheath is made from the same stuff as my suit, she thought. *I'd hate to go to a gunfight without a gun.*

Also not addressed in Taurik's marching orders were the countless other hazards that had awaited them—such as falling trees, winds powerful enough to hurl them about like leaves, or the complete lack of any visible point of reference. The only thing McEwan could see in any direction was more fire, another crash of sparks, a furnace blast of ash.

Now, less than forty-five minutes before the grimly anticipated Klingon invasion, she was certain they were lost in the inferno, with their suits rapidly running out of power.

She didn't see that Taurik had stopped until she had all but slammed into him. Pulling herself up short, she flailed her arms to recover her balance. Rao came to a stop on her left, and Mobe stumbled to an exhausted finish on her right. She felt bad for the Bolian engineer, who seemed to be having the hardest time keeping up with their mad dash through the firestorm.

"What's wrong, sir?" McEwan said.

Taurik turned to face her. "Nothing, Ensign. We are here."

Taking two steps forward through an inky curtain of smoke, she saw that they were standing directly in front of the main entrance to the firebase. The door was recessed into a small blockhouse meant to be camouflaged as part of a low knoll. Like soap removing a stain, the fire had scoured the structure of its disguise. The panel that opened the door was melted. "Controls are slagged, sir," she said. "Permission to blast them."

"Granted," Taurik said. "Rao, activate the signal jammer."

McEwan opened the polymer sheath on the back of her suit and drew her rifle. Figuring that the fire had done half her work for her already, she set her weapon to only half of full power. She steadied her aim and fired a single, short burst.

The control panel disintegrated. McEwan moved up to the door. Reaching through the white-hot gap where the panel had once been, she found the emergency release circuit and toggled it. The door opened with a pneumatic hiss, revealing a short stairway down to a small entry chamber, which was sealed off from the rest of the base by a second pressure door.

Looking around the corner first to confirm the chamber was clear, she waved the rest of the strike team forward.

Taurik entered the cramped space first, followed closely by the two engineers. McEwan stepped inside last and keyed the controls to close the outer door. Safe from the fire outside, Rao removed his tricorder from his shielded chest pack and scanned the room for a few minutes.

"Thirty-one degrees Celsius," the swarthy engineer said finally, closing his tricorder with a casual flip of his hand. "Suits are back to room temperature."

"Remove your pressure gear," Taurik said. "From here we use stealth." The team quickly shimmied out of the bulky, insulated pressure suits and recovered their tricorders, demolition kits, and weapons. They tossed their heavy boots by the outer door and kept only the lightweight, padded footwear they had worn beneath them. Taurik looked at the dim, pale-blue utility lights that lined the sides of the entrance chamber. "Mr. Mobe, disable these lights," he said, then added, "Quietly."

Taurik and McEwan crouched at the inner door. Mobe cut the lights, plunging the pressure lock into darkness.

"Open the door," Taurik said.

McEwan opened the control panel and disabled the maglocks. Wedging her fingertips between the door and its frame, she slowly pulled it open. The corridor beyond sloped downward. It was mostly dark, and illuminated by evenly spaced pools of harsh overhead light. A pair of sentries stood at the far end, near an intersection, talking animatedly.

Using hand gestures, Taurik made it clear he wanted McEwan to follow him, stay close to the wall, and grab the guard on the right; he would be taking the guard on the left. He signaled Rao and Mobe to hold position until he ordered them to do otherwise.

Adrenaline made her pulse race as she skulked in the half-shadow toward the inattentive guards. Conscious of her every step, her every breath, McEwan didn't dare let herself blink.

Matching the surprisingly stealthy Taurik step for step, she found herself only two arm-lengths from her target. She paused with her Vulcan team leader, who tensed, awaiting the prime moment. Watching him on the edge of her vision, she sprang forward a split second after he did.

His hand struck like a serpent and locked on to the sentry's neck, just above the shoulder. The guard contorted and collapsed under Taurik's deftly executed nerve pinch.

Her own target lunged at Taurik, noticing McEwan only as her arm wrapped around his throat. Planting her leg behind the guard's knee, she yanked his head back and toppled him easily to the floor, controlling his fall to prevent him from making noise. After a few seconds of expertly applied pressure, he lost consciousness. She released him and used his own manacles to bind him before gagging him with a strip of his own tunic.

Taurik, his own target similarly restrained, motioned Rao and Mobe forward while McEwan checked the intersection for other Tezwan personnel. *Two down,* she mused, *forty-three to go.*

As she followed the intense and undeniably skilled Vulcan assistant chief engineer deeper into the enemy stronghold, she decided those odds didn't look so bad, after all.

Chapter 40
Qo'noS

TENS OF MILLIONS OF PEOPLE lived in the metropolitan sprawl of the First City, but in the small hours of the morning the capital felt almost like a necropolis. The juxtaposed ancient and modern structures that lined the *wo'leng*—the main boulevard that extended away from the Great Hall toward the river—all had been dark and silent as cenotaphs, reinforcing Worf's impression that he was stepping farther and farther away from the world he had struggled so hard to become a part of.

Looking out from the end of the *qIj'bIQ* promontory, Worf watched the dark river surge past. Then, like a ghost emerging from the shadows, Lorgh was beside him, leaning against the railing and staring into the water. Worf had not heard him approach. The grizzled Imperial Intelligence agent was slight of build and far from the physical ideal of a warrior, but Worf knew his old family ally could be a skilled and dangerous foe.

"They say the river has no memory," Lorgh said.

"But Imperial Intelligence does," Worf said.

"You're up late, Worf. Or are you up early?"

"You were right about the concealed level in the embassy."

Lorgh glared with annoyance. "Did you—"

"And about Zeitsev."

Lorgh pounded his fist on the wide metal railing. "Damn you!" He half-turned away, then clenched his fists and leaned once again next to Worf. "Why?"

"I needed information. The kind only he could provide."

Lorgh shook his head. "That was foolish," he said. "I trusted you with that intelligence as a warning, for your protection in case he moved against you." He slammed his palm against the railing. "Now they know we've identified them."

Worf wondered who "they" were, but because he had less than forty minutes to get the master command codes to Captain Picard, he decided that was an inquiry for another time. "There was no other way," Worf said, hunching his shoulders against a chill wind blustering in off the water.

"Is that what you brought me here to tell me?"

"No. I need your help."

Lorgh snorted in disgust. "I've seen how you use my help."

"I need information. If I had time I could find it myself. But I need it immediately."

Lorgh remained cagey. "What kind of information?"

"Anything I can use against Councillor Kopek. The more damaging, the better. And I need it now."

That snared Lorgh's attention.

"Kopek, eh?" He ran his tongue over his jagged teeth. "He's been quite the *d'k tahg* in Martok's back, hasn't he?"

"Indeed."

Kopek, one of the newly elected members of the re-formed High Council, had made little secret of his disdain for Martok's commoner origins. In the short time since the pompous northern aristocrat's arrival in the Great Hall, he had done more to undermine Martok's leadership and thwart his political objectives than the rest of the council combined. Considering that more than half of the councillors were obstructionists par excellence, that was no mean feat.

"So, Kopek plans to use the Tezwa crisis against Martok."

"Not if I can prevent it." Technically, that was true. Worf would endeavor to prevent Kopek from transforming a national tragedy into an issue for personal gain. He conveniently omitted the fact that such a concern was currently secondary.

A malicious grin crept across Lorgh's face. "Are you here as the Federation ambassador? Or as Martok's kinsman?"

Worf chose his words with great care. "I am acting on my own authority. . . . For the good of the Empire."

"Aren't we all," Lorgh said. Worf detected a pronounced undercurrent of cynicism and world-weariness in the remark.

"How soon can you—"

"I haven't agreed to anything," Lorgh said. He let Worf stew for a moment before he added, "Yet."

"I do not have time to barter," Worf protested.

"Never tell someone that," Lorgh said. His tone was one of menace, not friendly advice. "It just lets them know you're desperate. That you'll do or say anything. You might as well stick the blade in your own heart."

Worf reminded himself that even though this man was an old family friend, he was still a lifelong spy. Lorgh had raised Worf's brother, Kurn, as his own son after Worf's parents were killed in the Khitomer massacre and Worf was adopted by a Starfleet noncommissioned officer named Sergey Rozhenko. Lorgh's bond of friendship with Mogh, Worf's late father, combined with his obviously paternal feelings for Kurn, had lulled Worf into thinking of the wily old spy as part of the family. It was an error he would not make again. "Make me an offer," he said.

"I can get you a dossier on Kopek that'll have his head on a *tik'leth* by midday," Lorgh said. "But I'll need information of equal value from you. Something only you can get for me."

"I will not betray the Federation or Starfleet."

"I wouldn't ask you to," Lorgh said. "But I'm sure you could share with an ally information the Federation has about a mutual rival?"

"Such as?"

"Eleven days ago, in the Ravanar system, Starfleet Special Ops personnel captured a Breen vessel, whose crew . . ." Now it was Lorgh's turn to select his words carefully. "Met with an accident," he continued. "The Federation Security Council denies any such incident took place. But we both know what their words are worth."

"And you want . . . ?"

"The schematics of the Breen vessel," Lorgh said.

"Get me its logs and I'll get you dossiers on the entire High Council."

"Tempting, but not necessary."

"You hope."

Worf scowled. "I will send the schematics in twenty minutes," he said. "Have the dossier ready."

Lorgh chortled darkly. "It's been ready for six years."

Worf turned to leave. He hesitated as Lorgh fired one last verbal shot across the weary ambassador's bow.

"This wouldn't have anything to do with the fact that your son is aboard one of the ships on its way to Tezwa?"

Worf did not dignify the question with a response, choosing instead to walk to his hovercar and make a swift departure. But as he raced back to the Federation Embassy, growing more anxious by the minute, his answer to Lorgh's query simmered in his thoughts: *It did not . . . until* now.

Chapter 41
Tezwa—Keelee-Kee

"THESE ARE FRAGILE TIMES, General," Kinchawn said.

General Gyero Minza wasn't sure how to respond to that comment. He stood at attention before the prime minister and speculated that he had not been summoned in the middle of the night to provide a status report. Kinchawn rose from his chair, stepped from behind his desk, and meandered around the perimeter of his lushly appointed office.

"We are on the threshold of a new era in our history," Kinchawn continued. "Wouldn't you agree?"

"Of course, Mr. Prime Minister."

Minza watched Kinchawn circle around him. The prime minister let his hand brush through the thick blue-green fronds of a clutch of potted plants that filled one corner of the room. Mixed with the *ilosk* ferns were dozens of tall flowers, with enough colors to win a rainbow's envy. Their fragrance was faint, but he had noticed it the moment he'd entered the room.

"As we take our first steps beyond our own solar system, there will be those who seek to thwart our efforts," Kinchawn said. "The Klingons. The Federation. Perhaps even elements from within our own government."

The prime minister continued his circuit of the room, moving behind Minza. Because the general remained at attention, he could not turn to keep his eyes on Kinchawn. Instead, he followed the lean *elininim*'s reflection on the glass of the framed print of Tezwa's Civil Charter, which hung on the wall between two red-and-gold Tezwan flags that were curled with ceremonial precision around their poles.

"I have reason to believe the Klingons will attempt another attack on our planet," the prime minister continued. "In fact, I am quite certain such a strike is imminent."

"All forces are on highest alert," Minza said.

"To threats external," Kinchawn said. "But are your troops prepared to defend our world from traitors? From a fifth column within our ranks that would seek to aid our enemies?"

"You know we are," Minza said.

"General . . . would you agree that, in times of war, a government divided against itself cannot hope to prevail?"

Minza saw Kinchawn's intent taking shape, and he found himself grateful to be part of such a momentous development in history. "I cannot see how it would be any other way," he said.

Kinchawn passed by the sliding doors to his balcony, beyond which the spires of Keelee-Kee sparkled like polished speartips. "Then how are we to respond to the dangerous elements in our midst?" As he continued, he waved his left hand one way, his right hand another. "Dissidents who fill the people's hearts with doubt. Instigators who provoke the masses into protest." Now that he was moving back toward his desk, Minza was once again able to watch him instead of his mirror image.

"In the best of all possible worlds," Minza said, "they would be turned to our way of thinking. Enemies would be converted into allies."

"I agree," Kinchawn said. "But there will always be those who refuse to negotiate. Who cannot see the value of reason." The prime minister stood in front of his chair and rested the tips of his slender, bony fingers on the desktop. "How are we to deal with them?"

"If they don't support the national good, they should be considered enemies of the state," Minza said, feeling bolder with each moment he spent in the prime minister's presence. "If they won't stand with us, they must be eliminated."

Kinchawn smiled warmly, radiating his approval. "Let me ask you a hypothetical question."

"Of course, sir."

"If I were to empower you—right here, right now—to take whatever measures were necessary to ensure the security of our political and civil interests . . . where would you begin?"

Minza hesitated to speak candidly. For as long as he could remember, as well known as the *Lacaam* Coalition's agenda was, it had been considered dangerous—even taboo—to say aloud what he was thinking right now. Was he being tested? Lured into the open so he could be disgraced? He could think of a few subordinates who would gladly have set him up to fail. But the prime minister's demeanor was relaxed and straightforward.

Minza decided that if this was a political ambush, it was too late to retreat now. Kinchawn was either looking to make Minza's career or end it. Either way, this was a threshold moment and there was no point in delaying the inevitable.

Mustering his resolve, Minza said, "I would kill Bilok and his inner circle of *Gatni* Party leaders."

Kinchawn took a deep breath, released it, and smiled.

"Excellent," he said. "And your second step?"

"Demand the loyalty of the other *Gatni* ministers, then disband the *Gatni* Party."

"History will remember you as a visionary and a patriot." The prime minister sat down. "How soon can it be done?"

"Two hours," Minza said. "Maybe sooner."

Kinchawn's eyes gleamed with hatred and delight as he gave the order that Minza had waited his entire career to hear.

"Kill them."

Chapter 42
U.S.S. Enterprise-E

PERIM FELT like a glorious impostor.

With Captain Picard in his ready room awaiting a vitally important, last-minute secret transmission, Perim was alone near the aft section of the bridge, seated in the captain's chair.

She had swelled with pride when he said "You have the conn, Lieutenant." From the moment she took the center seat, she began to understand the appeal of command. Once a vague, ill-defined notion, the essence of command had become a tangible commodity. The bridge looked a bit larger from here, and the rest of the galaxy felt just a little more manageable.

On the main viewer, Tezwa remained a minuscule flicker against the black backdrop of space. Maybe it was her pilot training, or the fact she was fretting about Jim Peart being down there risking his life, but even though Tezwa was nestled amid a million other points of light that looked all but identical, she still knew exactly which tiny white dot it was. No matter how many times she looked away, when she turned back to face the main viewscreen, her eyes found Tezwa's distinctive, vermilion-tinted twinkle every single time.

Ensign Le Roy swiveled away from the ops console to face her. "Lieutenant, sensors are detecting sharp power increases in the Tezwan spacedocks."

"They're powering up the fleet?"

"Looks that way," Le Roy said, turning back to her console. "I'm reading twenty-four unique engine signatures, all in prelaunch warmup."

"How long until they're ready to deploy?"

Le Roy checked her sensor readings. "Thirty minutes."

"Wriede," Perim said, glancing over to the tactical officer. "What's the Klingons' ETA?"

Wriede looked at his own console. Suppressing an awkward, lopsided grimace, he said, "Thirty-two minutes."

Perim sighed. "Wonderful," she lamented. In thirty minutes, this entire star system was going to turn into a shooting gallery, and two dozen Starfleet personnel down on that planet had front-row seats.

She calmly stood and moved back toward the first officer's seat; the golden aura of command had lost its luster.

"Captain Picard to the bridge," she said.

Chapter 43
Tezwa—Solasook Peninsula, 0337 Hours Local Time

DESPITE ITS INGENUITY and cunning, Data felt no sense of pride in the plan he had concocted.

The android officer vaguely recalled what pride had felt like, but when he tried to taste the emotion again from memory, its flavor eluded him. Cold equations, the records of the positronic pulses all were there, but they didn't add up to anything. Recollections of feelings both subtle and intense, from petty to sublime, resided in his neural storage matrix, software for a piece of hardware he no longer possessed.

He remembered thinking once—months ago, before Starfleet had demanded he give up his emotion chip— that to remember such feelings but not know what they felt like would be a tragedy, a loss worthy of terrible sorrow. *Perhaps I should feel sad now,* he ruminated. *Except that I cannot.* He acknowledged the irony of it, even though he could not appreciate its bitter humor.

He accepted the reasoning behind Starfleet's ultimatum, despite his reluctance to submit to it. After more than three decades of living without emotions, their sudden addition to his consciousness had changed his entire way of thinking—of *being*.

For a fleeting moment, he had considered resigning his commission rather than submit to Starfleet's order. But when forced to choose between keeping his long-sought emotions or continuing to serve beside his shipmates, he chose to surrender the gift his creator had labored to give to him.

He did not regret obeying the order; without the emotion chip, he was incapable of doing so.

However, he was eminently capable of completely dominating the poorly secured Tezwan artillery-control network. With only a fairly crude optronic patch into their communications system—and with a little help from his tricorder—he had accessed every major system in the Solasook Firebase. He dedicated an extra four-tenths of a second to a review of all the many variables that might impact the success of his plan, and he deemed the statistical probability of its success to be highly favorable.

He keyed his com. "Data to Bravo Team. Are you all ready?"

"Aye, sir," Parminder said. Her voice was almost drowned out by the howling of the arctic storm winds.

"All set on the west slope," Obrecht answered.

"Ready," Heaton said.

"Stand by," Data said, setting his scheme into motion.

Bypassing several security lockouts, he logged in to the antimatter-reactor control system. With a few quietly executed overrides, he altered the status readouts for several critical systems, all of which were, in fact, functioning within normal parameters. When he had pushed the meters' displayed states far enough away from optimal, he triggered the core-breach alarm.

Data tapped into the base's internal security network and observed the effects of his interference. The Tezwan core engineers hesitated, then stumbled over one another in a mad scramble to secure the reactor chamber and evacuate to a safer level. In response, the android hounded them with one phony failure alarm after another; cooling-system overloads, ventilator shutdowns, and radiation-shield malfunctions met them at every turn. After two minutes of unbridled chaos, one of the harried engineers did what any one of them should have done following the first core-breach alert: He sounded the evacuation alarm.

Beneath its protective shield of snow and ice, the main portal into the firebase opened. Even from nearly one hundred meters away, and despite the fury of the blizzard, Data heard the Tezwans' weapons blasting through the frozen barrier in their haste to escape what they believed had become a time bomb.

"They're coming out," Parminder said.

"Internal sensors show forty-nine personnel," Data said. "Wait until everyone has evacuated."

"Acknowledged," Parminder said.

Data tracked the evacuees' progress with the base's internal security network. Individuals who seemed slow or reluctant to comply with the evacuation order inevitably found themselves shepherded out of the complex by a cascading series of key-system malfunctions. Whenever they turned in any direction other than the one that led out of the base, a new critical-system failure threatened their lives.

Nine minutes later, Data confirmed that the last six Tezwan officers, most likely the base commander and his senior staff, were exiting the facility. "The last group is coming out now," he said into his com. "What is their position?"

A few seconds later, Heaton answered. *"They're congregating in the area immediately surrounding the entrance,"* she said.

"Ensign Parminder, are the Tezwans clear of your charge's blast area?"

"Barely," she whispered, most likely exercising caution to avoid being overheard by the nearby enemy troops.

"Detonate the charge."

A few seconds later, Data saw the golden-orange flash of the explosion a moment before he heard the crack of the blast wave. The plume of fire rolled majestically up into the sky, leaving behind an expanding cloud of thick, black smoke.

"They're retreating," Parminder said, her voice pitched with growing excitement.

"Lieutenants Heaton and Obrecht, stand by with your tricorders. Wait until the Tezwans pass your target markers."

"Here they come," Obrecht said. *"Clearing the markers in three . . . two . . . one . . . now!"*

"Activate tricorders."

The range of Data's hearing was barely broad enough to detect the hypersonic frequency the tricorders were emitting. Before he could verify with his own tricorder that their sonic pulses were properly collimated, a deep, rumbling thunder of collapsing snow and ice confirmed the two lieutenants had successfully sprung the trap he had instructed them to prepare.

"Report."

"Controlled avalanche went off exactly as planned," Heaton said. *"The entrance is clear, and all Tezwan personnel are alive and uninjured—and stuck on the other side of the snowfall."*

"Well done," Data said, disconnecting the optronic cables that linked his positronic brain, the tricorder, and the base's subspace signal buffer. "We have approximately thirty-four minutes before the Klingon fleet arrives. Regroup at the entrance in ninety seconds."

Pushing ahead through the clinging snow and driving wind, Data knew that capturing the firebase without a single shot being fired or anyone suffering an injury—on either side —was the optimally desirable outcome. His compatriots aboard the *Enterprise* would call it an achievement to be proud of . . . but he was no closer to remembering the sensation of pride in a job well done than he had been five minutes ago.

This did not seem unfair to him.

I am, after all, functionally immortal, he reasoned. *I will have time for pride later.*

Chapter 44

Tezwa—Mokana Firebase, 2350 Hours Local Time

"I SAID, the operations center is secure. We can move up."

Riker focused his eyes on Razka, who was crouched right in front of him. The first officer took a second to choke back the bitter bile rising in the back of his throat, so that he could reply without vomiting. "Okay," he said, his voice hoarse and his breath short. "Good."

Razka waved Tierney and Barnes forward. "Go do what you do," he told them. "We'll be right behind you." The two engineers tried to avert their eyes as they passed by, but Riker could see them casting sidelong glances at him. The Saurian security officer squelched their curiosity with a glare and a growl.

Riker tried to move forward, then clutched the wall as a wave of dizziness flooded his head, which already was caught in the grips of a fearsome, viselike pain.

Razka reached out and steadied him. "Hang on, sir," he said as he propped Riker against the wall, then opened his medical kit. He loaded a hypospray. "This should help reduce the fever."

The device's hiss just below his ear was loud enough to make Riker wince, but he relaxed as a cooling sensation extinguished the hot tingling pinpricks that had burned a swath across his neck and face, and calmed the manic pounding of his heart, which he was certain had been seconds away from splitting open his sternum.

"Can you hold a phaser, sir?"

Laboring to lift his rifle to a level position, Riker couldn't make his arms obey his wishes. There was no strength left in his hands. His suspicion that Razka could detect the difficulty he was having breathing was confirmed when the security officer injected him with a second shot from the hypospray. "Tri-ox," Razka said. "And some antihistamine."

Seconds later, Riker's sinuses and throat opened. Pulling in a much-needed breath, he felt some of his strength return. With a few moments of fierce concentration, he locked his hands around his rifle and held it steady. "Thanks, Chief," he said, not sounding at all like a man fit for combat. "Let's go."

Moving deeper into the base, they turned a corner at the end of the hall and kept to the shadows as they stole forward. After negotiating a short but steep downward flight of stairs, Razka led him into the firebase's operations center.

The room was small, had subdued lighting, and was packed on all sides with Starfleet-style technology. Modern adaptive interfaces had been modified to display readouts in Tezwan alphanumeric symbols.

Three unconscious Tezwan soldiers lay piled together in a darkened corner. Tierney and Barnes were at one of the consoles, resetting its display to Federation standards. Tierney looked over her shoulder as the first officer staggered in with Razka.

"I think we've compensated for the lost demolition kit," she said. "By linking the primary—"

"Can you blow the base or not?" Riker hadn't meant to sound so gruff, or cut her off so abruptly, but a riptide of sickness was surging through his gut, leaving him queasy and irritable.

She stiffened her posture and her tone. "Affirmative."

Subtly interposing himself between Riker and the engineers, Razka guided the first officer toward the main console. "You can monitor our progress from here," he said. "With your permission, I'll take them to their target." Leaning his weight against the console, Riker nodded and motioned for him to go. The Saurian noncom turned to the engineers and brusquely issued orders in Riker's name, then led them out to complete the strike mission.

Twenty-five minutes until the Klingons get here, Riker realized as he glimpsed his chronometer. *Hope that's enough time to do this.* New prickles of heat crawled across the back of his neck, and the relatively modest gravity of Tezwa suddenly seemed to increase its pull. He swallowed hard against a fresh wave of nausea churning inside his gut. *I hope I last that long.*

Chapter 45
Kolidos Firebase—0752 Hours Local Time

WHAT TOOK THEM SO LONG, Peart wondered cynically as he observed the advancing, regrouped Tezwan soldiers.

He and Sierra Team had stranded the enemy troops roughly eight kilometers away, just under an hour ago. T'Sona had escorted Scholz and Morello into the base, to capture ops and fence in the Tezwan base personnel.

Peart had stayed behind at the base's main entrance to activate the signal jammer, and serve as a one-man welcoming committee for the pursuing company of Tezwan grunts. From his prone position beneath his stolen hovercraft, he counted approximately one hundred enemy personnel moving in.

He began to wonder if facing them alone might be a mistake.

"Peart to T'Sona. Report."

"Scholz and Morello are preparing their demolitions. All secure inside the base."

"Well, tell them to hurry it up. The—"

"We are well aware the Klingon fleet is due in twenty-three minutes. . . . Sir."

Peart considered taking her to task for interrupting him, but seeing the Tezwans dodging from one protective dune to another, he decided the rebuke could wait. "Actually, I was going to say the troops we tangled with in the drop zone are on their way here, and looking to cut off our escape route."

That was met by a brief silence.

"I will join you shortly."

"Thank you. Peart out."

He removed his helmet to improve his peripheral vision. Searing, merciless heat hit him like a slap. The air was crisp and laced with windblown sand that tore across the back of his neck with scouring force.

He flipped open the holographic targeting sight of his phaser rifle. Aligning the crosshairs at center-of-mass height in a gap between two dunes, he took a breath and waited. He fired as a body blurred through his sights. The Tezwan soldier spun fully around and collapsed. Squeezing off another shot, Peart took down one of the two soldiers who had tried to duck past behind their braver comrade.

Taking his eye from the sight, he snapped his attention left, then right, with birdlike acuity. Enemy personnel scurried behind the dunes on either side of him.

Flanking me. Probably try to pin me down to defend a forward charge. This is gonna get ugly.

Choosing not to compare his tactical situation to that of Custer at Little Big Horn, or of Tirius at Arkalanna, he stunned two more Tezwans. Then the barrage began.

Shrieking blasts of radiant blue energy converged on his position. Bolts of charged plasma crackled across the firebase entrance, punched sizzling holes through his borrowed hovercraft, and turned long strips of desert sand into molten glass. Smoke and fumes spat from the hovercraft as a fire erupted in its engine.

Realizing that the hovercraft's antigrav system was about to fail—and drop the vehicle on top of him—he shimmied quickly backward on his belly, propelling himself through the sand with his knees and elbows. He cleared the hovercraft just in time to watch it fall the half-meter to the ground with a hollow bump and the clanging of its shoddily assembled metal chassis.

Flames roared up from the passenger area of the vehicle. Peart used the impromptu blaze as cover while he backed into the base entrance. Reaching for the door controls, he yanked his hand clear a microsecond before a Tezwan rifle blast fragged the panel in a shower of sparks. *So much for making them knock before they come in.*

Then he heard the oscillating whine of a damaged antigrav engine being pushed beyond its limits. The sound was getting louder and more distinct as it drew closer.

Poking his head around the corner, he saw a smoke-spewing, damaged hovercraft speeding toward his own wrecked vehicle—and the base entrance. It shook violently as it raced ahead, and it was obvious that it was barely functional. Regardless, Peart was impressed the Tezwans had been able to make sufficient field repairs to render the craft mobile at all.

Boosting his rifle to full power, he pivoted into the doorway, rifle stock braced against his shoulder, and fired. His phaser pulse flared as it struck the wobbling hovercraft, which lurched forward, gaining speed but suddenly veering off-center. Its sole passenger, the pilot, abandoned the controls and jumped overboard, rolling in a hard tumble across the sands.

The hovercraft's nose scraped the ground, initiating an uncontrolled roll that sent it tumbling like a burning boulder over the low dunes toward the base entrance.

Dodging a renewed fusillade from the Tezwan soldiers still hiding behind the dunes, Peart ran in a tight crouch back inside the base, just in time to see T'Sona racing toward him.

He motioned with his hands as he barked, "Get down!"

The Vulcan woman hit the deck. Peart hadn't intended to fall on top of her like a human shield, but the shock wave from the exploding hovercraft ramming the entrance behind him flattened him to the deck. A plume of fire and glowing-hot shrapnel-debris shot through the corridor over their heads.

Seconds later, as the blast impact wore off, Peart rolled onto his back, sat up, and surveyed the damage. The entrance and the corridor immediately behind it had collapsed and were blocked by the twisted wreckage of the hovercraft. Thick hazes of smoke and dust lingered in discreet layers. Chunks of broken metal and shattered stone littered the floor.

He looked at T'Sona, who was dusting herself off with casual aplomb. *Won't bother asking if she's fine. If she were hurt, she'd say so.* He keyed his com. "Peart to Scholz."

"Go ahead, sir."

"We've got a little snag in the plan. The Tezwans blasted our exit."

"Should we abort?"

"Negative. Finish rigging the charges."

"Sir? How do we get out after the timers are set?"

"Unless we find another exit, we don't."

T'Sona fixed Peart with a cold, reproachful stare. "Well put, sir. I am sure they found your words most inspirational."

He glared at her. "For the record, remarks like that are the reason no one likes talking to you."

Chapter 46
Tezwa—Linoka Firebase,
1955 Hours Local Time

TAURIK WAITED until the enemy officer was within reach, on the other side of the open doorway. Silently spinning on his heel, the Vulcan engineer pivoted around the doorjamb, reached in, and locked his thumb and first two fingers onto the man's shoulder, just below the neck.

He felt the reflexive twitch as the Tezwan officer's shoulder tensed and his nape feathers ruffled. To Taurik, the lanky humanoid seemed surprisingly lightweight as he pulled him off his feet and out of the room—all without making a sound to alert the two junior officers working at command consoles on the other sides of the room, their backs to the doorway.

On the opposite side of the doorway, lurking with him in the shadowy corridor, was Ensign McEwan. The delicate-featured human woman had proved quite adept at stealth tactics. Taurik gestured to her that they would wait in the corridor for the two junior officers to come looking for their supervisor.

The wait was brief. From inside the operations center, they heard the female officer ask, "Where's the commander?" A few moments later, the male Tezwan called out, "Commander Tregel?"

In contrast to Taurik, who remained relaxed and limber, McEwan seemed to tense as the two Tezwans' footsteps drew closer. *Perhaps I should offer to instruct her in V'Shan*, he thought. He surmised the ancient Vulcan art of self-defense—as demanding as it was graceful, and which many non-Vulcans mistook for a form of dance—would teach her patience and bestow greater fluidity to her technique.

Signaling her that he would strike first, he allowed himself to become one with the shadows. Dark and silent, his mind quiet and free of distracting thoughts, his breathing and pulse slowed almost to a standstill.

The male Tezwan stepped into the corridor, his female comrade only a long stride behind him. They turned in opposite directions, and the female officer stepped toward Taurik.

Before Taurik could attack, the male Tezwan spotted McEwan and shouted an alarm as he reached for his weapon. The female officer spun away from the Vulcan engineer, who lunged, grasped her trapezius, and dropped her to the floor.

McEwan, reacting with surprising speed and grace, ducked into a crouch and sweep-kicked the male Tezwan's legs out from under him. His weapon discharged as he fell, sending a deafening blast of painfully bright blue plasma into the ceiling. McEwan finished knocking the officer unconscious with a swift snap-kick under his chin.

Taurik sprinted into the operations center and immediately began locking down the facility. He was certain that many of the base's personnel had heard the officer's weapon being fired, and that one or more security personnel would come to investigate. McEwan followed him in a few seconds later, accompanied by the engineers, who moved to other consoles and reconfigured them as they began laying the groundwork for their sabotage of its reactor systems.

"The base personnel have been contained," Taurik said, turning to his teammates. "I have prepared an unobstructed path to your targets on sublevel five. You have twenty minutes."

Rao and Mobe acknowledged the order, finished their preparations, and headed for the door. Mobe checked the base floor-plan schematic on his tricorder, while Rao walked briskly ahead of the cautious Bolian, obviously confident that he knew where he was going.

McEwan watched them depart. "Sir, should I go with them?"

"Negative, Ensign. I require your assistance here."

"What do you need me to do?"

"Copy as many of the Tezwans' internal logs as possible to your tricorder."

McEwan patched her tricorder into the Tezwan firebase computer system. "Sir, almost all these files are encrypted."

"I am aware of that, Ensign."

"Beginning download," she said. "What are we looking for?"

"We are not seeking anything in particular," Taurik said. "We are gathering data for later analysis."

"But it's all encrypted."

"There is no such thing as an unbreakable code, Ensign." Reconfiguring the fire-control system to respond only to his commands, he noted how many Starfleet-standard protocols were in use at this facility. "If our foes' proclivity for using our technology without modification is any indicator, I suspect we will have little difficulty decrypting these files."

"I hope you're right, sir," McEwan said, brushing a stray lock of her red hair from her eyes.

Unlike many Vulcans, Taurik was not one to sing the praises of logic at every opportunity, but he made a point of skewering illogical outlooks as a matter of principle. "Hope has nothing to do with it, Ensign."

Chapter 47
Tezwa—Nokalana Firebase, 1157 Hours Local Time

FOUR MINUTES BEHIND, Vale noted. *This is gonna be close.*

Her tricorder indicated that the base was now completely flooded. Sakrysta and Spitale were cutting through the base's outer hull as quickly as their phasers were able, but the superdense duranium plating was harder to penetrate than they expected. "Vale to Spitale. How much longer?"

"Sixty seconds," the blond engineer replied.

Vale watched the two women work and tried to dispel her own impatience. Their amber-yellowish phaser beams were the only illumination in this deep-sea pit of eternal darkness. Fortunately, the light-intensifying filter on her pressure suit's faceplate had a smart circuit that prevented it from flaring when exposed to sudden increases in luminosity, otherwise she'd be unable to see anything at all right now.

She watched her chronometer. *Thirty more seconds*

until I can pester Spitale again. "Vale to Fillion. How're you doing?"

"Five by five, sir."

"So the Tezwans are playing nice and staying inside their submarine?"

"I think they've got the point now. As long as I'm here, they aren't comin' out."

"Acknowledged. Hang tough, we're almost done here."

Just as Vale had expected, after Sakrysta and Fillion had disabled the submarine's weapons, armed divers had tried to leave the vessel to inspect the damage and find the saboteurs. Waiting to greet them, however, was Fillion. The security officer had nestled snugly into a cluster of machinery casings on the roof of the Nokalana Firebase, his phaser rifle aimed squarely at the submarine's top hatch. Every time the Tezwan divers opened the hatch and tried to swim out, Fillion fired a warning shot that sent them scuttling back inside the ship.

Spitale and Sakrysta ceased fire as the ends of their respective semicircular cuts found the starting point of the other's incision. The irregularly edged, vaguely circular chunk of duranium succumbed to gravity and fell away from the overhanging angle of the outer hull, landing with a deeply muffled *whump* on the sandy ocean floor. Sheathing their rifles, the two engineers swam inside the base without even waiting for Vale's order. Given that the Klingon invasion fleet was now only seventeen minutes away, the security chief didn't mind the two women's initiative.

Following them through the meter-and-a-half-wide hole into an upper-level corridor, Vale was surprised to see the base so intact, considering that it was flooded. The engineers proceeded directly to a pair of turbolift doors. Although the original mission profile had called for avoiding the turbolifts in favor of using emergency staircases or access crawlspaces, that was now unnecessary. Working together, the engineers pried open the doors. Sakrysta checked the upper section of the turbolift shaft, while Spitale confirmed the lower portion was clear.

The three women swam straight down the turbolift shaft. Two levels down, Spitale stopped and motioned to Sakrysta to help her open the doors to another flooded corridor. Spitale said, *"The operations center is down this hallway, and to the right."*

"Good work. Proceed to your targets. I'll let you know when I reach ops."

"Aye, sir." Spitale resumed swimming downward, with Sakrysta following close behind her. Vale propelled herself down the corridor with quick kicks and wide forward strokes. Her muscles ached from the constant effort needed to move and manuever in the deep, high-pressure environment, and the exertion made her breathing even louder within the confines of her pressure suit.

Snaking around the corner, she saw the pale glow from the still-functioning consoles in the operations center. She moved inside and positioned herself at the master-control panel.

Only fifteen minutes to go, she realized. "Vale to Delta Team. I'm in ops. Spitale, report."

"We're almost there, sir," Spitale replied, her voice

wavering from her ongoing exertion. *"We'll be in position in thirty seconds."*

"Fillion, status."

"Little busy right now," Fillion said in an agitated tone. *"Our friends got clever."* Vale could hear the sound of Fillion's rifle firing repeatedly in short bursts while he spoke. *"Rewired their maintenance bots."* His next few words were mumbled too low for Vale to discern clearly through the phaser fire, but it sounded like he was cussing a blue streak. *"Little buggers are fast. And there's a lot of 'em."*

"Are you okay?"

"Yeah, I'm great," he groused. *"Hang on."* His phaser shots were repeating faster now. Vale knew that sound; Fillion had switched his weapon to rapid pulse-fire. *"Divers poked their heads out. Nice try, guys."* Fillion shouted his next string of expletives, which included a few choice words Vale had only ever heard Nausicaans use before. *"Score at the buzzer: Fillion twenty-eight, Tezwans zero."*

"And the crowd goes wild," Vale said. "Before you do your victory dance, do me a favor."

"Name it."

"Warn the sub to leave now, while it still can."

"My pleasure. Fillion out."

Vale noticed that the Tezwans, before evacuating their base, had taken the precaution of locking out all their system controls. Which meant that control of the six nadion-pulse cannons to which this base was linked had been automatically handed off to the two closest firebases. Three of Nokalana's guns were under the control of the Kolidos Firebase, and the other three were now under the control of the Ranakar Firebase.

"Vale to Peart and La Forge."

"Peart here."

"This is La Forge, go ahead."

"Nokalana Firebase handed off its guns to your targets. Can you both confirm control?"

"Affirmative," Peart said. *"I've got your guns online."*

"Commander La Forge?"

"Can't tell you that just yet." Vale sensed from the tension in his voice that the situation was worse than he was saying, but she decided to give him the benefit of the doubt.

"How soon can you confirm handoff?"

"I'll let you know once we get inside the base."

"You're not inside yet?" The words had just tumbled out of her mouth. La Forge had to know the Klingon attack fleet was only thirteen minutes away. Reminding him of it served no good. Nonetheless, if Piper Team had not yet entered its target at Mount Ranakar, then the Tezwan personnel manning that base had just been alerted that the Nokalana base had gone offline. If and when they attempted to contact Nokalana—or anyone else, for that matter—they were bound to realize their communications had been completely cut off, at which point they would go to full-alert status.

"We're working on it. I'll contact you as soon as we're in. La Forge out."

Unlike some notable Starfleet engineers, La Forge had never earned a reputation as a miracle worker. He was a brilliant engineer—methodical, precise, and scrupulously honest in his estimates and analyses—but he wasn't known far and wide as the one to turn to when you needed a rabbit pulled from a hat. Vale could only hope the chief engineer actually had a few magic tricks up his sleeve that he hadn't told anyone about.

"Spitale to Vale. We're in position and setting the charges."

"How soon until you're set?"

"Ten minutes."

"Make it eight," Vale said, watching the chronometer count down their rapidly dwindling time. "And swim quickly."

Chapter 48

Tezwa—Mount Ranakar, 1602 Hours Local Time

LA FORGE AND T'EAMA each gripped one of Braddock's arms and pulled the muscular young security officer up onto the summit plateau of Mount Ranakar. The fog had cleared, though the fearsome dome of charcoal-colored clouds drifting overhead had all but blotted out the midafternoon sun, leaving the area shrouded in a grim, unnatural twilight.

Taking a second to recover his breath, La Forge was acutely aware of the drenching, full-body perspiration that trickled across his skin. Scaling the cliff had taken a terrible toll on his palms and fingers, which were raw and sore. Falling chunks of jingle rock had left him with fat bruises on his clavicle and forehead, and all his muscles cried out for rest that he couldn't yet allow.

T'Eama and Braddock, who kneeled with him behind a small outcropping of thick brush, were also in poor condition. Despite his athletic prowess, Braddock looked like he'd just been run over by a Klingon *sark*. T'Eama, whose Vulcan biology had gifted her with tremendous strength and endurance, was the least exhausted, but even she was pulling ragged, tired breaths.

Disguised as a natural depression on the slope of the summit's rocky, rounded crest, the door to the firebase was less than fifteen meters away. Because of the many delays La Forge and his team had endured while scaling the unstable cliff, the Tezwan personnel on the other side had been forewarned by the shutdown of the Nokalana base that something was amiss.

So now the base was on alert. Piper Team was one man short, and the rest of the team was injured and exhausted. The Klingons were only twelve minutes away, and La Forge still had absolutely no plan for what to do next.

Braddock observed La Forge's intense scrutiny of the base entrance. "What's our next move, Commander?"

"Well," La Forge said. "We've lost the element of surprise. How would you feel about a direct frontal assault?"

"With ten-to-one odds? Against people who are shooting to kill?" Braddock looked dubious. "Not great."

"T'Eama? If you've got a suggestion, now's the time."

"Perhaps you can order them to surrender," she said dryly.

"That's not bad," Braddock said. "But what do we do *after* they shoot us dead?"

"Hang on a second," La Forge said. "I'm looking at this all wrong." Shifting the frequency range of his vision as easily as most people shifted their focus from near to far, he surveyed the land around the summit and the rock surrounding the entrance. Leaning over the edge of the cliff, he cycled through infrared and gamma wavelengths, searching for clues to which his normal luminosity-and-chrominance spectrum might be blind.

Looking back across the summit he saw a huge boulder, half his height but twice as wide, twenty meters away from the main entrance. Its heat signature was unlike those of the other rocks on the summit. He moved closer to it, and with his tricorder confirmed that it wasn't hollow, or artificial. Switching his synthetic eyes to maximum magnification, he discovered that its surface had been sealed with a concrete resin to hide the fact that the boulder was pitted with tiny cavities.

"This rock is volcanic," La Forge said. "But the nearest volcano is several hundred kilometers away."

Looking down at his feet, La Forge noticed the ground here by the boulder was covered in a thicker layer of dry sand than the rest of the summit. He kicked through the sand until he hit solid earth, and he kneeled down to run his fingers across it. He didn't need magnified vision to find the gouges in the ground; he could feel them, even with his torn-up fingertips.

"There's something under this rock," he said. "A door."

Braddock was at La Forge's shoulder, eyeing the scrapes.

"I bet they used volcanic rock 'cause it's lighter," Braddock said. "Easier to move."

"A logical assumption," T'Eama said.

"We need to move this thing," La Forge said.

Braddock shook his head. "It may be lighter than other rocks, sir, but it's still a rock. And a mighty big one."

"Stand back," T'Eama said. La Forge turned to see she had pulled her rifle from its sheath. She fired before he could tell her not to. The weapon gave off a low hum as its ruby-colored beam quickly and neatly sliced through the porous, low-density stone like a knife cutting a loaf of bread. Guiding the beam in slow, evenly spaced horizontal passes, she cut the huge rock into thin layers. She finished by cutting four vertical lines through the boulder. She gave the pile a swift kick, and the stack of diced rock collapsed before her.

"Divide and conquer," she said.

"Nicely done," La Forge said, then began chucking aside the now manageably sized rocks. Braddock and T'Eama joined him, and in less than a minute they had uncovered a recessed trapdoor hatch and a set of antigrav tracks on which the boulder had rested. After scanning the trapdoor, Braddock deactivated its security sensors and phasered through its lock. La Forge pulled it open while the security officer stood ready to blast anything that might pop out.

"All clear, sir," Braddock said.

Beneath the trapdoor was a ladder, which descended four meters to a landing at the top of a narrow stairwell. Braddock slung his weapon and climbed down first, then kept lookout for Tezwan security while La Forge and T'Eama climbed down. "Back door," Braddock whispered.

"More like an emergency exit," La Forge said. "Take point." Braddock sidestepped down the stairs in a half-crouch, leaning over the railing to watch and listen for approaching personnel. La Forge and T'Eama stayed close behind the security officer, stepping lightly, with their own weapons braced against their shoulders and muzzles pointed down.

Three flights down, Braddock stopped at an access door. "Ops should be through here, left down the corridor, then right." Looking up, he frowned. "Door's wired. Give me a second." Fishing through his suit's free-fall-secure pockets, he found the tools he was looking for. He worked with swift, practiced ease and bypassed the door's security before phasering through the lock bolt. "Ready, sir."

La Forge nodded his assent. Braddock cracked open the door and peeked through the sliver of space. Opening the door wider, he slipped through, dark and quiet as smoke on a moonless night. Creeping along in Braddock's footsteps, La Forge could almost hear crucial seconds ticking away.

As they neared the corner to ops, the sharp snaps of booted footsteps echoed off the walls, moving toward them. The middle of the corridor offered no cover, no other doors to duck into. Even if they pressed themselves against the wall and stayed silent as the grave, the hallway simply wasn't dark enough to conceal their presence. There wasn't enough time to retreat to the emergency stairwell.

La Forge confirmed his weapon was set for stun, lifted it to firing position, and held his breath. Braddock and T'Eama mirrored his actions, and readied their weapons.

Four Tezwan security officers, all carrying plasma rifles, turned the corner. The two in front blocked any kind of easy shot at the two behind. In less than a second, the two point men spotted the strike team and raised their weapons.

La Forge fired first, knocking the first security officer on the left backward onto the man behind him. Braddock and T'Eama fired in unison, stunning the two guards on the right. Sprinting forward, La Forge snapped off a quick shot at the pinned-under Tezwan, then rounded the corner into the hallway outside ops. He heard T'Eama and Braddock keeping pace behind him.

Tumbling past the open doorway of the ops center, La Forge felt the hairs on his neck and arms stand up as plasma bolts flew past him, searing hot scars onto the wall and floor. Braddock and T'Eama stopped on the other side of the doorway.

La Forge heard distant, running footsteps. Silent alarms had definitely been tripped, and Tezwan reinforcements would be here any second. Unless he and his team could capture ops in the next thirty seconds, this mission was about to meet a grisly end.

Setting his rifle to rapid-pulse fire, he quickly blasted all the light fixtures in the corridor, showering himself and his comrades in sparks and hot phosphors. Inching the muzzle of his weapon around the corner into the ops center, he squeezed off another few seconds of pulsed phaser shots at the ceiling. The corridor was now completely dark, and the only illumination in ops was the glow of its computer consoles.

Rolling to a prone position in the doorway, he gambled that the Tezwans' eyes would be unable to adjust to the rapid loss of lighting as well as his cybernetic eyes could. The three Tezwans opened fire in his direction, but all the plasma bolts passed nearly a meter above him. He returned fire with a quick strafe of phaser pulses that traced a path across the Tezwan officers, who fell backward and tumbled to the floor.

"C'mon," La Forge said as he scrambled to his feet and moved into ops. Finding the master-control screen, he reset it to Starfleet's default interface and initiated a base lockdown.

From the corridor outside, he heard grunts of pain and shock as Tezwan personnel, no doubt responding to the silent alarm, collided with the invisible security force-fields he had just activated. Behind him, T'Eama and Braddock scrambled to other terminals and made their preparations.

"The turbolift's clear," La Forge said. "I've opened a route to the targets. Go!"

Braddock and T'Eama sprinted out of ops. Their foot-falls grew fainter while La Forge began reprogramming the firebase's identify-friend-or-foe software and execut-ing the override commands on the nine guns this base now controlled.

Seven minutes till the Klingons arrive, he realized, glimpsing the chronometer. He chuckled grimly. *And I thought we were cutting it close.*

Chapter 49
Qo'noS

WORF TENSED BESIDE THE DOOR, lying in ambush.

Councillor Kopek's chambers in the Great Hall were far more lavish than those of Chancellor Martok. Unlike the chancellor, Kopek was a scion of a noble House, with generations of haughty expectations to live up to. Polished black marble floors, pillars of gleaming obsidian, and supple *targhDIr* furniture were all warmly illuminated by crackling, spice-scented *varHuS* candles housed in ornate carved-crystal sconces.

The councillor was also well traveled, as evidenced by the delicate paper ceiling tiles from Vulcan, and the gently burbling Betazoid water sculpture that dominated the wall to the right of the main double doors, which had been hewn whole from ancient Terran redwood trees.

While concealing Kopek's now-unconscious aide-de-camp, L'Vek, in the antechamber next to the councillor's desk, Worf had also noted the councillor's sizable and smartly tailored wardrobe. The councillor's *boQDu'* had posed no significant threat to Worf, who easily placed the man in a stranglehold and forced him to reveal his name, before knocking him out.

Using the dermal voice patch to impersonate L'Vek, Worf had summoned Kopek back to his chambers on "an urgent matter." After setting the security-jamming device, there was naught else to do but wait for the prey to walk into the trap.

Waiting, unfortunately, was the one thing Worf least wanted to do right now. With each passing moment the Klingon invasion fleet raced closer to Tezwa, and his son was among those who were about to be sacrificed on the twin altars of honor and futility. Also in jeopardy were Worf's old friends aboard the *Enterprise,* who, he was certain, were even now risking their lives to spare the Klingon fleet from the need to make a suicide attack on a target of admittedly little long-term strategic value to the Empire.

At least Lorgh was prompt, Worf reminded himself. The dour old Imperial Intelligence agent had been telling the truth when he'd said the dossier on Kopek had been ready for years. Lorgh also had been right about the Federation's capture of a Breen starship. To acquire its schematics, Worf had called in two favors and made four promises. He downloaded schematics the Federation government claimed it didn't have, from a ship it alleged it hadn't captured, less than ten minutes after he'd first requested it.

Being an ambassador sometimes has its privileges, he mused.

Moving the data through a series of encrypted, anonymous channels, he'd traded it to Lorgh for the Kopek dossier twelve minutes ago. Six minutes ago, Worf returned to the Great Hall. Four minutes ago, he opened the door to Kopek's chambers with codes that were conveniently annotated in his I.I. file. L'Vek unwittingly gave Worf his voiceprint three minutes ago.

The doors swung open.

Councillor Kopek, a beefy, broad-shouldered Klingon in the prime of his life, barreled in and slammed the doors. "L'Vek! Where are you, you worthless *petaQ!* What's so damned urgent?" Even from two meters away, Worf could tell that the councillor's expensive clothes reeked with the cheap perfume of whichever one of his mistresses he'd lain with before being summoned to the war council, and his breath was ripe with *warnog.* "L'Vek!"

Worf was grateful for Kopek's boorish bluster; it made it much easier to sneak up on him. Locking his right arm around Kopek's throat, Worf bent him backward at a sharp angle and jabbed a neural disruptor—one of the many cruel gadgets Zeitsev had left in his office—between his shoulder blades.

Worf whispered menacingly in the struggling man's ear. "I am not here to kill you, but if you force me to, I will."

Kopek continued to fight, but with less vigor. "Who are you?"

The question assured Worf that his voice-disguise patch was functioning perfectly. "That is not important," he said.

"I beg to differ," Kopek said, with the same mock courtesy Worf had come to associate with the Cardassians. Kopek's neo-Cardassian affectations were high on the list of things that Worf hated about the man.

With a single zap of the disruptor, Kopek went limp from the chest down. Worf let him fall like a sack of garbage, then kneeled over the paralyzed councillor and rolled him onto his back. The black balaclava that concealed Worf's face wasn't quite as high-tech as his voice patch, but it served its function just as well.

Kopek stared in horror at his motionless limbs. "You've crippled me, you *taHqeq*. If you had any honor, you'd kill me."

"You will recover in a few hours," Worf said. "If you cooperate."

"With an honorless *yIntagh?*" He spat at Worf. "Never."

Wiping the warm spittle from his mask, Worf removed an optolithic data rod from his pocket. "This may interest you." He inserted the rod into a small playback device, which projected a small holographic image in the air above Kopek's scowling face.

Long scrolls of annotated data flashed by, one densely packed screen after another. Every few seconds there was a brief image showing Kopek stabbing someone, shooting someone, or engaged in intercourse with someone.

The look of unmitigated terror on Kopek's face confirmed for Worf that the evidence had been worth his effort to acquire.

"Yes, Kopek, it is *all* here," Worf said. "The weapons

you sold to the Cardassians during their war against the Federation. The imperial supplies you smuggled to the Orion Syndicate, during the Dominion War. Your mistresses, your bastards—even your true firstborn, the one whose infant skull you dashed on Mount Vor so no one would know you sired him with a commoner woman." Kopek squeezed shut his eyes. Worf grabbed the traitor by his scalp and yanked his head back until his eyes opened. "You did these things with open eyes! Look at them now!"

Kopek tried to mask his fear with rage, but the micro trembles in his jaw betrayed his agitated state. "Who are you? Where did you get all this?"

"You are not asking the correct question."

Kopek glared up at Worf. His terror transformed into bitter disgust as he grasped the true purpose of this visitation. He narrowed his eyes and mumbled through gritted teeth. "What do you want?"

"Your command access code," Worf said. "Now."

Kopek's face twisted with furious disbelief. "Are you mad?" Worf continued to glare at him. Kopek shook his head. "No."

"If you refuse me again, this data rod will find its way to the chancellor. You will be executed, your House dishonored, and its holdings forfeited to the Empire. Your bloodline will end."

"You'll expose me anyway."

"I will not. You have my word of honor."

"Honor?" Kopek barked out an angry laugh. "What honor does a man with *no name* have?"

"More than you," Worf said, every word infused with

contempt. He turned off the holoprojection and held the data rod in front of Kopek's face. "If you tell me your command code, when you awake, this will be yours, to do with as you see fit. Refuse me—or lie to me—and you will not wake up at all."

Worf gave the councillor's scalp another firm twist, in case it might help extract his answer more quickly. If Kopek followed an honorable path, choosing to die rather than reveal his code, Worf would be out of options. Captain Picard and the *Enterprise* crew would have no way of stopping the Klingon attack fleet, which would almost certainly be destroyed over Tezwa. He thought it bitterly ironic that the only hope for the survival of thousands of honorable Klingon warriors was the fact that one of their highest leaders was an honorless, degenerate traitor.

As Worf unsheathed his *d'k tahg* and raised it to striking position over Kopek's throat, the councillor lived up to his reputation. "My code is Kopek *wej Hut baH Soch vagh loS taj.*"

"I hope so," Worf said. "For your sake." He reached into his satchel, took out a hypospray, and injected its contents into Kopek's jugular. The councillor faded almost instantly into anesthetized slumber, and Worf moved on to the next phase of his plan.

He unclasped the side loops of his satchel and unfolded it on the floor next to Kopek, revealing the full assortment of tools that Zeitsev had loaned to him, complete with a short set of instructions on a minipadd. Propping open Kopek's eyelids with his thumb and middle finger, he scanned the councillor's retinal patterns.

After changing the voice patch to mimic the man's hoarse baritone, he uploaded the scan of Kopek's retinal patterns into the holomask.

The holomask was a technology that Worf had never heard of before tonight, but he suspected it was the product of efforts to duplicate a mobile holographic emitter that the crew of the *Voyager* had brought back from the Delta Quadrant. He affixed the device to his tunic and activated it.

A few seconds of disorienting, static-filled vision later, he caught his reflection on the water sculpture. He was the perfect simulacrum of Kopek, from his clothes to his upturned cranial ridges—to his retinas.

Worf dumped the real Kopek into the wardobe antechamber, on top of the still-incapacitated L'Vek.

Sitting down at Kopek's desk, Worf spied the chronometer. *The fleet will be there any minute.* He pushed that concern from his mind. "Computer, activate holographic interface."

"Submit for retinal-pattern identification."

"Proceed."

A shaft of intense green light, projected from the ceiling, traveled up his torso to his face. *"Look into the beam."* The emerald flash scanned his right eye first, then the left.

"Identity confirmed, Councillor Kopek." A semitransparent image of the red-and-gold Klingon emblem appeared in midair above the desk.

"Connect to the Fleet Command Center."

"State access code."

"Kopek *wej Hut baH Soch vagh loS taj.*"

"Code verified."

The trefoil was replaced by a graphical display consisting of the Fleet Command Center insignia and a diagram of its hierarchical directory structure. Navigating swiftly through the holographic interface, Worf zeroed in on the master fleet command codes. With a few simple inputs, he began downloading the information to his tricorder.

He looked at the optolithic data rod on the desktop. The notion of surrendering it to Kopek enraged him. The man deserved to die, and very likely his House deserved to fall into ignominy with him. There was no way to know for certain how many Klingon lives he had betrayed with his profiteering during the Dominion War, or how many Starfleet personnel had been slain by arms he had provided to the Cardassians. Even if none of those crimes were worthy of being avenged, certainly the murder of Kopek's helpless child—whom he had slain, in cold blood, with his own hands—was enough to warrant his disgrace and death.

But I gave my word.

The classified files finished copying to his tricorder, and he terminated the connection. Rising from the chair, he picked up the data rod and clutched it in his fist. He thought of all the heinous misdeeds it documented, the honored blood with which its sordid tales had been written.

This might be my only chance to destroy him, Worf realized. *His opposition of Martok will only worsen. He will resort to murder, lies, bribery . . . nothing is beneath him. I could give this to Martok, to help him force Kopek off the council.*

He looked at the data rod in his hand. *I gave my word.*

He dropped the data rod on the desk and walked to the door. *I have offended my own honor enough for one day,* he decided.

Stepping into the crimson-lit corridor, Worf quickened his pace. The fleet was about to drop out of warp, and he knew full well the bloody price that would be paid if he was late.

Chapter 50
U.S.S. Enterprise-E

PICARD'S EARS STRAINED against the silence. The countdown timer had ticked down to zero, but all was quiet on the bridge.

Perim hovered for a moment over Le Roy at ops before resuming her circuit of the bridge's primary duty stations. She paused briefly at the helm, nodded to herself as she eyed Magner's console, then moved on to review the security and tactical stations.

The captain occupied his mind reviewing the latest status reports Perim had forwarded to him. Her damage evaluation indicated that the *Enterprise* remained without shields, and the Tezwan attack drone that rammed the primary torpedo launcher had turned the bulk of the ship's most sophisticated targeting sensors into mangled junk.

Dr. Crusher's latest report was more encouraging; the majority of the ship's personnel injured by the Tezwan sneak attack had been treated and cleared for duty. Only a handful of more serious cases remained in progress, and the medical staff had limited the number of crew fatalities to five.

Which is still five too many, the captain brooded.

Perim returned to her seat next to Picard. Keeping her voice down, she told him what he already knew. "No sign of the Klingon attack fleet, Captain."

Picard's eyes drifted across the ceiling. He could almost feel a deadly presence lurking beyond its fragile protective shell. "They're out there, Lieutenant."

Perim looked up, as if to see whether Picard was privy to some kind of clue she had overlooked. Picard sighed and pensively pressed his closed fist against his chin. There was still no word from Worf or from the strike teams on the surface of Tezwa. "Status of the Tezwan fleet," he said.

"Fully deployed," Perim said. "They've formed a defensive perimeter around the planet. I think they're expecting the attack."

"They'd be fools not to," Picard said.

Wriede turned toward Picard and Perim. "Captain," the willowy tactical officer said. "If the Tezwan fleet decides the Klingons aren't coming . . . they might come after us."

The worried looks that darted between the rest of the bridge crew loaned credence to Wriede's theory. Picard had already considered that possibility, more than an hour ago. It was a genuine risk; the Danteri-made Tezwan fleet was more than capable of keeping pace with the *Enterprise,* and their greater numbers might enable them to surround the Federation flagship.

"Ensign Le Roy, open a channel on secure frequency one-eight-alpha."

"Aye, sir," the ops officer said, tapping the command into her console. Picard didn't expect the Klingons to listen to reason, but the longer he could delay them in conversation, the more time Worf and the strike teams would have to complete their assignments. "Channel ready, sir," Le Roy said.

Picard stood, to better project his voice. "Attention, Klingon fleet commander," he said in his most authoritative manner. "This is Captain Jean-Luc Picard of the Federation Starship *Enterprise*. We request a parley, on behalf of the people of Tezwa. Please respond."

Several seconds passed. There was no reply. Picard felt slightly self-conscious standing alone in the center of the bridge, addressing an invisible entity that he couldn't truly prove was there, but for the benefit of morale he held his resolute stare at the viewscreen, willing a response to come.

He was met by silence.

Behind his shoulder, Perim's voice was low and soft. "Sir, what if the Klingon fleet isn't here?"

Picard held his ground. *I know you're out there.*

Perim kept her tone diplomatic. "Captain, maybe we—"

From the overhead speaker, a voice like broken glass cut her off. *"Attention,* Enterprise: *This is Fleet Captain Krogan. There will be no parley. You have three minutes to get out of the war zone. Krogan out."*

So much for diplomacy, Picard lamented.

"That answers that question," Perim said. "Orders, Captain?"

Picard sat down and fixed his gaze on the main viewscreen.

"Signal the strike teams," he said. "Let them know they have three minutes until Armageddon."

Chapter 51
Tezwa—Keelee-Kee

FOLLOWING MINISTER ELAZOL through the door to his office, Bilok recoiled as a sapphire blue flare of energy disintegrated the top of his friend's head.

The deputy prime minister stumbled backward, fumbling awkwardly beneath his robe to find his pistol. Even as he yanked the weapon free of his belt, age and panic combined to trip him over his own feet. He fell hard to the floor as the assassin inside the office appeared in the doorway, the military-issue blaster in his hand leading his way.

The killer was a young, physically fit *elininim*—one of Kinchawn's people. He had the hard, cold eyes of a professional murderer. In the fraction of a moment it took him to realize Bilok was below the level of his aim, the fragile statesman opened fire in self-defense.

The blinding azure beam of charged plasma killed the young gunman almost instantly. His lifeless body seemed to dance, suspended on the coursing stream of energy like a marionette on an inverted string. Bilok released the trigger. The slain would-be assassin slammed to the floor next to Elazol's corpse.

His weapon still clutched tightly, Bilok scrambled across the floor to Elazol. The room stank of burnt feathers and charred flesh. He took his friend's body in his arms. Tears of rage stung his eyes. There had been no reason for Elazol to enter Bilok's office ahead of him. He had always walked faster than Bilok, and they had known each other for so many years that they had long since abandoned the formalities of protocol.

An ancient Tezwan saying haunted his thoughts: *"A step early, a step late, we walk blindly to our fate."*

Running footsteps overlapped their own bright echoes in the corridor outside his office. Bilok turned and raised his weapon. Dasana halted at the sight of his pistol, and Itani lurched to a clumsy stop behind her. "Neelo's dead," Dasana said, her voice warbling with sorrow and fear.

Bilok lowered his weapon and looked down at the desecrated visage of his friend and ally of more than three decades. "They came for me, too." Dasana and Itani's eyes, already wet with tears, overflowed as they looked down in mourning on Elazol. Bilok knew there was no time now for sorrow-songs. The *Lacaam'i* had begun their endgame. "Who's left?"

"Unoro and Tawnakel," Itani said. "Edica's been shot."

"They're coming for us," Bilok said. "All the *Gatni*. Warn everyone. They must arm themselves." He gently laid Elazol on the floor. There was no time now to wait and consult with Azernal. The Federation was too far away to be of any help, and in any case it would almost certainly refuse to intervene, calling this an "internal matter." Rising to his full, imposing height, he turned to Dasana and Itani. "Come with me."

He marched past them, his pistol nakedly brandished.

"We have to call the constables," Itani said, blocking his path. "We can't—" He pushed her aside and kept walking.

"They're all part of the military," Bilok said. "Just like the one who came to kill me. Kinchawn's declared war upon us. Stand and fight, or stand aside."

Dasana fell into step behind him, her own plasma pistol shaking in her white-knuckled grasp. With her free hand she readied her personal com. "What should I tell the others?"

"Shoot to kill, and meet at Kinchawn's office. We're taking back the government."

Chapter 52
U.S.S. Enterprise-E

THIRTY SECONDS HAD PASSED since Krogan's warning. Picard felt a growing sense of dread, like a cold ache in his gut. In just over two minutes the Klingon attack fleet would begin its assault, turning all of Tezwa into a killing field. Adding insult to the injury, two dozen of his best personnel, including most of his senior officers, were standing on the front line of a war that didn't have to happen.

The tension gripping the young officers who surrounded him was tangible. He trusted all of them to meet the challenges of their duty, no matter what that might entail. He didn't share their anxiety. What haunted him, he realized, was loneliness.

To his right—where he expected to find the reassuringly solid presence of Will Riker—sat Perim, a Trill woman whose piloting skills were second to none, but who seemed ill prepared for the role of first officer. To her credit, she masked her awkwardness with quiet grace.

Looking past Perim, he saw Wriede at tactical, substituting for Vale.

Lieutenant Magner was only a semiregular face at the helm, and it was jarring to see Ensign Le Roy at ops when Picard had, after fifteen years, grown accustomed to the inimitable precision of Lieutenant Commander Data at that station.

He felt like a teacher whose star pupils had graduated, leaving him behind to greet a class of fresh-faced new students who had come to take their desks. All the old voices of counsel were absent now, and he felt terribly alone, surrounded by strangers while perched on the lip of the abyss.

The disaster was eighty-two seconds away when an alert chirped from Le Roy's console. The young officer couldn't conceal her rush of renewed optimism. "Captain, incoming signal from Commander Riker!"

"On speaker," Picard said. Le Roy nodded to him that the channel was open. "Picard here."

The first officer sounded badly fatigued; his pronunciation was a bit slurred. *"All teams ready, Captain,"* Riker said. *"Standing by for your order."*

"Well done, Number One. Target the guns on the Tezwan fleet. Let us know the moment you're ready to fire."

"Aye, sir. . . . Targeting now."

Picard was about to indulge in a moment of hope when Le Roy declared, in a voice for the entire bridge, "Sixty seconds."

Perim showed slightly more discretion, leaning close to Picard to whisper her concerns. "Captain, controlling those guns is only half the battle."

"Quite right, Lieutenant."

Sparing him the need to elaborate, another com signal beeped, this time on Wriede's console. "Captain," the tactical officer said. "Encrypted data coming in from . . ." He paused, in a moment of what Picard considered to be completely understandable shock. Wriede completed his sentence, even though he didn't sound like he believed it: ". . . from Qo'noS."

Picard smirked at Perim with the well-earned bravado of a man who'd made a career out of dodging bullets, both figuratively and literally. *"That* is the *other* half."

Chapter 53
I.K.S. veScharg'a

"CAPTAIN, the *Ya'Vang* is in attack position."

"Good." Fleet Captain Krogan of the *I.K.S. veScharg'a* made final adjustments to the deployment pattern of his attack fleet. Zurka, his first officer, waited at the tactical station for the captain's next order. "Order Captain Rota to decloak on my signal," Krogan said. "The honor of first strike will be hers."

"Yes, Captain," Zurka said.

Krogan was prepared to overpower the Tezwan ships by a comfortable margin. The planet's artillery presented a formidable challenge, but defeating it would only make his victory all the more glorious. He had spent the four hours en route planning a complex pattern of cloaking and uncloaking that he was certain would confuse the targeting systems on the planet. He didn't expect it to prolong any individual ship's survival by more than a few minutes, but in those few extra minutes he could inflict enough damage to lay waste to every gun on the planet. What little of Tezwa's natural resources and civilian population survived would be easily cowed and subjugated for the glory and enrichment of the Empire.

He downed the final tart dregs of bloodwine from his metal mug, then sucked loose a few savory chunks of *gagh* that had lodged between his razor-sharp incisors and canines. Unlike some flag officers, Krogan was no glutton, but he knew not to go into battle hungry. Some warriors believed that an empty stomach gave them greater fury; it was his opinion that it led to fatigue and slow wits.

He slammed his fist down on the intraship com. "Krogan to all dropships. Prepare for launch. *Qapla'!*" With another brusque slam of his palm, he closed the channel. "Zurka, report."

"All wings ready to attack on your order."

"Has Picard's ship left the system?" Like many of the elder soldiers of the Empire, Krogan considered the name of that ship to be an expletive, an ill omen, a curse best never said aloud.

"No."

"*Fek'lhr* take him, then." Raising his voice to a rough-edged bellow, he barked orders around the bridge. "Arm disruptors and torpedoes! Stand by to disengage the cloak! On my signal, order the *Ya'Vang* to begin the attack!"

He lifted his left hand, in anticipation of snapping it forward for emphasis as he issued the order that would deliver the Empire's icy revenge upon the upstart world below. *It is a good day to die,* he reminded himself as he prepared to speak.

Then his bridge turned darker than the deepest pit of *Gre'thor.*

The viewscreen, the overhead lights, even the com panels—all were offline, utterly without power. Dim, white emergency lights snapped on where the bulkheads met the deck, casting fuzzy and distorted shadows on the ceiling as it silhouetted the bridge crew. Krogan growled in disgust as he watched the younger officers hammering futilely at their consoles. From every station came the same frustrated report: All systems offline.

Goza, the communications officer, was the only one who had anything useful to report. "Emergency coms still functioning," she said. "The rest of the fleet is dead in space."

The crew's speculations multiplied faster than tribbles, but none of them added up to anything better than a wild guess. A new weapon? A natural phenomenon? Zurka turned to Krogan. "We're unable to restore main power, Captain," he said, both furious and ashamed. "We have no explanation."

Krogan was almost frothing at the mouth with irrational rage. "You don't?" He wore the darkness like a mask over his bitter dishonor. "I can explain it in one word!" A murderous growl propelled the obscenity that escaped his snarling lips:

"Enterprise."

Chapter 54
U.S.S. Enterprise-E

"THERE THEY ARE," Perim said.

Picard watched the Klingon armada emerge from under cloak. The battle group consisted of more than sixty vessels, all of which were now poised in strategic attack postures in orbit above Tezwa. Wriede had downloaded the data packet from Worf in barely enough time for Le Roy to configure the subspace signal and transmit the master command code to the still-cloaked fleet. The moment she confirmed that control had been established, she and Wriede coordinated the emergency shutdown of the entire Klingon invasion force.

Which now lay dead in space, helpless before the two dozen Tezwan vessels moving to take advantage of the Klingons' sudden incapacity. "The Tezwans are raising shields and charging weapons," Le Roy reported.

"*Enterprise* to strike teams," Picard said. "Fire at will."

Less than four seconds elapsed between the order and the action. Even though he knew the artillery was firing at reduced power, he still winced as he watched the fiery blasts streak up from the planet and inflict crippling blows on the Tezwan ships.

Seconds after the cannon fire began, it ceased. In orbit over Tezwa, two fleets lay immobilized—one by force, the other by sabotage.

"Ensign Le Roy, report."

"All Tezwan vessels are showing heavy damage to power systems," she said, running a confirmatory sensor sweep. "Several are ejecting lifeboats. . . . Five are signaling their unconditional surrender—to anyone."

Picard knew better than to gloat; a disaster of epic magnitude had only just been postponed—it was not yet avoided. He could only hope that in the next several minutes, before the Klingon fleet succeeded in overriding the command lockout, someone in the Tezwan government would take advantage of this momentary reprieve to sue for peace, at any price.

Until then, however, all Picard could do was continue to play his part in this imminent interstellar tragedy.

"Picard to strike teams. Well done, everyone. Destroy the artillery system and begin your retreat. Picard out." He returned to his chair and sat down. "Helm, move us into orbit over Tezwa. Let's finish this, and bring our people home."

Chapter 55
Tezwa—Keelee-Kee

"IT WAS OUR OWN ARTILLERY, Mr. Prime Minister."

"Damn!" Kinchawn swore, swatting a lamp off his desk. It smashed to the floor of his office and scattered broken glass over the feet of General Minza, who had personally delivered the bad news. "How much of the system is compromised?"

"All of it."

"By whom?"

"We're not yet certain. What we do know is that our fleet is dead in space, and more than sixty Klingon warships are in orbit, positioned to strike all our major cities."

Kinchawn's mind raced through the possible scenarios. Had a rogue faction risen up within the military— one loyal to Bilok? Or had the Klingons somehow sabotaged the artillery defense system? The latter scenario seemed implausible until he recalled the report of a suicide attack by a lone Klingon cruiser. *They sacrificed their ship to land strike teams,* he concluded.

"One more thing," Minza said. "Bilok's alive. I don't have all the details, but the *Gatni* ministers have armed themselves and are gathering right now."

Kinchawn pushed his skeletal fingers across his scalp. His skullfeathers ruffled with a brittle sound. His breath came only with effort, as if the air were suddenly thick as sap. *Sixty warships,* he thought. *Hundreds of thousands of Klingon warriors.* He pondered how long his now-crippled military would fare against such a fearsome war machine. An open conflict would be hopeless; the Klingons would annihilate the tattered remnants of the Tezwan army in days, if not hours.

He couldn't begin to fathom what horrors the Klingons would reserve for him personally. Public execution? Torture? He had heard blood-chilling accounts of the Klingons' rare gifts for painful retribution, which exceeded even his own tolerance for inflicting such measures. Would they assign some grinning demon to kill him by degrees, taking his life one piece at a time? It seemed likely; of all the things for which the Klingons were renowned, mercy was not among them.

Kinchawn stepped behind his desk and hurled the framed print of the Civil Charter from the wall. Behind it was a computer panel. He placed his hand on the genetic scanner and stood still as it scanned his eyes. "Initiate emergency protocol *Jee-lim ko'Cha,*" he said, triggering a silent alert that would summon his fellow *Lacaam'i* ministers to join his flight.

A circular design in the center of his office floor opened like an iris. A capsule-shaped turbolift, large enough for only one person, rose from the floor. Checking the wall panel, Kinchawn confirmed that his most sensitive personal data files had all been destroyed. He walked to the capsule and stepped inside.

"Put the army on a resistance footing," he said to Minza. "Gather the senior officers and rendezvous at the redoubt as soon as it's safe to travel."

"Yes, Mr. Prime Minister."

He pressed the switch and descended toward his executive escape shuttle. This emergency exit had been designed into the *Ilanatava* ostensibly as a precaution against foreign attack. But Kinchawn and the other *Lacaam'i* had long known that the greatest threat to them was not Tezwa's enemies, but its citizens.

Four minutes later, Kinchawn settled into his luxurious escape transport, surrounded by dozens of his political allies.

Their pilot guided the ship vertically out of its secret hangar, emerging from a now devastated park several spans from the *Ilanatava*. Rising above the city, the ship rocketed away into the night. Kinchawn watched the spires of Keelee-Kee retreat into the distance. *The Klingons will pay for this in blood and shame,* he vowed. *Today is theirs . . . but every day that follows will be mine, until they are gone.*

Chapter 56
Tezwa—Kolidos Firebase

"IN ABOUT SIXTY SECONDS," Scholz said, "we're gonna be up to our necks in Tezwans."

Peart eyed the glowing-hot wall of smoldering debris that blocked the exit. The pungent stench of burned wiring and molten polymers filled the narrow corridor. The rest of Sierra Team stood behind him, looking about as flustered as he felt.

Flipping through schematic details on his tricorder, the deputy chief of security searched frantically for another path out of the desert firebase, which was set to self-destruct in a few minutes, with or without them. He preferred it without, if possible.

T'Sona watched him, her demeanor disturbingly calm under the circumstances. "Logic would suggest," she began, in a tone of voice that made Peart's eyebrows furrow with contempt, "that in the event of emergency, there likely would be a—"

"A shuttle hangar," Peart interrupted. "One level down

and across to the north. Let's go." Pushing through the trio, he led the way, jogging at a pace just shy of running for his life.

All the corridors looked the same, and in Peart's haste to make his retreat they all blended together into a rolling backdrop of shadowy gray corners and flashing red emergency lights. The prerecorded alert he had triggered, in accordance with his orders to help the base's Tezwan personnel escape, ran on a short loop. The nasal voice, presumably speaking in one of Tezwa's many dozens of major languages, urged all personnel to "evacuate at once."

The hangar door did not open at Peart's approach. He slammed into it, and found himself pinned as Scholz and Morello collided with him as well as each other. Aloof and clearly more dextrous, T'Sona stood off to one side of the pileup.

Pushing back from the door, Peart lifted his rifle and blasted the door lock. Acrid smoke spewed beneath the shower of sparks, and the door opened with a grinding scrape.

The hangar was half the size of the smallest one on the *Enterprise,* and it housed only a single small shuttlepod. Sierra Team sprinted to the tiny craft and piled in. Peart slid into the pilot's seat while T'Sona secured the hatch.

The nasal voice reverberated in the empty hangar outside: *"You have three minutes to reach minimum safe distance."*

"The forcefields are down," T'Sona said. "The Tezwans should now be free to evacuate."

"Except we have their only shuttle," Scholz said.

"Sir," Morello said. "If we take the only shuttle, how will the Tezwans escape?"

"They will use the emergency exit," T'Sona said, trumping Peart's reply. Morello just sat there with his jaw open.

Scholz looked at Peart as if he had just shot the man's dog. "Is that true?"

"Yup," Peart said as he powered up the shuttlepod's engines and confirmed it was fueled and ready to fly.

Scholz quaked with aggravation. "Then why are we—"

" 'Cause I don't want to be standing in a desert with a hundred ticked-off Tezwans after we blow up their base."

The two engineers looked at each other and both silently conceded that there was some merit to that argument.

T'Sona, meanwhile, leaned forward and looked up at the hangar doors, which also doubled as its externally camouflaged roof. "Lieutenant," she said, "do you know the code to open the hangar doors?"

"Not exactly," Peart said. "I'm working around it."

She pointed out the cockpit windshield at a squad of armed Tezwan security personnel who had just entered the hangar. "You may wish to work faster."

Scholz was beginning to frazzle. "Let's blast it and go!"

"We don't have any weapons," Peart said flatly.

"Ram it," Morello said, clearly thinking on Scholz's level.

"And you call *me* crazy," Peart said. "Look at those doors. We'd be guacamole."

Scholz cringed as the Tezwans aimed their plasma rifles at the shuttlepod. Morello shut his eyes. T'Sona looked bored.

"Worth a shot," Peart said as he opened the throttle

and pointed the craft's nose at the roof. Flashing a maniacal grin, he fired the main engine. "Ramming speed!"

Everything was a blur and a jolt, followed by a lurch and a teetering, spinning escape from an airborne cloud of smoke and debris. The hull groaned and the engines screeched. Oily smoke puffed from the sizzling helm controls. Outside, electric-blue plasma blasts arced past the craft, doing no damage.

Scholz and Morello's stunned gasps of numb surprise overlapped in the tiny cabin. The view in front of the shuddering craft dissolved into wisps of passing clouds, which parted to reveal a cinnamon sky. Peart whooped with equal parts relief and excitement. "Yeah! Now *that's* a takeoff!"

"I can't believe you did that," Scholz said.

Morello muttered in a shocked monotone, "I was kidding."

"I don't apologize for being right," Peart said. "Now stop sweating, you're stinking up my shuttlepod."

Chapter 57
Tezwa—Mokana Basin

TIERNEY AND BARNES were the first ones out the door into the jungle, and the first to get shot by the sniper.

Riker wanted to help Razka pull them back to safety, but the cruel pounding in his temples was too powerful. His skull throbbed with an inner violence that sent waves of nausea roiling through him. While Riker lay on the floor and fought to breathe, Razka pulled Barnes back into the doorway and checked his vitals. The grizzled Saurian looked at Riker and shook his head "no," just as he had done moments earlier for Tierney.

He leaned protectively over Riker. "Can you walk, sir?"

Riker's limbs were leaden, little more than dead weights anchoring him in the doorway. He tried to shake his head, but merely succeeded in lolling it awkwardly to one side. Razka helped him sit upright. "We can't stay here, Commander. The base crew is coming out this way. Do you understand?"

Fighting against exhaustion, against the muggy wet

heat, against the siren call of surrender, Riker somehow nodded.

"We can escape underwater," Razka said. "Can you hold your breath for thirty seconds?"

Riker could feel the words inside him, but couldn't get his mouth to make the sounds. His jaw was slackening, and his tongue felt swollen and dry. In a huff of foul breath he slurred out, "Don't know."

Eerie animal calls haunted the tropical night and mingled with the reverberating, overlapping Tezwan voices growing closer from inside the base. A fever-tone of tinnitis rang in Riker's burning-hot ears. Razka wrapped his sinewy, scaled arms around him. "Don't worry, sir, I've got you. Take as deep a breath as you can, and hold it till I say to let it go."

Relax, Riker commanded his body. *Breathe.* Concentrating on the simple act of pulling air into his lungs, he inflated his chest slowly, measure by measure, until it refused to accept any more. Then, as he clamped shut his jaw and devoted all his will to holding that breath hostage, Razka pulled him across the muddy ground and into the warm, murky swamp.

It was like returning to the womb to find it polluted by a creeping, squirming foulness. Pulled along through the slime-laced shallows, he was concealed with Razka beneath a blanket of thick algal scum. Riker marveled at how blithely he'd halted the tides of his breathing, as if he could simply abandon the habit anytime he wanted. As if he could make life stop and permit him to recover from its relentless indignities—the shaming of his friends, the murder of his father, Data being robbed of his emotional soul. All these blows crashed over him like waves assaulting a beach, wearing him down by degrees, eroding his will with unforgiving repetition.

"Let go." His breath bubbled out of him as his head broke the surface. Algae and angelhair water roots clung to him like a new skin. Razka leaned close over him, covering his elongated reptilian jaw with a taloned finger. "Shh," he cautioned. He opened his medikit and loaded the last ampoule of medicine into the hypospray. Injecting it into Riker's throat, he whispered, "You'll be able to breathe a bit easier in a few moments."

Razka slinked back into the murky water, leaving Riker propped in the cradling bough of a tree that reminded the first officer of a Florida cypress. "I'm taking out the sniper," Razka said. "Then we can hide until the *Enterprise* comes for us." As he submerged, he added, "Stay here."

Unable to lift his arms, Riker ignored the specklike insects that swarmed silently around him, hovering millimeters above the water's surface. Though his head was still racked with pain, his thoughts cleared slightly as he once again was able to draw a normal breath and revel in its sweetness.

Choruses of flinty grackle-squawks and rasping croaks struck up a maddeningly loud musical duel, until a deep and terrible rumble announced the destruction of the Mokana Firebase and preempted the competitive duet. The blast wave faded, leaving only faint insect noise in its wake . . . and then the angry whine of weapons fire.

Harsh voices barked orders in the night, almost drowning out the muted *swush* of bodies wading through the swamp. Crisp, blinding-white shafts of light slashed through the wild undergrowth, crisscrossing one another in the darkness.

He recoiled as a hand locked onto his wrist.

"Hurry, sir," Razka said, firmly pulling him forward and down below the level of the search beams. "Follow me." Riker's legs wobbled like rubber with every step. He felt at every second as if he were about to pitch forward and sink. One of the Tezwans' search beams fleeted over Razka's back, exposing a fresh and gruesomely charred grazing plasma wound.

Riker stumbled as a new surge of vertigo robbed him of his balance and left him feeling like water circling into a drain. He spat out the swampwater that rushed into his mouth. Razka turned back and labored to pull him back to his feet.

"Keep going, sir," Razka urged. Riker couldn't answer him, not even to refuse; he had nothing left.

The Saurian leaned him against another tree, unsheathed his rifle, and hunkered down in front of him. He lowered himself into the swamp, until only the crown of his head and the muzzle of his weapon remained above the water, poised to strike. Riker listened for the approach of the enemy, but felt his focus soften as a soothing darkness took hold of him at last.

Riker awoke to the hard slap of a hand across his face. Two blurry shapes towered above him, silhouetted in the night by searchlight beams. "He's alive," said the medic who had hit him.

Finally, Riker thought. *The rescue team's here.*

His delirious perspective swish-panned in all directions. Then clarity returned for a moment, sharp and bitter. His gaze settled on the charred corpse of Razka, who floated facedown in the swamp. A cluster of Tezwan soldiers poked and prodded the slain Saurian with the barrels of their weapons.

The command officer behind the medic sounded impatient. "We need to get to the rendezvous," he said. "Just kill him."

Pulling open Riker's camouflage jacket, the medic pointed at Riker's uniform collar. "He's a high-ranking officer."

The commander gave an irritated sigh.

"You know what to do."

The medic slammed his rifle stock against Riker's head, delivering the first officer back into the arms of oblivion.

Chapter 58
Tezwa—Mount Ranakar

A HIGH-PITCHED, swooshing scrape whistled from the synthetic rope as La Forge's carabiner streaked across it. The metal ring rubbed taut against the line with each descending jump he made down the belaying line.

The mountain trembled from a percussive boom, which was muffled but still audible through several hundred meters of rock. Several dozen meters above, a sharp blast resounded and hurled debris into the overcast sky.

His shallow arc pulled him back toward the cliff face. Extending his feet, he bounced into the impact, and pushed off again without losing momentum. His drops were longer and wider than he was accustomed to; Tezwa's lighter gravity made the rapid descent easier to manage. T'Eama and Braddock were slightly ahead of him one moment, a few meters behind the next, but generally keeping pace on either side of him.

A humid gale blew in on the leading edge of a storm, then another sonorous blast hammered Mount Ranakar from within. Suddenly, and with a deafening thunder-crack of splitting stone, a fissure opened in the cliff face between La Forge and T'Eama.

Heavy chunks and jagged shards of jingle rock rained down around the trio as they quickened their pace, risking longer jumps and free falls to escape the disintegrating cliff face.

La Forge looked down at the swiftly nearing ground, which was now peppered with freshly shattered, razor-sharp broken rock. Bouncing into his last jump, he glanced upward. Several enormous slabs of the cliff face sheared away from the mountain, directly above the strike team.

No time to play it safe. La Forge released the breakaway clasp of his climbing harness and dropped the final six meters. He rolled into the impact, gritting his teeth as he tumbled across the jagged stone debris. T'Eama landed on her feet, with feline agility, and bounded away from the wall in a single graceful leap. Braddock tried to emulate La Forge's technique, but he landed on a mound of loose stone that sent him sprawling hard onto his side. La Forge heard the bones in Braddock's left arm break on impact.

Grabbing the stunned security officer by the collar, La Forge tossed him clear and narrowly dodged the massive blocks of shale that smashed down behind him, stinging his neck and the back of his head with tiny pieces of rocky shrapnel.

With T'Eama's help, Braddock got back on his feet and tenderly cradled his shattered arm. "Let's go," La Forge said. "We have to get back to Wathiongo."

Trudging back through the wiry scrub brush, La Forge palmed the blood from the back of his close-cropped head. Looking over his camouflage jumpsuit, he saw it was badly torn and marred with bloodstains, sweat, and dirt. Braddock was in even worse condition, while T'Eama merely had to brush the dust from her fatigues to look good as new.

As they neared the camouflaged shelter they'd hastily erected for Wathiongo, Data's voice scratched through the static on La Forge's headset com. *"Bravo Leader to all teams: Bravo Team is clear. All team leaders report in."*

La Forge walked and listened while Peart and Vale checked in. As Taurik confirmed that Echo Team had *"achieved its objectives and reached minimum safe distance,"* the team reached Wathiongo's shelter. T'Eama stepped inside and checked on the injured engineer with her tricorder. La Forge didn't need to wait for her report—the perfunctory manner in which she turned off and holstered her tricorder told him what he needed to know. "This is Piper Leader. Mission complete. We have one KIA."

"Acknowledged," Data said.

Braddock, who had been listening in, looked puzzled. "Wasn't Commander Riker supposed to do the check-in?"

"Yeah," La Forge said, his voice chilled with a cold, prescient dread. "He was."

Chapter 59
U.S.S. Enterprise-E

TROI STEPPED ONTO THE BRIDGE expecting to face the grim tension of a disaster's aftermath. Instead she was relieved to find the mood one of guarded optimism. The young officers who surrounded Captain Picard seemed to be drawing their calm surety from him.

"Counselor," Picard said. "Just in time."

She moved to her seat and nodded to Perim, who was seated in Riker's chair, on the other side of the captain from Troi. The planet Tezwa grew large on the main viewscreen as the ship dropped out of warp. The Klingon and Tezwan fleets all were posed in space, like a re-created image from a history text.

"We've entered orbit, Captain," Magner said.

At ops, Le Roy worked quickly, analyzing sensor readings. "The guns and firebases have been destroyed, sir. All effects appear to have been implosive, as predicted."

Picard nodded. "Mr. Wriede, any reports of casualties?"

The tactical officer peered at his console. "Scanning

Tezwan military frequencies now," he said. "Initial reports indicate limited injuries—but no fatalities, at the firebases or the artillery units."

"Very good," Picard said. Troi felt the captain's relief at the news, even though he was maintaining a steady, calm façade. "Open a channel to the office of the Tezwan prime minister. And raise Fleet Captain Krogan, as well."

"Aye, sir," Wriede said as he began hailing the surface.

Troi turned to consult privately with the captain. "What's our next move? . . . Reopening the dialogue between the Klingons and the Tezwans?"

"Not yet," Picard said. "There's something I need from the Tezwans first."

Troi shot him a questioning look.

With a wry smirk he added, "Their surrender."

Chapter 60
Tezwa—Keelee-Kee

KICKING IN THE DOORS to Kinchawn's office felt good.

The rudely opened double doors crashed inward and rebounded off the walls with a bang. Bilok strode in like a conqueror, his pistol held level, his eyes sweeping the room for a target.

The room was empty.

Dasana, Tawnakel, and Unoro followed him into the office, all of them likewise brandishing small plasma blasters. The room was deathly quiet except for a soft, repeating double tone.

The four ministers moved deeper into the room and gathered around the desk. Bilok examined the computer panel on the wall. The small panel was surrounded by a discolored area the exact size and shape of the now-shattered frame that lay on the floor, its torn print of Tezwa's historic Civil Charter trampled underfoot. The gently warbling double tone repeated twice more.

Minister Itani walked in. "They're all gone," she said.

Bilok needed a bit more information. "Who?"

"The *Lacaam'i* ministers," she said. "They've fled."

"Impossible," Unoro scoffed. "They couldn't all get out of the *Ilanatava* without being seen."

"Well, they did," Itani said. "If they're still here, they're very well hidden." The double tone sounded again.

"Do you think they had military help?" Dasana asked.

"Of course they did," Tawnakel said.

Bilok tapped a string of commands into the computer interface on the desk, calling up an overview of the planet's tactical situation. "Well, that's probably why." He swiveled the monitor to show the other ministers the satellite images of sixty Klingon warships in orbit above Tezwa. The double tone continued to chirp softly beneath their debate.

"Superb," Unoro said. "While we've been staging a coup, the Klingons have landed on our doorstep."

"It gets worse," Bilok said, his throat going dry as he kept reading the tactical reports that had come in during the past four minutes alone. "Kinchawn's invincible artillery's been destroyed, and most of the army has deserted." After a moment of grave silence, he added, "We're defenseless."

Tawnakel pointed out one additional detail from the satellite image. "Isn't that the *Enterprise?*"

Bilok finally paid attention to the singsong double tone as it sounded once more. Checking the com channel, he realized the incoming signal was from the Federation flagship.

"Quickly," he said, pointing at the bare spot on the wall where the Civil Charter had hung. "Cover that." He motioned to Tawnakel and Unoro. "Tawnakel, stand on my right. Unoro, on my left. Hurry!" Itani and Dasana lifted the flagpoles from their stands behind the desk and unfurled the flags. They held them up at matching angles, from opposite sides, in front of the empty spot on the wall. Looking around himself, Bilok took a breath.

As he pressed the switch on the desk that opened the com channel, he prayed to his ancestors that Captain Picard would be able—and also willing—to intercede on Tezwa's behalf with the Klingons. *If he's not,* Bilok knew, *we're all about to die.*

Chapter 61
U.S.S. Enterprise-E

"KINCHAWN HAS BEEN DEPOSED. *I am the new prime minister.*"

Picard's hopes for this discussion brightened at that statement. With the rabidly hawkish Kinchawn out of power, negotiating a peaceful end to the crisis might be remotely possible—assuming Bilok was better able to talk to the Klingons than his predecessor had been.

The main viewscreen was divided in half, Bilok on the left and Krogan on the right. Krogan's eyes burned with barely suppressed fury, like a man trying to pretend that his hand isn't on fire. Bilok was flanked by two other male Tezwan ministers, behind whom a pair of female Tezwans held up identical, diagonally overlapping flags.

"*I am ordering our military to stand down,*" Bilok continued. "*Captain Picard, at this time I would like to ask you to mediate our surrender.*"

Krogan bared his teeth at Bilok's request. "*There will*

be no mediation," he said. *"Your surrender will be unconditional."*

Picard hardened his expression. "I concur," Picard said. "But it will be to the Federation, not to the Klingon Empire."

"What!" Krogan's self-control collapsed as he bellowed. Spittle erupted from his fanged mouth like lava from a volcano.

"Starfleet personnel destroyed the Tezwan artillery," Picard said. "They also crippled the Tezwan fleet—and currently have control over yours. The field of battle is ours—on behalf of myself, the *Enterprise,* and the Federation, I claim the right of *batyay'a.* This world is now under Federation control."

The captain expected that his invocation of the ancient Klingon privilege—which granted him exclusive dominion over the conquered foe—would infuriate the Klingon fleet commander even further. Krogan sat, stunned, and with an angry look on his face, for several seconds. Then his mouth widened into a sinister grin, and he laughed, loud and deep. He tossed his head back, chortled toward the ceiling of the *veScharg'a* bridge, then recovered his composure. "MajQa, *Picard . . . you* petaQ'Doj."

Picard nodded to Krogan, then turned his attention back to Bilok. "Mr. Prime Minister, I await your surrender."

Bilok looked to his fellow ministers, who all gestured their assent. *"Captain Picard, on behalf of the people of Tezwa, I hereby offer our unconditional surrender to the United Federation of Planets."*

Bilok rose from his chair and stepped in front of his desk, then kneeled. *"Fleet Captain Krogan, on behalf of the government and people of Tezwa, I kneel before the glorious might and perfect honor of the Klingon Empire."* Bilok bowed his head. The other four ministers stepped from behind the desk and lined up behind him. In unison they kneeled and lowered their heads, and the two women laid their flags on the floor.

"Touching," Krogan said. *"Did you bow to our ships before you murdered six thousand Klingon warriors?"*

Bilok lifted his head and stood. *"That abominable crime was the work of one man, not this government."* He half-turned to the ministers behind him. *"Call up the record of the last Assembly,"* he said. *"Cue it to Kinchawn's order to arrest the negotiators."* As he continued, the gray-feathered statesman held his arms apart, as if to show he was empty-handed and not a threat. *"What you are about to see, Captains, is evidence that Kinchawn developed these terrible weapons in secret collusion with our military, revealing their existence to our Assembly only moments before he gave the order to fire. Equally important, you will see and hear that he acted alone, without a vote of the Assembly."* Motioning to the other ministers, he said, *"Play it."*

Picard watched the transmission and glowered at Kinchawn's brazen assertion of executive power. *"I control the majority vote,"* Kinchawn said in the recording, *"and if I say we're at war, then we're at war!"* They were the words of a power-drunk leader run amok, so convinced of his own moral authority and infallibility that he bordered on delusional.

Picard also noted, with a small measure of satisfaction, that the recording showed Bilok arguing the Klingons' case to the former prime minister—demonstrating that he understood both the idea of honor and the criminality of Kinchawn's actions.

The recording ended, and Bilok returned to the viewscreen, once again seated at his desk and surrounded by his allies. *"At this time, I am ordering a warrant for the arrest of former Prime Minister Kinchawn,"* Bilok said. *"He is hereby charged with the premeditated murder of six thousand Klingon citizens. This offense, because it was committed in the name of the government, will be prosecuted as a war crime, and is punishable by death."*

"I will show your evidence to the High Council on Qo'noS. And I will recommend they hold Kinchawn and his accomplices personally liable for the murder of our soldiers—if you vow to extradite them to the Klingon Empire," Krogan said.

"No," Bilok said. *"There will be no extraditions. Their crimes were committed here—they will face our justice, not yours. But I assure you—it will be swift, and final."*

Bilok's answer pleased Picard. Apparently the new prime minister could be diplomatic without being spineless; he seemed ready to make concessions, but not to kowtow. It boded well for the planet's recovery.

"Prime Minister Bilok, on behalf of the United Federation of Planets, I accept your surrender. . . . Fleet Captain Krogan, this star system is now under Federation jurisdiction. I must ask you and your fleet to withdraw immediately."

Krogan looked disgusted, but also weary. *"We'll be under way shortly, Captain,"* he said. His first officer started to protest, but Krogan cowed the man with a primal growl before continuing. *"Prime Minister Bilok . . .*

I will deliver your terms to the High Council. Krogan out." The Klingon transmission ceased.

"Captain," Bilok said. *"Now that we are under Federation control . . ."* The phrase seemed to give the Tezwan leader pause. *"I must ask—does that mean the Federation will assist us in rebuilding? The Klingons' counterstrike all but annihilated our military, which provided our cities' law enforcement. In addition, several of our cities suffered collateral damage from the attacks, as did our atmosphere."*

Even knowing that he was about to overstep his authority, Picard answered without hesitation. "Yes, Mr. Prime Minister, the Federation will assist in the rebuilding of your world. My crew and I will do what we can to contain the damage and provide relief, until more ships arrive. I'll ask the Federation Council to initiate a full-scale emergency relief effort."

"Thank you, Captain," Bilok said. *"We look forward to welcoming the Federation's diplomatic representative. Now, with your permission, I must attend to critical matters of state."*

"Of course, Mr. Prime Minister. Picard out."

The screen switched back to the orbital view of Tezwa. The Klingon fleet continued to hang impotently above the planet. "Ensign Le Roy," Picard said, striding back to his seat. "Guide the Klingon fleet to the edge of the system, then release their command lockouts."

"Aye, Captain."

Picard settled into his chair and savored the restored sensation of pride that had been absent for far too long. Months of self-doubt had weighed gravely upon him, but now that internally imposed burden was gone—displaced by the return of confidence.

"Picard to transporter room. Begin beaming up our strike teams from the planet surface."

"Acknowledged," said Transporter Chief T'Bonz.

Picard began compiling data for his next update to Starfleet Command. Minutes later, Perim looked up from her command console, clearly alarmed, and swiveled toward Picard. Apparently sensing Perim's distress, Troi leaned in, as well. "Captain," Perim said, glancing nervously at Troi. "Chief T'Bonz reports five of the teams are safely aboard."

He waited for her to elaborate. She didn't. *"Five* teams?"

"Commander Riker's team is missing . . ." Perim looked afraid to continue in front of Troi, but she steeled herself and finished her report. ". . . And presumed dead."

Troi looked like someone had slapped her.

His good mood immediately gone, Picard's left hand clenched over his knee, an irrational reaction, but it felt like what he had to do to hold himself together as his thoughts went flying apart. He hadn't felt so overcome with grief in years, not since the day he'd learned that his brother and young nephew had perished in a fire on Earth. But the truth was that this was worse. Losing Robert and René had grieved him deeply, but to even imagine that Will Riker was gone left him feeling hollow and hopeless. *Like losing a son* was all he could think—over and over, until he was unable to breathe.

Troi rose from her seat and marched to the turbolift.

Perim stood a moment later, then paused and looked at Picard.

"Go," he said.

Perim followed Troi into the turbolift. The doors swished shut, leaving Picard again surrounded by strangers.

Chapter 62
Tezwa—Kinchawn's Redoubt

"OUR SITUATION is already improving."

Kinchawn sat at the head of the long table, flanked by several dozen of his most senior military commanders and backed by two dozen of his *Lacaam'i* ministers. The underground command center was barren and felt more like a dungeon than the seat of a government-in-exile, but he didn't plan to be here for long.

"Not only are the *Gatni* still hopelessly disorganized," he said, "but we now have the additional boon of contending with the Federation and its Starfleet, instead of the Klingons. The Federation has no tolerance for violence. At the first sign of serious resistance, they'll withdraw—leaving us free to deal with the *Gatni* traitors on our own terms."

"When do we strike?" asked General Minza, who sat to Kinchawn's immediate right at the head of the table.

"We need to wait for softer targets," Kinchawn said. "The Federation will send civilians to help Bilok and the

Gatni make repairs. We'll let them . . . for now. Let them put out the fires, restore communications, distribute food. Then, as soon as we have enough vulnerable targets, we attack."

"Someone will need to coordinate the cells in person," said General Yaelon, an older officer who did not look like a man who was suited to sitting at meetings; his sun-bleached feathers and rough, cracked skin bore the stamp of a veteran battlefield officer. "I would like to volunteer."

"You'll be directing the cells in Arbosa-Lo, General," Kinchawn said. "However, General Minza will be masterminding the insurgency. You'll report to him."

"As you command, Prime Minister."

"I want deployment estimates by midday," Kinchawn said to the room. "Continue to follow the chain of command. General Minza, keep me informed of any changes in the situation."

"Understood, sir."

"Meeting adjourned. *Aleem no'cha.*"

"*Aleem neel'ko,*" the room replied with one sonorous voice.

The generals and the ministers dispersed, and Kinchawn retired to his private sanctum. Forcing the Federation to abandon his world would be costly, but the alternative was to watch Bilok and his *Gatni* miscreants permanently subordinate Tezwa to that soulless political juggernaut.

Azernal betrayed me . . . thought he could use me for a pawn, then toss me aside. Now he's recruited Bilok to help mop up his mess, all to protect his sanctimonious Federation. Kinchawn pondered what kind of endgame would inflict an appropriately devastating retribution upon the Federation. It would not be enough merely to spill their blood on Tezwan soil; he needed to guarantee that neither the Federation nor the Klingons would come calling on his people ever again.

Of course, he realized. *It's so simple.* He gloated over the malicious elegance of the answer to his dilemma. *I'll get them to destroy each other.*

Chapter 63
U.S.S. Enterprise-E

DATA WATCHED the medical staff tend to the injured strike-team personnel. Nurses Ogawa and Weinstein aided Lieutenant Commander La Forge and Lieutenant Braddock. Dr. Crusher finished patching up Lieutenant Peart, who sat up and grabbed his jacket from the adjacent biobed. On the other side of sickbay, Dr. Tropp sealed a dark blue body bag around the corpse of Ensign Wathiongo.

Taurik and Vale had gone on ahead to the briefing room; the other uninjured strike-team personnel had been dismissed to their quarters. As the senior-ranking strike-team leader, Data was required to assemble and debrief the remaining team leaders once their injuries had been attended.

The door swished open. Troi rushed in. Her face conveyed what Data recognized to be distress. Perim entered behind her and went directly to Peart, who caught the slender Trill woman in a familiar embrace and kissed her passionately.

"Data," Troi said, her voice unsteadied by grief. "What happened? Where's Will?"

"I do not know, Counselor."

Her eyes brimmed with tears. "Is he dead? Tell me."

"His personal transponder went offline shortly after the Mokana base imploded. He and his team might not have reached safe distance in time." Troi grabbed Data's uniform jacket and twisted handfuls of its fabric in her white-knuckled fists. Her lips curled into a tight, horrible grimace as tears rolled down her cheeks. His social-courtesy subroutine guided him to say something else, something that might suggest an alternative conclusion regarding the commander's fate. "However, that is only one possible scenario."

His conversational gambit did not have the desired result. Troi pressed her face against Data's chest and sobbed.

He wanted to comfort her, but without his emotion chip he found empathy difficult. He knew that an acceptable behavior in this circumstance was to place one's arms around the grieving individual. Calculating the precise application of pressure to be firm without causing discomfort, he embraced her.

He tried to remember sorrow. It was a dim memory, vague and imprecise. His positronic mind could see its mathematical values with perfect clarity but could do nothing with them.

Awkwardly bereft of feelings, unsure of what to do or say, he stood silently, closed his eyes, and held his weeping friend.

Chapter 64
Qo'noS

"I SHOULD KILL YOU MYSELF," Martok said, his rasping growl of a voice echoing even in the modest space of his private chambers.

Far from hanging his head in shame, Worf defiantly returned the chancellor's fearsome, one-eyed glare with equal intensity. "I admit nothing."

"You don't deny it, either." Martok said. "Who else would have stolen our fleet's master command codes and given them to the *Enterprise?*"

"There could be many suspects."

"I disagree," Martok said. "And so will the council."

"Then let the council bring charges."

He had to admire Worf's unrepentant bravado; like any true warrior, Worf was not one to apologize for his victories.

Martok snorted, then walked away from him, toward the liquor cabinet. "Very clever," he said, taking a bottle of *warnog* and a carved onyx goblet from the shelf.

" 'Bring charges.' When you know damn well they have no evidence."

Worf said nothing. Martok poured himself a drink and put away the bottle without offering to pour one for Worf.

"Not that they need evidence," Martok said. He sipped his bitter drink. "Once the council starts lobbing accusations, the truth won't matter. They'll stain us both with the same lies."

"Your allies on the council could prevent such an inquiry."

Martok's voice became quiet. "Allegiances falter when the storm comes. You should know that better than anyone, Worf." Stepping from the shadows into the low, flickering firelight, Martok felt far older than his years. "Forced to choose between honoring our pact and increasing their own power . . ." He knew that Worf would understand the implied end of his sentence.

"Then you must eliminate your vulnerability," Worf said. "Accuse me yourself."

Martok shook his head and stepped closer to Worf. "You'd still be my kinsman. Your dishonor would still be mine."

"Then you must disown me. Force me to accept *web'ghIm.*"

"Never!" Martok hurled his goblet, which smashed against the wall, splattering one of his old war banners with *warnog.* "You're my family. I'd rather face an eternity in *Gre'thor* than deny you." He grasped Worf's shoulders. "Let the council come. If they want a battle, we'll give it to them."

"I thought you wanted to kill me yourself," Worf said, the hint of an impudent smirk tugging at his mouth.

Martok returned the gesture with his own lopsided half-grin and a grunt of amusement. *For what?* Martok mused. *Saving three hundred thousand Klingons from a pointless slaughter? Preventing the start of an occupation that would have consumed more time and lives than it could ever repay?* Martok wondered sometimes whether he was being unduly polluted by Worf's way of thinking.

"Honor is our way of life, Worf," he said. "But to blindly confuse honor with pride . . . that just might be the death of us."

"Indeed."

"Your role here will be harder, from now on. People are going to resent the Federation—and you—for some time. And you'll find the council less willing to cooperate than before."

"I expected as much." Worf really didn't seem fazed by the hostility that was certain to await him, both on the streets of the First City and in the treacherous corners of the Great Hall. Martok couldn't openly approve of Worf's actions, but he still admired the younger warrior's fearless conviction. A bitterly ironic thought made him chortle.

"This is just like old times for you, isn't it?"

Worf looked puzzled. "How so?"

"Once again you've saved the Empire from itself," Martok said, placing his hand on the back of Worf's neck in a fraternal clasp. "And once again, you'll be vilified for it."

Chapter 65
Earth Orbit—McKinley Station

"WE DON'T HAVE MUCH TIME," Azernal said, his voice echoing in the chilly close quarters of the airlock.

Quafina, who was almost folded in half above Azernal, blinked his bulbous eyes slowly, a gesture Azernal had come to recognize as a pensive expression among the Antedeans. "All is in motion," Quafina said, his words seeming to tumble back down his own throat as he spoke. "I have opened the channels. I need presidential approval to move the cargo off Earth."

He handed a special secure-encryption padd to Azernal.

Azernal reached into his pocket for a data rod, which he plugged into the socket on the back of the padd. The red symbols that indicated the classified shipping orders were pending were replaced by different blue-and-white emblems, which verified the orders now had presidential approval.

"I thought only the president could do that," Quafina said.

"The less he knows, the better," Azernal said as he handed the padd back to Quafina.

"True," Quafina replied, casually tucking the device back under his robe. "Better for all of us."

"When will the cargo get to Tezwa?"

"Freighters are not so fast," Quafina said. "Four weeks."

"Cover your tracks."

"Always." Quafina opened the inner airlock door and strode away, his footfalls slapping loudly in the echoing corridor.

If Picard's stunning success against ridiculous odds had convinced Azernal of anything, it was that the single most explosive variable in the Tezwa equation would be the presence of Starfleet personnel. The Admiralty had just deployed several ships to the beleaguered planet, and those were soon to be followed by tens of thousands of civilian relief workers.

He wasn't certain how to keep Starfleet in check while he worked his political damage control on Tezwa, but he still had a few days to iron out the details. *If anyone's going to turn this into a fiasco,* Azernal worried, *it'll be Picard.*

Then he imagined how Kinchawn might retaliate for being sent into exile with his military leaders. *If we give him a big enough target,* the crafty Zakdorn surmised, *he just might provide my distractions for me. . . .*

It was a reprehensible strategy; it would produce thousands of casualties—but ultimately it would save billions of lives.

In Azernal's icy calculus of life and death, that was good enough.

Chapter 66
Qo'noS

NOT ONLY WAS THERE NO TRACE of Zeitsev or his Andorian guard, there was no evidence that anything had ever been there at all.

Worf stood in the empty shell of the subbasement below the Federation Embassy. Less than twelve hours ago, this had been a high-tech underground intelligence center, with surveillance equipment capable of peering into every shadow on Qo'noS. But as he scanned it now with his tricorder, he found no traces of the technology or people he'd encountered here.

No power signatures. Not even a single dangling wire.

No biological residue. No organic matter of any kind.

Even the interior walls had been removed.

It was precisely as Worf had expected. Before answering Martok's summons to the Great Hall, he had concealed in his office the satchel of spy tools Zeitsev gave him. When he returned from the meeting, the tools were gone. The embassy's internal security monitors showed no one entering or leaving his office. No one had seen or heard anything unusual.

Like Zeitsev, the tools had simply vanished.

Worf trudged back to the turbolift. *Good riddance.*

Chapter 67
Tezwa—Keelee-Kee

"YOUR TERMS are more than fair. On behalf of a grateful people, I offer you our thanks."

Bilok bowed his head and wore a serene expression that belied his anxiety. The salty grit of raw shellfish on his back teeth mingled with the tart aftertaste of *jeefa;* together, they tasted like shame. *My people are starving,* he chastised himself, *and I'm sharing delicacies with our conquerors.*

He corrected himself: The Federation had shown no interest in behaving like a conquering power. Seated on the other side of the negotiating table were Federation Ambassador Lagan Serra and Starfleet Captain Picard. Lagan was a statuesque and regal-looking Bajoran woman whose steely eyes hinted at a past steeped in suffering. Similarly, Picard's affable manner and practiced courtesy were marred by an unspoken sadness. They both had shown Bilok every courtesy, and their generosity on behalf of their government was more than he would have dared to hope for.

Gathered behind them was a retinue of diplomatic hangers-on that included Commander Deanna Troi, who had accompanied the captain to the previous day's disastrous—and, in hindsight, fraudulent—peace negotiations. Standing beside and behind Bilok were numerous *Gatni* ministers, and a handful of moderate *Lacaam* Coalition ministers who had quickly distanced themselves from Kinchawn after he fled the capital. Bilok had named Tawnakel as his deputy prime minister, and he had promoted Unoro to serve as the new minister of state. The rest of the senior ministry posts were still in flux, left vacant due to internecine squabbling.

"The *Enterprise* will remain in orbit for the next several weeks," Lagan said. "More starships will arrive within the next forty-eight hours, to provide security for the civilian vessels that will bring supplies and relief workers."

"We look forward to welcoming them," Bilok said.

Lagan affixed her signature to the aid agreement, and applied an embossed stamp of the Federation emblem next to it. She slid the oversized document across the table to Bilok, who signed it and marked it with the Tezwan double-winged crest. They both stood and shook hands, completing the ritual that had been described to him before he'd entered the room.

"Mr. Prime Minister," Picard said as Bilok returned the agreement to Lagan. "With your permission, I'd like to pose a delicate question." Behind Picard, the rest of the Federation personnel were slowly moving en masse toward the exits.

"Please, speak candidly, Captain."

"The artillery that you say Kinchawn developed in secrecy . . . it would have required a significant number of personnel to assemble, would it not?"

"Yes, I imagine it would."

"It would be difficult to keep so massive a project secret, don't you think?" The captain's tone was civilly neutral, which Bilok knew was the preferred tenor of seasoned verbal assassins.

"Kinchawn's influence over the military was profound, Captain," Bilok said. "But I agree—the scale of this deception was truly shocking."

"Do you have any theories on how Kinchawn acquired that kind of technology? Was it developed here? Or did he acquire it off-world?"

"I wish I knew, Captain. But I fear its origins are as much a mystery to me as they are to you." That answer seemed to satisfy Picard, who said his farewells and departed with the rest of the Federation contingent.

Bilok didn't enjoy lying to Picard; he genuinely liked the man. But Koll Azernal's warning was still fresh in his thoughts. Only hours ago, the Zakdorn had contacted him in secret, both to congratulate him on his rise to the top of the *Ilanatava,* and to enlist his aid in a covert effort to disguise the origins of the now-destroyed nadion-pulse cannons.

The plan was hardly as simple as Azernal liked to make it sound. Its logistics were complicated, but the gravest threat to its success was its need for absolute secrecy. It would take only one misstep, one rumor to unravel the entire scheme.

Bilok had questioned the need for such elaborate measures. "Why not simply have Starfleet help plant your new 'evidence,' " he'd asked Azernal. "They're under your command, aren't they?"

Azernal had grimaced. *"You obviously don't know much about Starfleet,"* he'd said glumly.

Bilok stood alone at the enormous table, situated in the center of the cavernously empty, ornate banquet hall. Plates of half-eaten food and glasses smeared with oily fingerprints littered the dozens of small tables spread along the room's perimeter. Outside the wall of towering windows, the midday sky was stained dark with the smoky aftermath of the Klingons' anger. Beyond the protected environs of the capital, Bilok knew that his world lay in ruins. He felt exposed and vulnerable.

Yesterday I feared the Klingons' revenge. Today I'm waiting for Kinchawn to take his. I was better off with the Klingons.

More than the petty bickering of his fledgling administration, more than the heartbreaking environmental devastation that threatened his people with starvation, Bilok worried about the return of Kinchawn, who now was safely at large and backed by a private army of his loyalist partisans.

He knew the exiled *Lacaam'i* would come back, seeking retribution, desperate to reclaim the reins of power at any cost. Not right away, by any means; and not all at once. *No,* he brooded, *they'll leave us be long enough to put out the fires of their carelessness. They'll hide while we tend the wounded and feed the hungry, bide their time while we house the homeless. When they decide we've repaired enough of their damage to make this a world worth ruling . . . that's when they'll strike.*

The new prime minister was too adept in the black arts of politics to believe that peace would reign for long; Tezwa's current, placid state of affairs was doomed not to last. But he had not aspired to leadership without accepting its inherent risks. He had waited years for the chance to lead his world out of Kinchawn's militarized dark age, and into a new era of individual liberty and modernity. Azernal's dark bargain was Bilok's best chance to effect real change on Tezwa. And what did Azernal ask of him in return?

Some simple lies. Some smuggled contraband. Partnership in a conspiracy to frame the Tholians as the source of Kinchawn's artillery. A few buried secrets to help avert an interstellar war that would shatter the quadrant.

It was an ignoble agenda—but if it gave his people freedom, Bilok would call it his finest hour.

Chapter 68
An Undisclosed Location

"MOST IMPRESSIVE," Zeitsev said. "And resourceful."

"Their efforts were adequate," L'Haan said, clearly not as awestruck as Zeitsev by the eleventh-hour triumph of Ambassador Worf and Captain Picard. Dietz, for his own part, marveled at the joint effort, which had made a moot point of L'Haan's invocation of an Armageddon order.

Zeitsev and L'Haan stood behind Dietz as he manipulated the data feeds to his monitor array. At Zeitsev's request, the lights in the surveillance room had been dimmed and the rate of updates to the various monitors increased to match his heightened perceptual acuity. The swiftly changing images bathed the room in a peculiar, almost hypnotic flicker.

The two senior operatives loomed over Dietz as they studied numerous surveillance images from Tezwa, from the *Enterprise,* and from Earth. "Of course, the Tezwa situation is still in play," Zeitsev said.

"Indeed," L'Haan said. "I do not think events there will transpire as Chief of Staff Azernal expects."

Zeitsev tapped Dietz's shoulder. "What's Quafina doing?"

"Back to the Orions," Dietz said. "Looks like he's planning on using the *Caedera* again."

Zeitsev *hmmphed.* "Do you have someone in place this time?"

"We've activated the Orion Sleeper," L'Haan said.

"Good," Zeitsev said. "Well done. How do you see the Tezwa situation playing out?" Dietz knew that Zeitsev was talking to L'Haan, not to him. Zeitsev rarely deigned to solicit opinions from subordinates.

"Once again," L'Haan said, "Azernal proceeds from a flawed wargame scenario. It is highly probable that his smuggling of forged evidence will be compromised by rogue political and military elements on Tezwa."

Zeitsev nodded. "Kinchawn's guerrilla campaign."

"Yes," L'Haan said. "He will target Starfleet personnel and Federation civilians, hoping to force a withdrawal. When numerous escalations of violence fail to achieve this result, he will attempt to depose Bilok by force and order Federation personnel to leave."

"He'll probably succeed," Zeitsev said.

"Unless Starfleet gets involved and defends Bilok," Dietz said. Zeitsev and L'Haan looked down at him. Their coldly dismissive stares made it perfectly clear that he should refrain from injecting himself into the conversation.

"Indeed," L'Haan said. "However, Starfleet will likely treat the uprising as an internal matter and withdraw from the conflict. Kinchawn will easily reclaim power."

"At which point he'll be looking to punish the Federation," Zeitsev said. "He'll try to reveal Zife and Azernal's deal to the Klingons."

Dietz expected to be reprimanded for not minding his own business, but he decided this was worth mentioning. "Question," he said cautiously. "What if Kinchawn reveals the plan to the Klingons right now? If we end up at war against the Klingons, we'd almost certainly have to abandon Tezwa—giving him a free hand to depose Bilok."

"If Kinchawn could get a signal to the Klingons without giving away his own position to the *Enterprise*, he probably would," Zeitsev said, apparently not upset at the query. "But right now he's underground, probably regrouping and avoiding signal traffic that would draw attention."

"The question remains," L'Haan said, "how will we respond when Kinchawn returns to power?"

Zeitsev half-shrugged; he clearly thought the answer was obvious. "We kill him and blame it on the *Gatni* faction. Or the Klingons. Or whoever. Bottom line—that man has to die before he gets us *all* killed."

Chapter 69
Tezwa—Mokana Basin

DEANNA TROI STARED FORLORNLY into the crater, which was filled with murky water. Much of the surrounding swamp had drained into the chasm after the firebase imploded, leaving the flooded pit bounded by a slick, muddy ring. Starfleet rescue divers were surfacing from the crater pool, dragging two bodies between them. As the watery muck sluiced off the corpses' faces, she recognized them as engineers Kelly Tierney and Matthew Barnes.

She resisted her worst impulses . . . fought to banish from her mind the image of Riker's body trapped beneath all that darkness—crushed and broken, drowned . . . dead. Even in the absence of any proof to the contrary, she refused to believe he was gone. *I can feel it. I know he's not down there. He can't be.*

A man's voice called out from behind her. "Counselor!" She turned to see Lieutenant Gracin from security striding toward her. "We might have something. Come with me."

She followed Gracin into the eerily quiet jungle, where they joined security officers Lofgrin and Clemons. They moved quickly across the slippery mud. Blinding blue-white search beams swept through the trees and thick jungle foliage, some from search teams on the ground, some from the Starfleet runabouts hovering overhead. Groups of Starfleet security personnel and Tezwan civilian volunteers moved in carefully blocked sweep patterns.

More than a hundred meters from the implosion crater, Troi and her escorts reached Peart and Ensign th'Chun, who were both scanning the area with tricorders, looking for any trace of the missing Starfleet personnel. Peart looked sympathetically at Troi. "We think we have a lock on his transponder," he said. "It's offline, about ten meters that way, past those trees."

Troi followed Peart's gesture. The other search teams continued sweeping the area around them. Peart moved a little bit closer to her and kept his voice down. "You can wait here," he said. "You might not want to see what we see."

She had to trust her own eyes. Shaking her head, she swallowed hard to force back the nervous acid fountaining up from her stomach. "No," she said. "I have to know."

Peart nodded. "All right. Stay with me."

He led her forward, flanked by a large team of *Enterprise* security personnel. As they clambered over some fallen tree trunks, Troi saw a mud-crusted humanoid form lying facedown in the murky slime of the exposed swampbed. Its legs were twisted at grotesque angles; one arm was stretched above its head, the other flailed out to one side.

Ensigns Liryn and Carmona kneeled beside the body and gently lifted it free of its muddy shallow grave. They rolled it over slowly, revealing the unmistakably Saurian features of Master Chief Petty Officer Razka. His torso was scorched and blasted apart, his garments nothing but filthy rags.

Troi turned away from the gruesome sight, expecting to see something much worse behind her.

Peart watched his tricorder as Danilov and Weathers carefully extracted a torn and mangled set of camouflage fatigues from the mud. "It's his all right," Peart said. "Danilov, check the left chest pocket." The security officer opened the pocket and reached inside. He turned it inside out to reveal the damaged Starfleet transponder. "Bingo," Peart said.

"The rest of the teams have finished their sweeps," Gracin said to Peart. "There's no trace of him, sir."

Peart tapped his combadge. "Peart to *Enterprise*."

Vale answered. *"This is* Enterprise. *Report."*

"We've recovered the bodies of Lieutenants Tierney and Barnes, and Chief Razka. We also have Commander Riker's transponder."

"His transponder?"

"Aye, sir." Peart glanced over his shoulder at Troi, who remained fixated on the torn, muddy fatigues. "It's my opinion that Commander Riker has been captured."

Troi walked over and took the shredded uniform from Danilov and Weathers. They resisted at first, until Peart silently gestured for them to let go. Troi held the tatters in her hands, felt the greasy mud against her fingers, pressed her fingertips against the fabric.

My Imzadi *is alive,* she told herself, her grief burning away, consumed by a fiery anger that walked hand-in-hand with her renewed hope. *And I'm not leaving this planet without him.*

Acknowledgments

It's difficult for me to decide who I should thank first, because so many people deserve my gratitude. I'm sure no one will hold it against me if I choose to begin by praising my lovely wife, Kara, whose patience during the long months that I spent holed up in my home office writing this book and its companion volume, *A Time to Heal,* was indispensable. She tolerated my long absences, my insanely late nights behind closed doors, and my rambling digressions about plot points and characters about whom she knew not a thing.

Next, of course, I must tip my hat to my longtime friend, John J. Ordover. It was John who, in the summer of 2003, invited me to step into the breach and take on this two-book assignment. Prior to this, my published prose work for *Star Trek* had been limited to technical and reference volumes (the *New Frontier Minipedia* and *The Starfleet Survival Guide*) and the S.C.E. eBook novellas (*Invincible,* which I cowrote, and *Wildfire,* my solo-prose debut). Making a jump from writing eBooks to signing a two-book paperback deal, as I explained to some of my more sports-minded relatives, was akin to a minor-league pitcher being called up to the major leagues and asked to pitch a playoff doubleheader as his debut. John guided me as I molded the story and counseled me as I hammered it into shape over the next several weeks.

Heartfelt thanks are due also to Paula Block at Paramount Licensing, for helping to curb some of the story's early, more irrational excesses. Some of the best ideas for this book were the product of her suggestions during the story-development phase. Not only did she help prevent this tale from going badly astray, she pointed it in narratively fruitful directions that I certainly would otherwise have missed.

Let me also heap kudos upon the other authors in this series: John Vornholt, who released this Sisyphean boulder and challenged the rest of us to push it back up the hill; Dayton Ward and Kevin Dilmore, who raised the bar on the rest of us yet again, with their gripping mix of action and character work; Robert Greenberger, whose two novels proved to be a gold mine of dramatic possibilities and set the stage for my own efforts; and the indefatigable Keith R.A. DeCandido, whose boundless energy (and remarkably fast typing skills) inspired and dared the rest of us to keep up with him. Keith deserves special bowing and scraping from yours truly, because he went above and beyond to help me out—answering frantic instant messages and e-mails (about Klingon society and customs, *Star Trek* continuity, his *I.K.S.*

Gorkon books, and many other, more obscure matters) at all hours of the day and night, gently coaching me out of the corners I wrote myself into, and generally talking me down off my metaphorical ledge.

I would be remiss if I did not express my gratitude to my family—both my blood kin and my unofficial tribe. Offering encouragement from the faraway land of New England are my parents (a.k.a. David and Yvonne), and my brother, Stephen, his wife, Elizabeth, and their little ray of ever-inspiring sunshine, Julia. Keeping the fires lit for me here in the Big Apple, of course, is the increasingly infamous Malibu crowd, especially my long-suffering best friend and fellow *Star Trek* author, Glenn Hauman, and his indubitably better (looking) half, Brandy. Also, a belated *muchas gracias* to founding Malibuvian and jill-of-all-trades Kim Kindya, who verified a Spanish translation of the "Hail Mary" for my eBook novel *Wildfire*.

Penultimately, a sincere *merci beaucoup* to the fans who lurk and post at PsiPhi.org's *Star Trek* Books BBS and the characters over at the TrekBBS Literature Forum, for making me feel so instantly welcome in the *Star Trek* books online community.

And lastly, my thanks to you, the reader—for making this effort worthwhile. Enjoy.

About the Author

David Mack is a writer whose work spans multiple media. With writing partner John J. Ordover, he cowrote the *Star Trek: Deep Space Nine* episode "Starship Down" and the story treatment for the *Star Trek: Deep Space Nine* episode "It's Only a Paper Moon." Mack and Ordover also penned the four-issue *Star Trek: Deep Space Nine / Star Trek: The Next Generation* crossover comic-book mini-series *Divided We Fall* for WildStorm Comics. With Keith R.A. DeCandido, Mack cowrote the *Star Trek: S.C.E.* eBook novella *Invincible,* currently available in paperback as part of the collection *Star Trek: S.C.E.* Book 2: *Miracle Workers.* Mack also has made behind-the-scenes contributions to several *Star Trek* CD-ROM products.

Mack's solo writing for *Star Trek* includes the *Star Trek: New Frontier Minipedia,* the trade paperback *The Starfleet Survival Guide,* and the best-selling, critically acclaimed two-part eBook novel *Star Trek: S.C.E.—Wildfire.* His other credits include "Waiting for G'Doh, or, How I Learned to Stop Moving and Hate People," a short story for the *Star Trek: New Frontier* anthology *No Limits,* edited by Peter David; the short story "Twilight's Wrath," for the *Star Trek* anthology *Tales of the Dominion War,* edited by Keith R.A. DeCandido; and S.C.E. eBook #40—*Failsafe.* He currently is working on an original novel, developing new *Star Trek* book ideas, and writing a new S.C.E. novella titled *Small World.*

A graduate of NYU's renowned film school, Mack currently resides in New York City with his wife, Kara.

The saga continues in September 2004 with

STAR TREK®

A TIME TO HEAL

by
David Mack

**Turn the page for an electrifying
preview of *A Time to Heal*. . . .**

Dusk settled upon the city of Alkam-Zar. Rays of deep-crimson sunlight flared through the seam of the horizon, casting a fiery glow across the sullen, steel-gray clouds. Wind like a mournful cry twisted between the towering husks of buildings both ancient and modern—all sinking now into decay and history.

Starfleet Ensign Fiona McEwan stood on the edge of a rubble-strewn plaza near the center of the battered metropolis. Alkam-Zar, like many other Tezwan cities, was still smoldering more than two weeks after it had been racked by a shockwave from a Klingon torpedo, which had destroyed a military starport several dozen kilometers away from the urban center.

These people probably thought the base's presence made them safer, McEwan mused. *It just made them a target.*

Behind the petite, red-haired young officer, a Federation relief team coordinated the distribution of food, clean water, and medicine to local Tezwans, who had lost most of their basic utilities because of the Klingon barrage. The relief group was composed of civilian workers and physicians. McEwan was one of six Starfleet security personnel assigned to protect them. Some relief groups, working in similarly war-torn urban areas around the planet, had been nearly overwhelmed by Tezwan refugees, whose suffering and desperation had led to food riots; other groups had been ambushed by Tezwan military insurgents still loyal to the deposed prime minister, Kinchawn.

Today things had been quiet in Alkam-Zar. Most of its people were still in shock. Tezwan adults and children wandered the streets like gangly, looming phantoms. Their feather-manes were pale with dust and matted with neglect, their arm feathers tattered and scorched and stained with blood. Shuffling footsteps crunched across boulevards dusted with shattered glass and pulverized rock. Broken beams of metal crusted with ancient stone had impaled the ground and dotted the thoroughfares and side streets like monuments to a quiet despair.

So far, the Federation's efforts had focused on providing these people with the essentials of survival— food, water, shelter, and basic medical treatment. Just two days ago the Starfleet Corps of Engineers had arrived, to direct the monumental task of rebuilding this world's ravaged cities.

For her part, McEwan was in no hurry to see the streets swept bare. If a Loyalist ambush were aimed at her squad, she would be grateful for all the cover she could get.

Thirteen more days, she reminded herself. *Then I rotate back shipside.* She had just begun her two-week deployment to the planet surface and was already looking forward to her return to the *Enterprise.* Because she had risked her life during the commando mission that neutralized Tezwa's ground-based anti-ship artillery, she had been lucky enough to miss the first, grueling two-week rotation. Danilov had told her the reeking, insect-infested carnage in the major cities had left him with nightmares. Jae had described—in a haunted monotone that made his nauseatingly vivid details all the more unsettling—a guerrilla ambush in Anara-Zel that killed four security officers from the *Republic.* Danilov and Jae were front-line veterans of the Dominion War, so McEwan took their warnings seriously.

A keening cry, anguished and beautiful, cut through the heavy hush. Turning toward its source, McEwan looked up, toward the top of a twenty-story building rendered by war into a gutted frame. Standing like an emperor atop the structure was a lone Tezwan singer, his arms flung wide as if to embrace the sky. Nasal and piercing, his voice reverberated off smashed, hollow edifices painted with the dying light of day. McEwan's heart stirred with his projected grief, ached as it grasped the terrible emptiness of his operatic wails.

Without taking her eyes from the singer, she grabbed the sleeve of a young Tezwan boy who was walking past her. Holding him with one hand, she pointed with the other at the singer. "What's he singing?"

Following her gesture with stunned, distant eyes, the

boy seemed utterly unmoved by the singer as he answered. "It's a sorrow-song. We sing for the dead."

McEwan stood, transfixed by the singer. His voice was like a majestic wolf cry, despondent beneath a shadowy dome of gray, casting on her an enthralling spell of mourning. The boy pulled away from her, and she let go of him. "Who's he singing for?"

The boy glanced up at the singer. As he turned away, he answered with an ominous emotional flatness, "The world."

She glanced at the boy, who plodded off, his daily ration of Federation emergency nutrition packs tucked under one arm. Then the singer's tune crested, pulling McEwan's eyes back to the top of the tower. For a fleeting moment the singer's voice filled every corner of Alkam-Zar. Then his music dropped away like a dying breath. A faint and tragic note rose and vanished into the heavens, like his soul taking flight, as he leaned forward and pitched headfirst off of the building.

McEwan's cry of alarm stuck in her throat as she watched the singer plummet to earth. He neither flailed nor cried out, but fell as if it was his destiny to do so. Empathetic dread swelled inside her as the singer's body accelerated.

He hit the ground with a dull, thick, wet crunch.

McEwan's horrified gasp was tangled up in her choking sobs. Burning tears ran from her eyes.

Fighting to compose herself, she turned slowly back toward the plaza. Behind her, the other Starfleet personnel watched in shock. A civilian woman with the relief team covered her mouth and began to weep. Many other relief workers turned away. A young doctor sprinted across the plaza with a surgical kit in his hand, apparently undeterred by the futility of his impending efforts. A Federation News Service reporter ran after him.

But all McEwan could see were the Tezwans, who continued to wait for their food packets and water rations, oblivious of—or indifferent to—the singer's gruesome end. Even more than his suicide, their numb disregard of it frightened her deeply.

Wiping the tears from her cheeks, she counted the days until she could leave this world and never see it again.

KNOW NO BOUNDARIES

Explore the Star Trek™
Universe with Star Trek™
Communicator, The Magazine of
the Official Star Trek Fan Club.

Subscription to Communicator is
only $29.95 per year (plus shipping and handling)
and entitles you to:

- **6 issues of STAR TREK Communicator**

- **Membership in the official STAR TREK™ Fan Club**

- **An exclusive full-color lithograph**

- **10% discount on all merchandise purchased at
  www.startrekfanclub.com**

- **Advance purchase preference on select items
  exclusive to the fan club**

- **...and more benefits to come!**

So don't get left behind! Subscribe to STAR TREK™
Communicator now at www.startrekfanclub.com

STAR TREK

THE EPIC STORY OF PICARD'S
FIRST COMMAND CONTINUES...

STARGAZER: MAKER

PICARD MUST RELY ON A WOMAN WHO
HAS BETRAYED HIM IN THE PAST TO SAVE
HIS SHIP—AND THE ENTIRE GALAXY.

DON'T MISS THE OTHER BOOKS IN THE
STARGAZER SERIES BY
MICHAEL JAN FRIEDMAN:

STARGAZER: GAUNTLET

STARGAZER: PROGENITOR

STARGAZER: THREE

STARGAZER: OBLIVION

STARGAZER: ENIGMA

AVAILABLE NOW